The Executioner drilled two rounds into his adversary

The rapid gunshots sounded like a double thunderclap inside the crowded subway car, eclipsed at once by frightened shouts and screams.

Mack Bolan grabbed the bag containing the sarin gas canisters and strode toward the exit at the end of the car. The door swung open when he threw his weight against it, and he cleared the noisy coupling, bursting into the next car back.

A hundred faces swiveled toward him, all gaping when they spotted the gun in Bolan's hand. He bulled his way forward and watched them scramble, taking advantage of their fear, painfully conscious of the fact that he was running out of time.

They were all running out of time.

Other titles available in this series:

Stony Man Doctrine
Terminal Velocity
Resurrection Day
Dirty War
Flight 741
Dead Easy
Sudden Death
Rogue Force
Tropic Heat
Fire in the Sky
Anvil of Hell
Flash Point
Flesh and Blood
Moving Target
Tightrope
Blowout
Blood Fever
Knockdown
Assault
Backlash
Siege
Blockade
Evil Kingdom
Counterblow
Hardline
Firepower
Storm Burst
Intercept
Lethal Impact
Deadfall
Onslaught
Battle Force
Rampage
Takedown
Death's Head
Hellground
Inferno
Ambush
Blood Strike
Killpoint
Vendetta
Stalk Line
Omega Game
Shock Tactic
Showdown
Precision Kill
Jungle Law
Dead Center
Tooth and Claw
Thermal Strike
Day of the Vulture
Flames of Wrath
High Aggression
Code of Bushido
Terror Spin
Judgment in Stone
Rage for Justice
Rebels and Hostiles
Ultimate Game
Blood Feud
Renegade Force
Retribution
Initiation

DON PENDLETON's

MACK BOLAN®

Cloud of Death

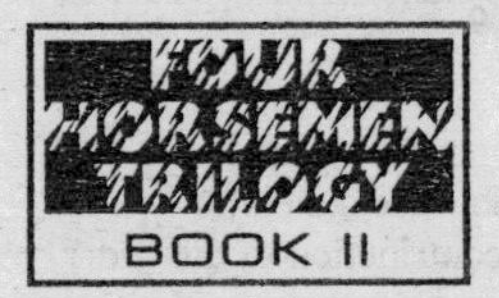

TORONTO • NEW YORK • LONDON
AMSTERDAM • PARIS • SYDNEY • HAMBURG
STOCKHOLM • ATHENS • TOKYO • MILAN
MADRID • WARSAW • BUDAPEST • AUCKLAND

First edition April 1999

ISBN 0-373-61465-9

Special thanks and acknowledgment to
Mike Newton for his contribution to this work.

CLOUD OF DEATH

Printed in U.S.A.

Faith may be defined briefly as an illogical
belief in the occurrence of the improbable.

—H. L. Mencken

Prejudices, Third Series

Faith consists in believing not what seems true,
but what seems false to our understanding.

—Voltaire

Philosophical Dictionary

Misplaced faith is a dangerous thing, often utilized
by fanatics. I can't stop them all, but I can teach one
group, one time, to fear the Executioner.

—Mack Bolan

To General Henry Shelton,
commander of the U.S. Joint Chiefs of Staff

CHAPTER ONE

"Two minutes till they're all in place."

FBI Special-Agent-in-Charge Greg Underwager caught himself whispering, even though he knew there was no need. Inside the command vehicle, parked half a mile from the scene of the action, none of the enemy was likely to catch a glimpse of him, much less hear his voice.

The enemy, he thought, and frowned. He was supposed to think of them—his targets—as "subjects," maybe even "suspects," but the term he automatically applied to those he hunted would be frowned upon at headquarters. It was miles away from what the brass would call politically correct, but Underwager couldn't help the way his mind worked. He had played the deadly game too long, spent too many years on the front lines, to start going soft this late in life.

"No contact with the sentries yet?" Tom Wakefield asked the young man with a plug in his left ear, eyes scanning half a dozen mini-TV monitors arranged in a console in front of him.

"No, sir," the young agent replied, without taking his eyes from the screens.

"They may not have men posted," Underwager told his counterpart from ATF. It was unusual, to say the least, for the FBI to join forces with Alcohol, Tobacco and Firearms on an active field operation. They served different departments in Washington—the Bureau working out of Justice, ATF out of Treasury—and it was much more common for one to pick up where the other's jurisdiction ended. The FBI, for instance, sometimes inherited terrorism cases from ATF when the T-men finished their preliminary investigation of firearms and explosives violations, and the Bureau's hostage rescue team had been called in to clean up ATF's mess at Waco.

Even thinking about the Waco debacle set Underwager's teeth on edge. It was bad enough that four federal agents had died in the initial assault, but the fiery climax, fifty-three days later, had been even worse, and that was squarely in the Bureau's lap. Not that Greg Underwager took responsibility for the fire that leveled Rancho Apocalypse; far from it. Multiple investigations had shown the Branch Davidian cultists set the fire themselves, with many of the victims stabbed or shot at point-blank range before they fried, but there were still fanatics in the land who viewed the incident as "government assassination," aimed at subverting "religious freedom."

Never mind that David Koresh and company had stockpiled illegal weapons and threatened cult defectors with death. Never mind that the "Sinful Messiah" himself was having sex with anything that moved, including children well below the age of consent. Never mind that the initial raid—however poorly planned—had been conducted in accordance with the rules of law, and that the cultists had fired first, killing four federal agents in performance of their duty. It was all a plot, according to some spokesmen for the rabid right, and Underwager cringed at the thought of replaying that disaster.

Especially with the big man from Washington sitting ten feet away, watching every move he made.

"They'll have guards out," the big man said. "Bank on it."

Hal Brognola his name was, flown out special from D.C. to supervise the raid. It was a long way from the seat of government to Colorado, and the big brass didn't roll out every day.

"If you know something we don't," Underwager said, "I don't think you should keep it to yourself, sir."

Brognola frowned at that, as if considering his answer for a heartbeat. "Nothing special," he replied. "I know this crowd, is all. They *always* have guards out."

"Keep checking," Underwager told the agent seated at the console.

"Yes, sir."

Fifty agents on the ground, with twenty in reserve, made this the largest, most potentially explosive operation Underwager had commanded in his five years as special-agent-in-charge of the Denver field office. For the first time since his promotion, he found himself wishing the rank had gone to somebody else—someone in St. Louis, for example. If the Missouri field office had been on the job, these bastards never would have slipped through the net in the first place.

"Thirty seconds to jump-off," Wakefield said, glancing up from his watch with a sour look on his face.

Thirty seconds, Underwager thought. It wouldn't be long.

One way or the other.

MACK BOLAN LAY AWAKE, staring at the ceiling overhead. Almost forty-eight hours had passed since the raid in Missouri, and nearly a full day since his return to the Millennial Truth compound outside Boulder. The television in the camp's command post had been playing constantly since his arrival, tuned in to the all-news channel, following developments in the national manhunt.

Thus far, there had been no mention of Millennial Truth, a.k.a. The Path, in connection to the hostage situation at the Mormon temple outside St. Louis. Justice knew the connection, of course, Bolan had no doubt of that: he had been assigned specifically to infiltrate and break the cult, a role that had involved him in the hostage-taking, with a narrow last-minute escape from a quick-trigger SWAT team. It made good sense for the Feds to hold back what they knew until they had dropped a net over the rest of the cult, but upstairs Bolan still felt edgy, like a nervous sleeper waiting for the other shoe to drop.

His cover was solid, as far as he knew. No other members of the raiding party had survived, according to the CNN reports, but only two or three of them had been identified so far, and news reports were inconsistent on the number of bodies recovered. Twelve men, counting Bolan, had gone on the raid, and reports of the aftermath cited hostile body counts ranging from nine to eleven.

And where were the Feds?

Brognola knew about the Boulder compound. Bolan had no doubt of that, since he had passed the word along himself. Why was the hideout not surrounded, then, by federal guns?

"The Two"—cult leaders Galen Locke, a.k.a. Hermes, and Helen Braun, a.k.a. Circe—were gone, having made their escape when news of the Missouri temple snafu first broke. Bolan didn't have a clue where they had gone, but there were still plenty of rabbits in the pen, including Dillon Murphy—cult name Ares—who served as The Path's resident enforcer and commander of its military arm, Thor's Hammer. If the Feds got off the dime—

He caught himself, with a silent reminder that *he* was in the pen, as well. One narrow escape from the law was enough, in any given week. He should welcome the breather.

There was a pistol underneath his pillow and, while Bolan had stripped down to shorts and T-shirt, his clothes and boots were no more than an arm's length away. If he was forced to scramble, years of living-on-the-edge experience would see him dressed in seconds flat, ready to fight or flee, whatever was required.

If it was Feds, he knew flight would be the only way to go. Bolan had vowed that he would never drop the hammer on a lawman, and he didn't plan to break that solemn promise to himself, particularly not in the defense of cultists who were bent on pushing the United States—indeed, the world at large—into the fires of Armageddon.

If the Feds came, he would try to slip away. Failing that, he would be forced to trust Brognola, stay alive until his old friend found a loophole somewhere in the law for him to wriggle through.

Meanwhile, he still had other problems on his plate. Ares had looked askance at Bolan—known within the cult as Nimrod, a.k.a. Mike Belasko—when Bolan had returned alone from the fiasco in Missouri. There had been countless questions, but he had survived the inquisition by telling the truth, more or less. He had described his escape from the temple as it had occurred, simply omitting the fact that one or more of the raiding officers might have been instructed to look the other way.

Bolan still had no idea if that was true; it made no difference now, in any case. What mattered to him most was finding some way to get back in touch with Brognola, let him know what was happening inside the cult.

As for what Thor's Hammer and The Path had planned for their next move, to follow up the snafu in Missouri, well, the Executioner would simply have to wait and see, like everybody else. He had no pipeline to the scattered leadership, and, for all he knew, still might be regarded with suspicion as the sole survivor of the temple raid.

Whatever happened next, though, Bolan meant to

stay on top of it, be ready for it, if he could. Preparedness was second nature to him after years of living by his wits and martial skills.

Whatever happened next, Mack Bolan meant to give it everything he had.

JEFF GOINES HAD SPENT exactly thirty seconds in the woods before he wished he had night goggles. Damn, it was dark in there! No moon to speak of, and the trees cut off whatever light might have reached the ground anyway. He could, in fact, see a hand held in front of his face, but not a great deal more.

The others were behind him; Goines knew that much without trying to spot them. His five-man team had drilled specifically for situations such as this one, working in the dark, in pouring rain, inside a warehouse filled with pepper gas—you name it. Achuff, Weaver, Danks and Blair would stick behind him all the way, depending on their team leader to lead. Goines, for his part, had the contour maps fresh in his mind, a compass on his wrist in case he somehow went astray.

Within the Bureau, troops like his were known as HRT—the hostage rescue teams. The FBI refused to call its paramilitary units SWAT teams: first, because the SWAT label had been introduced by LAPD at a time when L.A.'s brass was feuding with the late director Hoover over jurisdictional issues; and second, because in the modern, politically correct age, "special weapons and tactics" sounded too damned aggressive and hostile for delicate sensibilities to stomach.

Still, it all came down to the same thing—Kevlar helmets and flak vests, steel-toed boots and combat harnesses, gas masks and flame-retardant clothing—midnight black—with an array of weapons that included CAR-15 assault rifles, MP-5 submachine guns, 12-gauge riot guns and .40-caliber semiauto side arms. The stun and smoke grenades were extras, sometimes used and sometimes not. The Ka-bar combat knives each agent carried was—at least in theory—regarded as a "tool," with no antipersonnel applications intended.

When the shit came down, though, Goines knew from grim experience that he would use whatever came to hand. If necessary, he would lob bricks at the bastards, or anything it took to finish another shift alive and well.

Goines and his team had been flown in from Phoenix for the raid on Millennial Truth. They hadn't been involved in the Missouri temple action, but were tuned in to the basic facts of what had happened. More to the point, they knew that certain members of the cult were armed with modern military hardware, including both full-automatic weapons and explosives. Booby traps were possible, although the team hadn't encountered any, yet. The likelihood of armed resistance, Goines and his people had been told, was somewhere in the neighborhood of eighty-five percent.

Tough odds.

Goines calculated that they were within a hundred

yards of the compound when he froze in his tracks. Behind him, the soft rustling sounds of his soldiers in motion instantly ceased. Goines pulled back the Velcro cover on his wristwatch, wincing at the muffled ripping sound it made. Velcro had been adopted as an improvement over metal snaps, but no one yet had found a way to silence it completely. In the present instance, now, it seemed to make no difference, since they had the woods all to themselves.

Two minutes remained before H-Hour.

They would have to pick up the pace if they wanted to get to the party on time. Goines recovered his watch, half turned toward his team and raised his left fist in the air, pumping it twice up and down, the signal for cautious haste—an oxymoron if there ever was one. They wouldn't double-time through the woods, but they could still make better time. As for silence, well, there was only so much one could hope for in a virgin forest, the ground beneath your feet carpeted with dead leaves, fallen twigs and branches, loose rocks and scurrying wildlife.

The team shaved another forty yards, Goines perspiring freely in spite of the late-night chill, and they were almost close enough to see the compound, when it all fell apart. The sentry seemed to come from nowhere, rising from a hideout on the ground, perhaps, or dropping from the lower branches of a tree, off to the left. Wherever he had come from, though, the guy was planted squarely in their path, some twenty feet away.

Worse yet, he directly faced Jeff Goines. It was impossible to see his eyes—the whole face was in shadow—but the way he moved, swinging his weapon toward the hostage team, left no doubt he had spotted them.

It was too late for silence, now. Goines saw the wink of muzzle flame and shouted, "Down!" before he hit the dirt. Bullets were rattling overhead as Goines found the trigger on his MP-5 and fired a short burst in return. The target staggered, pumping out another six or seven rounds before he ducked behind a giant tree.

"We're under fire!" he told the cordless microphone that had been clipped onto his helmet. "I repeat, we're under fire!"

And Goines wondered whether he would make it home alive this time.

DILLON MURPHY, known as Ares to his fellow members of The Path, was on his feet, clutching a weapon in his hand, before the first echoes of gunfire died away. He had been working at his desk, and three long strides brought him to the light switch. He slapped it with an open hand and plunged the office into darkness.

Better.

More gunfire erupted, and as he reached the doorstep, Murphy realized that it was coming from the forest on the west side of the compound. Those were automatic weapons firing, at least two submachine guns and one rifle, by the sound. That meant it was no accident, a careless lookout triggering a careless burst. If night-hunting poachers had tangled with one of the sentries, likewise, any return fire should have come from civilian arms—deer rifles or shotguns, for instance, but not automatics.

Which, in turn, could mean only one thing: they were under attack.

Murphy had been expecting it. TV reports about the screw-up in Missouri had omitted any mention of The Path, but that could simply be a dodge, the Feds manipulating coverage, lulling their target into a sense of false security before they struck. It was one of the oldest tricks in the book.

Murphy was ready for them, though. He had begun to subtly fortify the compound from the moment it was occupied, turning a former Girl Scout camp into a base his soldiers could defend. Not that he cherished any thoughts of holding off the government indefinitely; that was a pipe dream, and had never been the plan. Rather, defense of the camp was meant to be a stall for time, a tactical delay that would permit any cult leaders in residence to escape before the trap inextricably closed.

As luck would have it, Ares was the only officer of any rank on site. The Two had left within an hour of the first CNN reports from Town and Country, Missouri, well before the St. Louis SWAT team entered the temple. By the time it was discovered that the raid had failed, The Two were safely hidden at a site unknown to the authorities.

Now all that Ares really had to think about was looking out for number one. Before he left, though, there was work to do.

More firing sounded from the west, and a sputter of shots from the north. Ares retraced his steps to the desk, where his computer monitor provided the only real light in the room. A half-dozen keystrokes were enough to start the classified files erasing themselves, a process that required no more than ninety seconds, and which, once begun, was irreversible. Nothing was lost, per se—the same material was backed up on other computers at three different sites—but the Feds would find nothing of value when they stormed the command post.

To be doubly sure, Ares took the five-gallon gasoline can that he kept beside his filing cabinet, uncapped it and tipped it over on its side. The fumes filled his nostrils, bringing instant tears to his eyes, but he ignored the momentary discomfort. He removed a highway flare from the top drawer of his desk, and, striking it into life he retreated through the doorway. When he tossed the flare into the center of the spreading gasoline pool, it exploded into searing, hungry flame.

Ares was backlit by the fire as he emerged from his CP into the compound now swarming with bodies, sidestepping the doorway, cautious with the silhouette despite the fact that no invaders had reached the compound proper, yet. Discipline was only effective if you maintained it consistently.

Ares scanned the camp for soldiers, his own men, ignoring the rank and file who ran this way and that, some of the women crying, while men shouted questions that no one could answer. His troops—Thor's Hammer—had trained for this eventuality before any other, getting strong on defense before they started working on offensive measures. This would be the test for him to see how well they understood their lessons and applied them to real life.

Except that Ares didn't mean to stick around and watch.

No coward, Ares knew he was essential to the effort that was underway, moving the world toward Armageddon in accordance with the prophecies that would, as they came true, insure the return of the Ancients. There was nothing he could do to help the movement from a jail cell or a grave.

Holding his compact MP-5 K submachine gun ready, Ares struck off toward the corner of the compound where the vehicles were kept. Feds would be covering the road, but he had other plans. If all went well, he would be through the hostile lines before the pigs knew what was happening.

If all *didn't* go well... He shrugged it off. In that case, Ares told himself, then he would take as many of the bastards with him as he could.

BOLAN HIT THE GROUND running, shrugging into the Galco shoulder rig and sheathing his Beretta, snatching up a lightweight jacket as he cleared the doorstep of his quarters. There was never much light in the compound after sundown, and the scattered floodlights had been switched off now, in accordance with the camp's emergency defense plan. "Civilian" members of the cult—meaning the bulk of them, nonmembers of the paramilitary wing—had been through certain drills, rehearsed sporadically, but the sound of close-range gunfire had a miraculous way of wiping such plans from the average mind.

As far as Bolan knew, there were about 150 cultists in the compound, fewer than two dozen of them armed members of Thor's Hammer. Close to half of the compound's inhabitants were out of their quarters, milling about, some running here and there, without direction. Some were shouting questions, all of which had so far gone unanswered. From the woods on two sides of the camp—now three—gunfire echoed through the night.

He took for granted that most of them would be swept up in the federal dragnet, a few of them wounded or killed if the fighting continued. Those caught without weapons or other evidence of criminal activity would soon be released from custody without charges. Some might respond with civil lawsuits for false arrest or some other charge, but none of that was Bolan's problem.

His main concern was getting out.

Granted, he had a job to do, a niche to fill in Dillon Murphy's defense plan, but Bolan wasn't about to fire on federal agents, nor was he prepared to let himself be captured in the raid, if there was any way on earth he could avoid it. Getting out was problematical, but it could be done.

And Murphy, he knew, would be one of the first to bail out.

It crossed his mind to look for the man, but the general confusion in the camp would make the search a losing proposition, damaging his chances of escape. Whatever Bolan chose to do, he had to do swiftly and decisively.

A runner came at Bolan from the shadows, rushing

blindly at him, Bolan dodging to his left a heartbeat short of collision. The man sped past him, panting like an overweight contestant in a marathon, and vanished in the shadows off to Bolan's right.

The soldier left the Beretta in its holster, swiftly working out the details of a plan to save himself. He took for granted that the raiders would be staked out on the only access road that served the compound, so he couldn't go that way. The motor pool had ATVs and off-road motorcycles, however, in addition to the standard pickup trucks and four-wheel-drives, and Bolan wondered if the extra speed would compensate for the attention engine noise and headlights would attract from any raiders coming through the woods.

He had his mind made up to chance it, when a flash grenade went off across the compound near the single women's quarters. It was bright enough to sting his eyes and loud enough to make his ears ring, even detonating in the open, and he knew it meant the raiders were within fifteen or twenty yards, at most.

His time was running out.

So be it.

Bolan turned and struck off through the darkness toward the compound's motor pool. If he was cut off there, he could attempt to navigate the hostile lines on foot, evade them in the dark, but he would try for speed first before staking his life on stealth.

He needed just a little time, but would he have it?

Bolan put the question out of mind and ran on through the dark, with sounds of battle closing in on every side.

CHAPTER TWO

Jeff Goines saw the shooter lurch back into view, his automatic rifle spitting ragged bolts of fire. The bullets zipped above his head like lethal insects out for blood, and Goines grimaced as he heard a cry of pain somewhere behind him, knowing the slugs had scored against some member of his team, despite the vests they wore.

Cursing, he stroked the trigger on his submachine gun, tracking with the muzzle, firing for effect. He didn't try to wound the rifleman or shoot the weapon from his hands, none of the crap that was standard fare in Hollywood productions. In a combat situation, when you had to shoot you shot to kill. There were no warning shots fired in the air to fall on innocent bystanders, and no trick shots meant to wing a target, leaving him alive but properly subdued. In mortal combat, if you shot a man and he survived, it either meant your aim was bad, or you were dealing with a hard case who could soak up punishment and still keep fighting back.

Or maybe it was pure dumb luck.

This time the guy on the receiving end of Goines's fire had used up all his luck. Full-metal-jacket Parabellum rounds stitched him from left to right across the chest and slammed him backward in his tracks. His index finger clenched around the automatic rifle's trigger as he fell, emptying the weapon's magazine, but those rounds were expended on the trees and sky above, no danger to Jeff Goines or his team.

"Report!" he snapped, still holding steady on the prostrate body of his enemy, alert to any other movement in the shadows. He could hear more firing now from other points around the camp, and had a grim impression of the whole thing coming down around him.

"I'm hit," Blair told him, speaking through clenched teeth.

"How bad?" Goines asked, eyes still focused into the hostile night in front of him.

"Left arm," Blair answered. "In and out. It missed the bone. I'm losing blood, though, and it hurts like hell."

A backward glance showed Achuff working on a tourniquet, between Blair's shoulder and the elbow. Jesus! If the brachial artery was severed—even nicked—Blair could bleed to death in a matter of minutes.

"How bad?" he asked.

A pencil flash winked on and off. "Can't say for sure," Achuff replied. "Could be arterial."

"All right, you take him back," Goines said, making up his mind at once. "Weaver and Danks, with me. Let's move!"

Nobody argued. They were trained to follow orders, even if those orders seemed to make no sense, or if their lives were placed in danger by a word from Goines. It was what the HRT commandos had signed on for, after all—the chance to see some action, above and beyond the call. Each member of the team knew this assignment—or the next one, or the next—could be his last. Goines could only hope that Blair would make it back all right, that he would live; but he couldn't allow the thought to dominate his mind, when he had deadly work to do.

The three men moved through the trees, the sounds of battle drawing closer by the moment. Goines could smell gunsmoke now, not only from his brief exchange with the cult sentry, but from other firing, somewhere up ahead. He heard a flash-bang detonate, its sharp report buffered by trees and distance. Goines took heart from the sound, presuming that his comrades from the FBI and ATF had closed to pitching distance with the enemy.

How many guns against them remained? That question was among the most important of the operation, and he had no answer. Going in, the agents had been told there were between 150 and 200 cultists in the compound, with an unknown "fraction" of that number armed and dangerous. In concrete terms, that meant the raiders were outnumbered three or four to one, and they had no idea, in fact, how many of their enemies were packing guns and grenades. Ten percent would mean fifteen to twenty armed defenders in the camp; twenty percent would mean thirty to forty, and so on. All Goines knew, at the moment, was that he was in a fight for his life, and the strength of his team had already been cut by forty percent.

He had no choice but to proceed. It was the job they paid him for, but there was more to it than that. Goines believed in what he did, enforcing laws, holding the line against a world of savages that preyed on helpless citizens.

No matter what the cost.

Ahead of him, he saw the buildings of the compound, shadow figures rushing here and there, some muzzle-flashes winking on the fringes of the action.

"Heads up, men," he told the two remaining members of his team. "We're going in!"

THE CAMP COMMAND POST was in flames. Bolan assumed that Dillon Murphy set the fire himself, since it didn't appear that any of the raiders were close enough, yet, to be lobbing incendiaries.

Whatever its cause, the fire cast an eerie light on the chaotic scene in the compound. Frightened runners pursued—or were pursued by—long, grotesque shadows, monstrous distortions of themselves. Faces blushed red and orange by firelight, barely recognizable as people Bolan had communed with on a daily basis over several weeks.

He felt regret that most of them were caught up in the middle of such chaos, facing sudden danger that they barely understood, despite their so-called preparations for "The Final Days." Most of them were deluded seekers after cosmic truth, praying for peace of mind—a chance to look outside themselves, their daily grind of ordinary problems and believe in something greater, some transcendent meaning in the universe. They had been caught up in a current of fanaticism, swept along until they reached the present point, and now, without a moment's warning, they had all been cast adrift.

Most of them would survive, though, Bolan told himself. The federal raiders would be pros, well trained—as well as anyone could be, in any case—to deal with such chaotic situations. As for soldiers of The Path, his fellow members of Thor's Hammer, those who stood and fought would have to take their chances. Some might slip away in the confusion; others, Bolan could have bet the farm, would die this night—if they weren't, in fact, already dead.

A sudden rattle of automatic weapons' fire from his left drew Bolan's attention. He could make out muzzle-flashes at the tree line, darting shadow-shapes that might be raiders or defenders. In a different situation, Bolan would have run to join the battle, but he faced a deadly lose-lose situation now, if he allowed himself to get involved. He wouldn't fire on the officers, nor could he risk his cover by attempting to assist them—an assistance they would never recognize, in any case.

The best thing—hell, the only thing—for him to do was get away as quickly and as quietly as possible.

Bolan was halfway to the motor pool when someone started shooting at him. His first warning was the sharp, insectile whine of bullets zipping past his face. He hit the deck and rolled immediately to his right, seeking the shadows of the nearest bungalow, where he wouldn't be silhouetted in the firelight.

He scanned the compound, spotting muzzle-flashes here and there, but he spotted nothing in the nature of an immediate, personal threat.

Stray rounds? Coincidence?

It was a possibility, of course, and while he didn't like the feeling of uncertainty, Bolan refused to let himself be pinned down by a phantom. After thirty seconds passed with no incoming fire, he wriggled backward deeper into shadow, rising from his prone position only when he had the bungalow between himself and any unseen shooter who might still be waiting for him to appear.

It was a brief detour, nothing more.

One key to living through a combat situation was the gift of flexibility. It meant a great deal more than simply watching for the unexpected. Anyone could stay alert, given life-or-death alternatives, but some still missed the point of going with the flow in battle, never learned the trick of changing tactics in a heartbeat to accommodate new, unexpected threats. You didn't use a hammer on mosquitoes, but it always paid to keep the hammer handy—just in case a giant bird spider turned up.

Bolan continued toward the motor pool behind the bungalows, darting across the firelit open spaces in between. He drew no fire from the direction of the compound proper, but he had to stay alert to the threat of federal raiders coming through the woods. In Bolan, they would only see a fugitive intent on breaking through their lines, and while they probably wouldn't cut loose with deadly fire on sight, he had no intention of submitting to arrest if he could help it.

He reached the last building in line before the compound's motor pool and hesitated in the midnight shadows there. Behind him, on the fringes of the camp the sounds of gunfire had been picking up. With fewer than two dozen armed defenders in the camp, the increased firing told him that the Feds were closer now. There was a chance their field commander had committed his reserves to smother armed resistance in the camp.

Whatever, Bolan knew that he was running dangerously short of time. He edged around the corner of the bungalow, face toward the motor pool, and froze again, spotting another figure there ahead of him.

It seemed to be a man, judging primarily from size and bearing, since the cult's unisex fashion and haircuts made gender difficult to pick out from a distance. This figure—this *man*—was bending over one of the camp's four dirt bikes, checking the fuel tank, perhaps. When he had satisfied himself, he cleared the bike's kickstand and wheeled the bike out from under the long, common roof that shielded vehicles from rain and snow. He glanced toward the compound and the sound of guns before he turned his chosen mode of transportation toward the dark tree line, guiding the bike with both hands on the handlebar grips.

The tall man's face was turned in the direction of the firelight for only a moment, but it was enough.

Shadows and all, Bolan immediately recognized the cult's enforcer, Dillon Murphy.

The chief was bailing out, and who could blame him?

Bolan only wished that he would hurry up and clear the motor pool to give the Executioner a chance.

ARES RELAXED A LITTLE, as he slipped around the east end of the motor pool, an open shed-type structure sixty feet in length, that sheltered several types of vehicles. It made fair cover for him now, as he pushed the Honda off-road motorcycle toward the tree line. He hadn't switched on the engine or the headlight yet, intent on putting ground between himself and his pursuers first.

He still had no idea how many raiders were involved in the attack, how well they were positioned to surround the camp. The first thing that was always done, in any situation of the kind, was to cover the obvious exits—doors and downstairs windows, if the target was a building; roads and well-known trails, in any kind of rural situation. That was basic common sense, and Ares had a hunch that he could beat his enemies at this game, if he put his mind to it, showing audacity enough to take them by surprise.

But first, of course, he had to clear the obvious perimeter of the attack.

He walked the bike into the forest, balancing haste and caution, breathing through clenched teeth as he kept himself alert to any sound that would betray the presence of an enemy. If he was braced by federal officers before he got the Honda up and running, he would have to use his submachine gun, and to hell with stealth. Ares was hoping he could manage to avoid a confrontation, though, since any showdown in the forest would reduce—if not eliminate—his odds of breaking out.

An old familiar couplet came to mind, about the man who runs away and lives to fight another day. Ares wasn't embarrassed by his choice, the action he was taking. No one who had ever really known him would consider him a coward. He wasn't afraid to fight or die—particularly for the cause that had become his life—but neither was he hot to simply throw his life away for nothing, when he knew it could be put to better use another time, another place.

There was a world of difference, he quickly learned, between walking through the woods and pushing a motorcycle, all the while watching for unseen enemies. The Honda wasn't all that hard to handle, but it still took muscle to propel it over rugged ground through darkness, by brute force alone. Whatever problems normally arose from trying to walk quietly by night, were multiplied tenfold as Ares pushed and manhandled the dirt bike over rocks and ridges, through dense underbrush, with ferns and thorny bushes grabbing at him as he passed.

The Feds were bound to hear him if he passed too close. His only hope lay in a skirmish line spread thin, with raiders struggling over unfamiliar ground. Ares himself wasn't a woodsman, in the sense that he spent any great amount of time communing with the forest, but he knew his way around this property, had checked out the escape routes for himself against the time when an emergency like this one might arise. He knew where he was going, more or less, though he had never run the course in darkness under hostile fire.

It would take luck as well as skill, he realized, to make it through the dragnet in one piece.

Three times along the way, he froze with one hand on his weapon and the other on the bike, waiting for unknown sounds to be repeated or explained. The voices that he heard on one occasion turned out to be real enough, but they were carried to him on a night breeze, from a point off to his right. As he listened, Ares judged the sounds were coming from a point some fifty yards or more away, the distance making shouts sound more like muffled whispers to his ears. Twice more, he hesitated at the sounds of something's crashing progress through the woods: once, he identified the runner as a panicked white-tailed deer; the second noise wasn't explained, but as no human enemies appeared, Ares proceeded cautiously along his way.

With every yard he covered, the commotion from the compound faded, growing more remote. The sounds of gunfire hadn't slackened much, as yet, but Ares gained confidence from distance, content in the knowledge that his soldiers were holding the line, distracting the enemy who might otherwise be tracking him.

When he had covered something like a quarter of a mile, Ares decided it was safe for him to start the motorcycle's engine. Flicking on the Honda's headlight, he settled on the vinyl-covered seat and shifted into gear.

The headlight was a necessary evil. It would pinpoint his position for the enemy, if anyone was watching, but he dared not risk a headlong race through darkness, great trees pressing close on every side, with logs and jagged stones a constant hazard. He would wreck the bike before he made a hundred yards, and maybe break his neck while he was at it. That was wholly unacceptable to Ares; he would rather take the risk of being spotted by his enemies too late, outrunning them on his machine, than risk a smash-up in the dark.

A voice called out from somewhere to his right, still far away, as Ares aimed the bike downhill and pushed off with one foot, simultaneously twisting the throttle. Low-hanging branches whipped at his face, making him regret the omission of goggles from his list of emergency flight equipment, but there was nothing to be done about it now. He squinted, hunched his shoulders and leaned forward with his elbows bent, like a speed racer bending over the handlebars. In fact he wasn't breaking any kind of record; Ares didn't risk a glance at the speedometer, but he guessed that he was traveling at something less than forty miles per hour. Still, the combination of the downhill slope, the darkness and the apprehension that had tied his stomach into knots made him feel like he was rushing toward a brick wall in a rocket sled.

A few more minutes, Ares thought. He needed

only five more minutes, maybe ten. Once he had reached the old logging road that was his destination, he could circle back to reach the highway, well removed from any federal roadblocks.

He could make it yet, unless he crashed and burned. In which case, he decided, it would make no difference after all.

Head down, tears streaming from his burning eyes, he rolled on through the darkness toward escape and freedom.

Toward the next phase of his war.

BOLAN EMERGED FROM COVER after Murphy disappeared, giving the cult enforcer time to reach the tree line with his motorcycle. It wasn't part of Bolan's plan to chase the fugitive right now. Assuming he caught up with Murphy in the darkness, it would only bring further suspicion upon himself for bailing out, instead of standing fast at his assigned position and resisting to the bitter end. This way, if he was able to escape the dragnet, he could always regroup with the cult another time, explain his breakout from the compound in more acceptable terms. It would be dicey, even so, considering his near-miss in Missouri, but at least he had a chance to sell the story. On the other hand, if Ares caught him running from the battle prematurely, well, his ass was grass.

A motorcycle still seemed like the way to go, for all of that, and as he started for the motor pool, Bolan spotted black-clad warriors closing on the long shed from the other side. He didn't need to see their backs, the "FBI" or "ATF" that would be stenciled there, to know exactly who they were. Cult sentries at the compound dressed in camouflage fatigues and didn't wear flak jackets or helmets, while the raiders came equipped with both.

He gave up on the motor pool at once. There was an outside chance that he could grab a bike and make it to the trees, but such a move would court disaster, risk a shooting confrontation with the Feds that Bolan was determined to avoid. Cut off from any motor vehicles, he retreated into shadow, turned back toward the tree line and in another moment vanished from the camp.

He had drawn sentry duty twice a week while staying at the Boulder compound, and he was familiar with the forest in at least a general sense. He knew the basic contours of terrain, and could have sketched a rough map of the area from memory. He knew the unpaved access road, and felt assured that he could find the two-lane county highway. As far as slipping through the federal lines, that would depend as much on hostile numbers and dispersal as it did on Bolan's skill.

He didn't draw his pistol as he struck off through the trees. If there were G-men waiting for him in the dark, he wouldn't use the gun, regardless; on the other hand, if he should meet a "brother" cultist, any shots he fired would simply draw the hunters to him.

He would have to take his chances either way.

He had proceeded perhaps 150 yards when he heard the muffled sound of voices dead ahead. Bolan froze in his tracks, fixed on the sound, and made out two men coming toward him on a rough collision course.

What should he do? There was a chance that he could dodge them in the dark, but any move he made right then was perilous, the slightest noise sufficient to betray him if the hunters were alert. Another course of action was to hide as best he could and hope they passed him by. That, too, was dangerous, since it meant he had to find a hiding place: more furtive movement, more prospective noise.

There was a third alternative, and Bolan weighed the odds before deciding that it was the only way to go.

He stepped behind a looming tree trunk, standing with his back against the rough bark, waiting. In another moment, cautious footsteps made their way around his left side. Two men, by the sound of it, although he knew he could be wrong.

The black-clad agents were about to pass him when Bolan made his move. There were, in fact, only the two of them, and he had no idea if they were separated from their fellows, somehow, or if the assault was being carried out by two-man teams. It made no difference now, when all that mattered was his speed, precision and the force behind his blows.

The first strike was an elbow to the nearest G-man's face. It came in from his blind side, slammed into his cheek below one eye and rocked him on his heels. Before the agent could so much as gasp a warning, Bolan had a firm grip on his submachine gun, twisting sharply, letting physics and anatomy take over, disarming the stunned man in black.

That done, he swung the SMG butt-first into the reeling agent's face. A breathless grunt and crunch of cartilage rewarded Bolan's move, but he ignored the tumbling form, already focused on the second man, intent on nailing him before he had a chance to use his weapon.

It was close, with the muzzle of a riot shotgun swinging toward his chest. No way he could survive a charge of buckshot at that range, but Bolan beat the clock, another short chop with the liberated stutter gun against the second G-man's clavicle effectively disarming him. The agent gave a startled bleat of pain, but it was cut off instantly, as Bolan struck a second time, bare-knuckled, and the guy went down.

He checked the first man briefly, found a steady pulse, and left the agents there to sleep it off. They would survive and spend some time with doctors, doubtless suffer some embarrassment, but he had kept his private vow to take no lawman's life.

And in the process, Bolan realized, he had slipped through the hostile lines.

Now all he had to do was reach the highway, thumb a ride or walk back down to Boulder, find himself another set of wheels and make fresh contact with the cult.

But before he hooked up with The Path again, he had to get in touch with Hal Brognola.

Carrying the submachine gun underneath one arm,

he moved off through the darkness, letting his built-in direction finder take him to the highway.

He would take it one step at a time.

"HOW MANY CASUALTIES?" Brognola asked. His voice was grim, matching the expression on his face.

"We've got three people hit," Greg Underwager told him, "but they're stable, nothing serious. Two others are missing, and I won't know what the hell that means until we find them."

"What about the other side?"

"Four dead we're sure of," Underwager reported, "plus six or seven minor wounds. We're working on a head count now. Of course, we don't know how many were in the camp to start with. Working out how many got away may take some time."

"It might take forever," said Tom Wakefield, scowling from the sidelines. "What I'm hearing, so far, is we've got a clean miss on the brass."

"We didn't know if they were here to start with," Underwager replied. "We've got a watch on alternate locations."

"Right," Brognola said. "They're bound to show up now, maybe take out an ad in *USA Today*."

"Now, just a minute, Mr.—"

"I'll need access to the subjects you arrested," Brognola said, cutting off Underwager.

"Arrested, or detained?" Wakefield asked, speaking for the first time.

"Both. Whatever. Set it up, ASAP."

Underwager frowned at that. "I don't know—"

"What? You mean to say there's something *else* you don't know?"

Underwager's face flushed brilliant crimson, but he bit off any smart replies that came to mind and settled for a simple, "No, sir."

"Good," Brognola said. "It won't take long."

"Perhaps," Wakefield began, "if we—"

"No, thanks. I won't need any help. I'll need to see the dead ones, too," he added, as a grisly afterthought.

"The dead—"

"Just do it!" Brognola snapped, turning on his heel and leaving them to glare at his retreating back.

The man from Washington was in a foul mood, and he didn't care who knew it. Part of it was missing Galen Locke and Helen Braun, along with their gorilla, Dillon Murphy. Most of it, however, was the simple, galling fact that he had no idea where Bolan was and had missed the single phone call from his old friend since the bloody foul-up in Missouri. There had been a cryptic message on the answering machine that served his private line, Bolan's anonymous voice reporting that he was on his way back to "that place in the mountains, out west." The big Fed had assumed he meant the Boulder compound; it had seemed to be the only logical conclusion.

Brognola tried to pull in the reins on his personal anxiety, but calm eluded him. He was afraid that Bolan might be one of those already zipped in body bags, en route to Denver's morgue. If he was still alive, but wearing handcuffs, Brognola could doubtless manage to finagle his release by hook or crook, but what would then become of Bolan's mission to destroy the cult? Could he rejoin them, after having been in custody? Had all their effort been in vain?

Brognola yearned for a cigar and settled for a stick of gum instead. It didn't do the trick, and he was scowling, grumbling to himself as he approached his borrowed federal vehicle. He slid into the driver's seat and fumbled the ignition key into its slot.

The best scenario that he could hope for now, Brognola realized, would be if Bolan didn't show up anywhere among the dead or those in jail. In that case, the big Fed would know that he was still at large, that he had slithered through the net somehow, assuming he was even at the compound when the raid went down, but it was still no guarantee of Bolan's safety. There would be more raids, more roundups executed by the Feds. And in the meantime, thought Brognola, every moment Bolan spent inside the cult could spell disaster, bring him that much closer to an unexpected death sentence.

And there was nothing Hal could do to help him.

That much, at least, brought them back to business as usual in the hellgrounds.

CHAPTER THREE

Arizona

Regrouping with the cult turned out to be a relatively simple matter after all. Each member of Thor's Hammer had a shortlist of telephone numbers, memorized for use in the event of an emergency. One was a toll-free 888 number, while the other two were pay-as-you-go locals—one with a San Diego area code, the other in Milwaukee—that cult commandos were instructed to call collect if they found themselves short of coins. Bolan assumed all three telephones utilized cutouts to protect the flunkies on duty, but the technical arrangements were of no concern to him, as long as they worked.

In fact he got through on his first attempt with the toll-free number—no great surprise, all things considered, if the other members of the small team at the Boulder compound were in custody or dead. He used the password he had memorized—star child—and listened briefly to a gruff voice that could just as easily have been a man or woman. Bolan guessed the voice was altered with some manner of security device, but once again, he didn't care.

The robot voice directed him to Sawmill, Arizona, in the northeast corner of the state, roughly two miles from the New Mexico border. Bolan rented a non-descript sedan in Boulder and drove west from there on Interstate 70, leaving Colorado behind a few hours later, crossing over into Utah. At Crescent, in Grand County, Bolan stopped for gasoline and a meal of burgers at a drive-through before he aimed the rental south on U.S. Highway 191. That road would carry him 150 miles through towns like Moab, Monticello, Blanding, Mexican Water, Round Rock and Many Farms. At Chinle, in Apache County, Arizona, Bolan left the main highway and followed his road map for another twenty-five miles, rolling through majestic red-rock desert, until he reached the little town of Sawmill.

It had probably been named for its main feature, once upon a time, but there was nothing to suggest a major logging industry—or any other source of wealth—today. A faded highway sign claimed 400 residents for Sawmill, but fewer than twenty were visible as Bolan drove through town, scanning faded storefronts with painted-over windows, the For Rent or Lease signs sun-bleached and forlorn, attracting only flies and ants, their desiccated corpses strewed on dusty windowsills.

Bolan's instructions called for him to check in at a gun shop called the Sawmill Sporting Center. He parked out front and scanned the street for enemies, marking a solitary stranger two blocks west, slumped on a bench that would have been a bus stop, if there was a bus in town. The man wore shades below a droopy cowboy hat, and might have been unconscious—even dead—for all the life that he displayed.

The Sawmill Sporting Center didn't look too sporty, nor did it appear to be the center of anything. Three other shops on that side of the street were vacant, whitewashed windows partially blocking their failure from the outside world. Bolan pushed through the gun shop's door, a tarnished cowbell mounted overhead producing one listless *clank* as he entered.

The shop was all he had expected from a town like Sawmill: dust and faded advertising posters on the wall, their edges frayed and curled. A glass display case facing the door contained a sparse array of knives and pistols, several fishing reels, a lonely pair of vintage Zeiss binoculars. A gun rack mounted on the wall behind the counter boasted something like a dozen shotguns and rifles, several of the latter preban semiautomatics of the military style. A freestanding book rack to the left of the doorway featured dated volumes on hunting, fishing and camping.

The man behind the counter looked as tired and dusty as his stock. What little hair he had was dirty gray, a fringe above his ears; the two-day stubble on his cheeks and throat was white. Dark pouches underneath his eyes and flabby jowls gave him the general appearance of a basset hound. His flannel shirt and blue jeans had been washed so often that they looked like something from a bowery thrift store. He was smoking an unfiltered cigarette, and left it in his mouth as he addressed the new arrival in his shop.

"He'p you?" the old man asked.

Bolan responded with the code phrase that he had been given on the telephone. "I'm hoping you might have a Peacemaker in stock."

The old man blinked at him and frowned. "No Peacemakers today," he said. "Might know where you can get one, though. I'll have to make some calls."

"I'll wait," Bolan said, turning to the rack of books, perusing titles, while the old man shuffled through a doorway leading to a back room. The muffled sound of a one-sided conversation reached his ears, but he couldn't make out the words. A moment later, the proprietor returned.

"I can't get what you want, myse'f," the old man said. "But here's where you can find it." As he spoke, he slid a scrap of notepaper across the countertop, then reeled his hand back in and stowed it in a pocket of his blue jeans.

Bolan crossed the small shop to retrieve the note. He had it in his hand before the old man spoke again.

"Can't take it with you," he remarked. "Man likes 'is privacy, I reckon. Have to mem'rize that, you will."

It wasn't difficult. There was no address, just a rough map drawn in blue ink, lines that represented highways marked with names or numbers. Bolan's destination was a small blue *X*.

"You get there, ask for Smith," the old man said. One corner of the narrow gash that served him as a mouth twitched upward, something like a smirk.

Smith, Bolan thought, as he retreated to the sun-baked sidewalk. That was original.

The sketchy map directed Bolan west of town, a left turn on the first road he encountered, after crossing disused railroad tracks, then left again—this time on gravel—when he met a sign for Baker Station Road, pockmarked with rusty bullet holes.

The "road" barely deserved its name, and Bolan took his time, hearing loose gravel rattle against the undercarriage of his rented car. He would have felt more comfortable in a four-wheel drive, but there was nothing he could do about it now.

The gravel track dead-ended at the doorstep of a mobile home that should have been condemned ten years ago, squatting approximately where the *X* had been located on the old man's map. There was no name or number on the mobile home, nothing that would identify the occupant.

The trailer's only door swung open as Bolan emerged from his vehicle. A buzz-cut, twenty-something man emerged, his baggy clothes and track shoes standard issue for The Path.

"You're Smith?" Bolan asked.

"Close enough," the other said. "You're Mike Belasko?"

"Right."

"Stay where you are," the cultist said, leaving the trailer's door ajar as he moved toward the car. "We need to take a ride."

ARES WAS STEAMING. He had made it through the woods and out with nothing more than minor cuts and scrapes, one eye bloodshot and achy from a pine bough that had whipped across his face before he saw it coming. Merthiolate was painted on his facial wounds, and while the sting of it had long-since faded, Ares looked as if he had the world's worst case of measles.

None of that had worked him up into his present state, however. It had been the call relayed from Nimrod, the report that he would soon be face-to-face with a survivor of the Boulder raid, that made him wonder what in hell was going on. How had Nimrod wriggled through the federal net? More to the point, why had he left the compound when he had a duty to remain and fight?

The hell of it was waiting for an answer, but the wait wouldn't be long now. Ares checked his watch against the wall clock in the Flagstaff safehouse. Anytime, now, he would have a chance to ask those questions for himself.

A little time, at least, before they had to go.

As if in answer to his thoughts, he heard a car pull up outside. Two of his Arizona soldiers moved to intercept the new arrivals, Ares staying where he was. He stopped his restless pacing in the makeshift office that he occupied, stood facing toward the open doorway.

Waiting.

Moments later, two young soldiers armed with automatic rifles ushered Bolan in. One of them had a pistol tucked into his belt. He tapped it with an index finger, nodding toward Bolan, and said, "He's clean."

"All right," Ares said. "Leave us. Close the door."

When it was just the two of them, Ares faced Bolan squarely. "So," he said, "what brings you here?"

"Your man," Bolan replied. "I got directions from the contact number that you had us memorize. He did the rest."

"I mean, why aren't you still in Boulder?"

"Why aren't you?"

Ares could feel his hackles rising. "I suggest that you remember who you're talking to."

"I'm not forgetting anything," Bolan replied, his voice and gaze rock-steady.

"So? I'm waiting," Ares prodded him.

"Okay. The shit was coming down before I cleared my quarters. By the time I got to my station, it was obviously too late for a save. I started looking out for number one."

"In other words, you ran away."

"Damn right. Once I found out you were gone—"

"Who told you that?" Ares snapped, interrupting him.

"One of the troops," Bolan said with a shrug. "I'm not sure if I even knew his name. What difference does it make?"

Ares responded with a question of his own. "What did he say?"

"He told me you jumped on a dirt bike and took off. It sounded like a good idea to me."

"That's how you got away?" Ares asked.

Bolan frowned and shook his head. "I didn't get

the chance. Some kind of SWAT team took the motor pool before I got there, so I made it out on foot."

"To Boulder?"

"Right. I called the contact number when I got to town, and here I am."

"Your car?" Ares asked, nodding vaguely toward the yard out front.

"A rental in a phony name," Nimrod replied.

"You had ID?"

"The Boy Scouts taught me I should always be prepared."

The story added up, as far as Ares could determine. It might also be a lie, but there was no way he could check it out in detail, short of hooking Nimrod to a polygraph, and there was simply no time to arrange that sort of thing. Other arrangements had been made, and he was on the clock.

He eased up on the frown that had been carving furrows in his face. "It's lucky that you showed up when you did."

"How's that?" the soldier asked, belatedly remembering to add the "sir."

"I've got a date to meet some people later this evening," Ares told him. "If it all works out, we may be able to make up for that embarrassment we suffered in Missouri. You'll be coming with me."

"What's the story, sir?"

"Are you familiar with the Peacekeeper Militia?" Ares asked.

"It doesn't ring a bell," Bolan replied. "You've got so-called militias all over the map these days.

Most of them drill on weekends, shoot some targets and complain about the Jews."

"That covers most of them, all right," Ares agreed. "The Peacekeeper Militia is a bit more...shall we say...aggressive than the competition."

"Meaning?" Bolan asked.

"Meaning they've taken certain actions in the past," Ares replied. "They're not in tune with us, of course. But there's a possibility that we may find a common cause."

"When is the meeting, sir?"

"A few more hours," Ares told him. "After sundown. You've got time to catch a shower, change your clothes, eat something. We'll be driving to the meet out in the country. If we leave at five o'clock, we should have ample time."

"Yes, sir."

"That's all, for now," Ares said. "You're dismissed."

He watched the soldier go and wondered if he was a fool for taking Nimrod back. He wasn't fully satisfied with the report of Nimrod's near miss back in Boulder, but if *he* had managed to escape, why shouldn't someone else? What other explanation was there, after all, for Nimrod's presence? He had definitely been in camp, just back from the abortive action in Missouri, when the shit came down.

Ares had been intent on punishing the soldier for abandoning his post and fleeing under fire, but his resolve had weakened after Nimrod mentioned hearing of his own escape from Boulder. It shouldn't have been a problem—Ares knew damn well he had every right in the world to pull rank and save himself for later service to the Ancients—but it still made him feel awkward, almost embarrassed, somehow.

And besides, the story that Nimrod had told him could well be true, after all. Jarred awake by the sounds of gunfire and stun grenades, there was at least a fifty-fifty chance the man had been disoriented, arriving too late on the scene to make any difference in the outcome. As if there had been any doubt, Ares thought. Why shouldn't Nimrod save himself?

And, yet...

Any lingering doubts he might have about Nimrod's courage or devotion to The Path could be answered by watching the soldier's performance on the new mission. It had been on hold for weeks, a "possible," approved by The Two but held in abeyance while they waited to see how the raid in Missouri went down. With that pathetic failure—and now, with the roundup in Boulder—Ares was convinced they needed a victory, and soon, to boost morale and get the program back on track.

It was his decision, with The Two in hiding, and he was determined to proceed. Nimrod would be a part of it, and if he failed...

Ares believed that he would soon know what the soldier was made of, either way. And if the new guy didn't pass the test, his execution would become another training exercise.

Ares was pleased with his decision.

Nothing ever went to waste.

VERN PACKER SPIT a stream of brown tobacco juice into the sand and watched the headlights coming toward him, still at least a half-mile off, across the desert flats. His choice of meeting places, in the looming shadow of the Coconino Plateau, had been no accident, any more than the decision to meet after dark. Heat aside, the night made it that much easier to see his so-called friends—and any enemies—approaching from a distance, while the desert wasteland left no place for them to hide.

Not that an ambush was impossible, of course. As founder and commander of the Peacekeeper Militia, Packer reckoned he knew everything there was to know about black helicopters, covert listening devices and the microwave devices used by agents of the federal government to addle brains and keep the population stewing over bullshit, while the more important matters went over their heads. He even knew about the ultrasecret earthquake machine, developed in conjunction with Russian-expatriate scientists. It could level whole cities, from what Packer understood, but there was nothing to fall on him, out here in the middle of nowhere. The bastards could shake, rattle and roll until Phoenix lay in ruins, and wouldn't make a damn bit of difference to Packer.

"Ready, men!"

He heard the clacking of weapons being primed, as those behind him took their places. Packer knew he had a high-pitched, childish voice, but if he took his time and worked out what he had to say, he could produce an almost normal pitch. The last man who had dared to laugh in Packer's face, right there in front of God and everybody, had suffered an untimely, fatal accident.

Two vehicles approached across the flats, running side by side where the land was smooth and clear enough for the second car to go off-road. Packer was edgy, standing in the high beams of their headlights, but his soldiers had the two cars covered. At the first sign of a threat from either vehicle, both would be riddled by automatic weapons fire.

Packer relaxed his face muscles, opening his eyes a trifle wider, as the headlights were switched off. Doors opened on both of the newly arrived cars, and Packer counted seven heads as the passengers climbed out.

No problem, the militia leader thought. He had eight men himself, their weapons trained on the cars in a rough semicircle. His visitors had come down to two simple choices: they could deal, or they could die.

Packer recognized the cultist known as Ares. It was weird, he thought, the way these suckers took the names of stars or characters from ancient myths. Packer had nearly laughed at them, the first time; then, he had recalled the five or six years he'd spent as a member of the Ku Klux Klan, where everybody called each other kleagle, kligrap, kludd—some crazy shit like that. He didn't feel like laughing at the space folks anymore, as long as they could help him carry out his latest plan. If they decided not to help him, he would scratch them off the list and look for someone else.

But if the bastards tried to mess with Packer's plans, get in the way…

"Good evening, Colonel," Ares said, as he approached the lineup of militia vehicles, with two men flanking him. Packer knew one of them by sight from their last meeting, but the other one was new. The new man had a grim, no-nonsense look about him, and was carrying some kind of side arm underneath his windbreaker.

No matter. If the shit went down, he'd never have a chance to draw and fire.

Packer shook hands with Ares, and the cultist said, "You brought enough guns with you, Vern."

"I always do, son. Are you ready to talk business?"

Ares glanced around him, at the others. "Can we take a walk?"

"Suits me."

"You don't mind if my associates accompany us?"

"No sweat off my ass," Packer said, and snapped his fingers at a gunner standing near. The soldier fell in step behind them, with his AK-47, as they moved beyond the vehicles and started off across the moonlit desert.

"So," Packer said, when they had covered close to fifty yards, "what's on your mind?"

"I've thought about that plan of yours, and talked it over with The Two," Ares said.

Packer nearly laughed at that one, too, until he thought about the little runt who used to call himself "grand dragon" of the Arizona Klan, reporting back to an "imperial wizard" somewhere in Tennessee. Packer had quit the Klan for good after the wizard was arrested down in Chattanooga for molesting little boys. Last time he heard, the dragon had been tending bar in Bullhead City.

"And?" he prompted.

"We want to help you," Ares told him. "Tell me what you need."

Packer was on the verge of smiling, but he bit his tongue. The Peacekeeper Militia had been short of cash and arms from the beginning, and he needed all the help that he could get, but Packer also realized that there was no such thing as a free lunch. Whatever he accepted from The Path, it would come with a price tag attached. Whatever deal he made with Ares would be give and take.

"We're always short of cash," Packer told him honestly, "and various supplies."

"You've checked out the target?"

"Six ways from Sunday," Packer told him. "It'll be a wake-up call, all right."

"The preparations?" Ares asked.

"Waiting on you. There's no deadline. Damn thing ain't going anywhere. I didn't want to go without you, if you're coming in on it."

"We're in," Ares assured him. "How much money will you need?"

Packer had been waiting for the question, had the figures worked out to precision in his head. And he had tacked on a modest profit, to make the operation worth his while. Why not?

"Ten thousand ought to cover it," he said.

"Ten thousand," Ares repeated. "That shouldn't be a problem."

Packer had expected him to haggle at the very least—maybe laugh in his face and tell him he was dreaming. It wouldn't have been the first time a prospective sponsor of the militia balked at parting with some hard-earned, badly needed cash. If all the sunshine patriots Packer knew had opened up their wallets nice and wide, the Jew-run government in Washington, D.C., would lie in smoking ruins now, and real Americans would have their country back in strong, white hands.

"There is one thing, though," Ares added.

"One thing?"

"I'd appreciate it very much," Ares said, "if a couple of my people could assist you on this project. It would help them with their training, add new skills."

Packer blinked at him, surprised. "That's it? You just want two men on the job?"

"That's all."

"Hey, no problem," Packer said, relieved. "Who did you have in mind?"

"These two," Ares said, with a nod in the direction of his silent shadows. "That all right?"

"Suits me."

"When can you start?" the cultist asked.

"As soon as we have cash in hand. We'll need a day or two to set things up, put it together. Call it Monday, at the latest."

"Monday," Ares said, as if repeating it would make it true. "Sounds good to me."

"About the money..."

"Let's head back," the cultist stated. "I've got it in the car."

Goddammit! Packer could have kicked himself. If Ares had the money with him, and he had agreed to ten grand without batting an eye, it could only mean he had more in the car. Maybe much more.

It crossed Packer's mind to simply take the cash by force and have his gunners dump this lot somewhere, but that would only make things worse, bring lawmen sniffing all around the neighborhood if someone found the bodies. And for what? Packer had a profit coming to him as it was, but he was more concerned about the mission. When they pulled it off, his little wake-up call would do a damn sight more than wake up the Jewboys in Washington.

It would, Packer assured himself, be the beginning of the end. And when the smoke cleared, when histories of the Second American Revolution were written, Vern Packer's name would rank beside Washington, Jefferson and Adams in the holy honor roll.

So what if people had to die before that happened? He was in the middle of a war, lamentably unrecognized by most Americans, but they would recognize it soon enough. And they would thank him afterward.

At least, the ones who managed to survive.

BOLAN STOOD WATCHING while the cash changed hands. Ares removed it from a duffel bag that still looked fairly heavy when he tossed it back into the car. Ten thousand dollars wasn't all that much, in concrete terms, but it was seemingly a fortune to the leader of the militia.

Bolan still had no clear fix on what the mission was to be, the object of desire that Packer termed his "wake-up call." He would be finding out, though, and his soldier's instinct told him it wouldn't take long.

Murphy's suggestion that he join the militia team, along with a companion known as Canis in the cult, had been arranged before they left the Flagstaff safe-house. Bolan had agreed at once to Murphy's plan, for two distinct and separate reasons. First, he knew that any effort to avoid the job so soon after "abandoning" his post in Boulder would have raised intense suspicion, jeopardizing Bolan's place within Thor's Hammer and the cult at large. Second—and more compelling—was the thought that if he played along, he might devise a way to contact Brognola, or even find out where The Two had gone to ground.

Once that was done, he would be that much closer to the end.

Bolan watched Murphy and the others drive away, leaving him and Canis with the small group of militia troops. Vern Packer waited for the taillights to recede before he spit tobacco juice, addressing Bolan and his comrade in a voice that sounded like a twelve-year-old's.

"You boys are with us for a while, I guess."

"Looks like," Bolan replied.

"Experience?" Packer asked.

"Army Rangers," Bolan said. "We had a difference of opinion. Here I am."

"You know some demolitions, then," Packer stated.

"I've handled my share."

"How 'bout you?" the militia boss asked Canis.

"I'm checked out."

"Checked out." The tone of Packer's voice and the expression on his face showed his disdain for any preparation Canis might have had within the cult. "So, how's your gardening?" he asked.

"I don't know what you mean," Canis said.

Packer turned to Bolan. "Right. Do *you* know what I mean?"

"I wouldn't be surprised," Bolan said. It was still a guess, but he was getting there.

"So, share," the squeaky voice demanded.

"Would it be a fertilizer bomb, by any chance?"

Packer spit out another stream of murky juice. "The spaceman shoots and scores," he said. "The Oklahoma City special is exactly what I got in mind, except we won't be leaving anyone behind to take the fall...or talk his fool head off."

Canis was glaring at him, still fixated on the spaceman gibe. "It's rude to denigrate another person's faith," he said.

"No disrespect intended, boy." The sneer on Packer's face spoke louder than his words. "Y'all ready for a little road trip?"

"Ready as we'll ever be," Bolan replied.

"Ready," Canis said, as if to second the decision.

"That's just fine." The squeaky voice came close to sounding satisfied. "Let's us be on our way."

Bolan was right behind him, as they started toward the waiting four-wheel drives and vans.

CHAPTER FOUR

The first item of business after breakfast, was a shopping trip. Packer had been considering a Ryder rental truck, but Bolan had reminded him of Ryders being used in both the Oklahoma City and the World Trade Center bombings.

Bolan convinced the militia leader, over scrambled eggs and bacon, that it might be wiser to obtain a vehicle by other means, without a glaring rental logo painted on both sides. He still had no idea what the target was supposed to be, but he convinced Packer to have his soldiers steal a truck—some kind of a delivery van, perhaps—that they could then repaint and fit with different license plates.

It was a stall, of sorts, although he knew it wouldn't buy much time. They could obtain a truck within an hour or two in any major town, and painting it was no great problem. A few spray cans from a bargain store, enough to change the color superficially, would do the job all right. Packer assured him that the paint job wouldn't have to weather any rainstorms en route to the target zone.

Bolan didn't accompany the pickup team that Packer sent to find a truck. Instead, he and Canis were sent with three militia members to purchase the ammonium nitrate fertilizer needed to construct the bomb. They made eleven stops in Flagstaff, spreading the business around, picking up half a dozen fifty-pound bags at each nursery or garden shop along the way, driving each new load in turn to a tumbledown ranch on the outskirts of town. They rotated vehicles, using three different pickup trucks and a primer-gray van, in case the Feds had any reason to ask around afterward, comparing notes on bulk purchases. At each stop they paid cash, disdaining checks and credit cards that would have left a paper trail.

Bolan recalled the aftermath of Oklahoma City, when a number of alarmists had suggested federal laws to limit ownership of nitrate fertilizers, but the move had never gotten off the ground. It was the kind of senseless, knee-jerk move that often followed tragedy in the United States, off-loading personal responsibility onto inanimate objects, attempting to save man from himself by banning *things.* It hadn't worked in 1934, when Congress slapped a tax on Tommy guns in an attempt to do away with gangsters, nor had 1958s ban on switchblade knives succeeded in eradicating juvenile delinquency. The common-sense approach would have involved reeducating millions, but Americans preferred quick fixes, ballyhooed on prime-time television with the polish of a Wall Street ad campaign. Long-term results, somehow, were always secondary to a piece of good PR.

The diesel fuel was something else. No one had

ever seriously advocated banning that, although you couldn't build a fertilizer bomb without it. Banning diesel would have brought the country's transportation network to a grinding halt. No trucks delivering the produce, frozen food and auto parts, high-fashion clothing, toys, household appliances, and several million other things society would never voluntarily forgo.

Two tons of fertilizer meant they needed close to fifty gallons of the stuff. That added up to nine more stops at widely separated service stations, filling a five-gallon can at each. Again, the shoppers paid in cash, and no one raised an eyebrow as they made their purchases.

Bolan tried twice to telephone Brognola, each time from a different filling station, but he never got the chance. The first time that he split off from the group, allegedly to use the men's room, but one of the militiamen had decided to join him, and Bolan was forced to bypass the pay phone. The second time, while one of Packer's men was paying for the diesel fuel, the soldier had drifted toward the telephone wall-mounted in the corner of a Kwik-Stop, but Canis had shown up before he could drop a quarter in the slot, and Bolan wound up settling for a can of soda pop. It was frosty going down, but it did nothing to resolve his problem at the moment.

Bolan wasn't worried, yet. He couldn't have explained the situation fully to Brognola, even had he been allowed to make the call. Without some knowledge of the target, all that he could do was give directions to the ranch where Packer's men were going to construct the rolling bomb and hope the Feds arrived before it was dispatched.

Meanwhile, he would consider some alternative scenarios.

If there was no chance to alert Brognola, then it would be Bolan's job to stop the bomb—wherever it was going and whomever it was meant to kill. If it came down to that, of course, he would be called upon to make the save in such a way that his already shaky cover would be shattered in the process.

And that, Bolan knew, would be the real challenge.

In the meantime, there were still appearances to be preserved.

Bolan and Canis held themselves apart from the militiamen, for the most part, although they dined with Packer at the ranch, whenever meals were served. The menu ran toward beans, creamed corn and hash from cans. The squeaky-voiced commander loved to talk about "The Movement," but his vision for a New America was nothing Bolan hadn't heard before from various fanatics. What it all boiled down to in the end was one man's dream of power and authority, grabbing the brass ring that had always been an inch or so beyond his reach, and lording it over the people who had always made him feel less than a man. The payback came down to destruction, fire and blood.

In that way, Bolan realized, Vern Packer was no different from Hermes and Circe. He had changed the names of certain enemies, and he proclaimed a very different goal, but when you shoveled out the bullshit, it was really all the same.

A cry for help? Not even close.

A primal scream of rage? Perhaps.

Whatever it came down to on the psychiatrist's couch finally made no difference in Bolan's world. He dealt in hard and fast realities, a life where predators revealed no mercy for their prey and never got enough to eat.

They kept on feeding ravenously up until the very moment that they died.

CANIS—BORN James Garret Hobbs, in 1969—wasn't at ease among the members of the militia. He was there because Ares had ordered it, and Ares spoke for The Two. Canis assumed they knew what was required to bring the Ancients back and guide the faithful through the coming days when earth was purged by fire.

He didn't trust the militiamen. He saw the way they looked at him and smiled among themselves, the way they laughed behind his back, knowing he could hear them. None of them believed in prophecy, or, if they did, it was a different kind, a different message. When they opened up their Bibles, what they read between the lines was hatred—for the blacks, Jews, Catholics, "liberals," whomever they were *told* to hate by men they chose to follow.

Still, for some reason Canis wasn't entirely sure he understood, The Two had chosen Packer and his "soldiers" to assist in the advancement of a cause that served The Path. No one in the militia understood, nor would they have cooperated if they had, but it would make no difference in the end. Canis despised them for their ignorance and bigotry, but he didn't mind using them. He understood that certain people would be sacrificed along the way, and many more once battle had been joined at Armageddon. Earth wouldn't be cleansed through peace and prayer.

The Two had told him so.

The fertilizer bomb was something new. He learned by watching, while Nimrod and the militiamen fixed it up, pouring the fertilizer into fifty-gallon oil drums, adding diesel fuel to make it volatile, the recipe determined in advance. They worked inside the truck to avoid shifting drums with the mixture already inside. The cooks, as Packer called them, wore bandannas tied around their faces to help block the diesel fumes, using stout wooden sticks to stir the mix without striking sparks that would blow them apart.

The detonator was constructed with a kitchen timer and a blasting cap, a twelve-volt battery and insulated wire. They only needed one, attached to one of twenty loaded drums. When that one blew, the rest would go off in a savage chain reaction. The drums were capped with special care, the cooks employing rubber mallets and taking their time, no unseemly haste on this job.

The bomb wouldn't go off until it was intended to.

The recipe's final ingredient was rusty, jagged scrap iron salvaged from a junkyard, shoveled into gunnysacks, fifty pounds to a bag, wedged in around the loaded drums. The truck itself would serve as shrapnel, but the extra scrap could only help increase the body count.

Canis tried not to think about that, as the truck's tailgate was closed and padlocked. When they reached the target, one of them—perhaps himself or Nimrod—would unlock the tailgate, set the timer for enough lead time to let them clear the blast zone, and the rest was preordained.

"Where do you think the target is?" he asked Bolan that afternoon, when they had finished lunch and extricated themselves from Packer's odious company.

"I couldn't tell you," Bolan answered, "but it won't be all that far away."

"How do you know that?" Canis pressed him.

"Common sense, for starters. Also, something Packer said."

"What's that?"

"No rainstorms." Bolan glanced at Canis, saw the total lack of understanding in his eyes. "The truck. He told us that the paint job wouldn't have to stand up in a rainstorm."

"So?"

"That means he's got the weather at the target figured out. It's dry, and that spells desert. If we had to travel very far to reach the target, Packer wouldn't be so confident on that score. Also, what I hear, the Peacekeeper Militia has been sticking close to home, so far. They've never been connected to a job outside of the Southwest—specifically Nevada, Arizona and

New Mexico. One hit in Southern California, but it didn't work out well.''

Canis frowned, a twinge of suspicion making his left eyebrow twitch, a nervous tic. ''How do you know that?'' he demanded.

''I keep up on current events,'' Bolan said. ''Is that a problem?''

''Not for me,'' Canis replied. ''I'm just surprised, is all.''

Bolan favored him with the ghost of a smile. ''Somebody tell you that I couldn't read?''

''Nobody told me much of anything,'' Canis replied. ''I knew you were Army. That's about the size of it.''

''The Army reckoned they could do without my services. I figured it was mutual.''

''Bad feelings there?''

''No feelings,'' Bolan told him. ''Things just changed. The rules changed.''

''Everything is changing,'' Canis said. ''That's why we're here.''

Nimrod said nothing, but he nodded after several seconds, frowning to himself. Canis couldn't begin to guess what might be going through his mind.

''First time I saw The Two,'' Canis said—no reason he could think of, just a sudden urge to share, ''I thought they were insane. That lasted for about five minutes, till I really started listening. It started making sense, you know? Like something I'd been looking for, and didn't even know it. Once you know the truth, what can you do but go along?''

"I know some people who would swear we've got it wrong," Bolan replied.

"They haven't seen it, man. They haven't met the Ancients, seen the ships. They can't know what they're missing."

Bolan's eyes bored into him. "You're telling me you've seen them?" he inquired.

"I think so," Canis said. "I mean, I'm pretty sure."

"What happened?"

"It was three or four months after I found The Path," Canis said. "I was at the retreat, near Big Sur. Still learning, you know? One night, we had a group thing there, and offered up our energy. The Ancients take to that, sometimes, and answer if they feel like it. That night, we saw a ship."

"What was it like?"

"They're like nothing you imagine, nothing from the movies. Mostly light and sound, like energy, you know? I have a theory about how they travel, but I'm still not positive. The rest of it...um...that came later."

"Rest of what?"

"The grays," Canis said. "Later on that night—next morning, really, but still dark outside—they came to me."

"So, you were...what? Abducted?"

"No," Canis replied, shaking his head. "I was transformed. They filled me with such understanding, I could never tell you how it feels and make you understand. It's something you have to experience for yourself."

"I guess that's right." Canis didn't see doubt behind his eyes, but neither could he put a name to what *was* there. This man wasn't the average convert Canis had come to expect in The Path. His background, the experiences he had undergone before he found The Two, set him apart.

But they were brothers now. Canis hoped he could learn from Nimrod, that the soldier's skill would help him stand his ground and do his part in the final conflict, without fear or hesitation. It didn't matter if he lost his life, this earthly shell of flesh. The Ancients would restore him if he fell on their behalf. They had the power to resurrect him, make him better than he was in the beginning.

That being understood, Canis could only wonder why it was that he felt so afraid.

HAL BROGNOLA PEELED the tinfoil from a second stick of gum and rolled it up before he popped it in his mouth. It was his favorite brand, but it didn't seem to do the trick. At a time like this, he missed the soothing effect of the cigars he had enjoyed once upon a time, before his doctor and his wife joined forces to make him swear off. He was healthier now, they insisted, but he didn't always feel that way.

Today, for instance.

It would be a week tomorrow, since Brognola had flown to St. Louis to oversee the action at the Mormon temple in suburban Town and Country, Missouri. Thor's Hammer, the paramilitary arm of Millennial Truth—a.k.a. The Path—was supposed to seize the temple and hold its employees hostage, demanding air time to explain the cult's view of the coming ''Last Days.'' Brognola had planted agents inside, disguised as staff, and Bolan was part of the strike team. It was set to be an easy takedown, nice and smooth, before a local SWAT team captain turned the whole thing into a jurisdictional pissing contest and pressed an assault over Brognola's objections. The end result: ten dead terrorists, plus half a dozen police officers wounded.

And no trace of Bolan.

Brognola was still unclear on how his old friend had escaped, but gratitude had nearly leveled out the anxiety that helpless ignorance produced. Nearly, but not quite. He still had no idea where Bolan was, or why the soldier had been out of touch so long. Had he managed to rejoin the cult, somehow? And if so, had the characters in charge swallowed whatever story Bolan devised to explain his escape from the trap in Missouri?

For all Brognola knew, his old friend might be dead now, lying in a shallow grave somewhere, but he had faith in Bolan's proved ability to beat the odds. No one was perfect, of course. Even the toughest, smartest warrior ultimately ran out of luck.

The big Fed simply couldn't picture Bolan dead. There had been far too many hopeless situations in the past, where Bolan had surprised him and blitzed his way out of tight corners, with no aid in sight. Each time he had triumphed, leaving shattered schemes and bodies in his wake, the enemy in bloody disarray.

With nothing better to do, Brognola had coordinated a raid on the cult's Boulder compound, hoping he might bag Galen Locke and Helen Braun. With Hermes and Circe in custody, the cult would be a headless viper, thrashing in its death throes, and whatever damage it managed to inflict before the bitter end would be marginal, at best. Ideally he would have liked to bag Dillon Murphy as well, depriving the cult army of its commander in chief, but his luck had gone sour since the gig in Missouri. He had dead and wounded at Boulder, including some federal agents, but most of those arrested had already been released with no charges filed.

It wasn't, after all, a federal crime to camp out in the woods. Except for two or three of the cultists who were caught with weapons and bound over on local misdemeanor charges, the rest claimed ignorance of where their leaders had gone, and Brognola was inclined to believe them, for once. "The Two," as they were known within the cult, wouldn't have advertised their itinerary before bailing out. If nothing else, Locke and Braun had displayed a talent for evading the authorities when there was reason to make themselves scarce. As for Murphy—a.k.a. Ares, the ancient god of war—a dozen cultists agreed that he was in the camp the afternoon before the raid, but no one could remember seeing him that night, once the shooting began.

Again, Brognola believed they were telling the truth. Murphy was the heart and brain behind Thor's Hammer, presumed responsible for multiple acts of terrorism over the past couple of years, and he was clearly smart enough to keep his mouth shut around his subordinates, where escape plans were concerned.

Two ATF agents reported hearing a motorcycle somewhere behind them the night of the raid, and one thought he had glimpsed a headlight rapidly receding through the trees, but he couldn't be positive. There had been two dirt bikes among the vehicles seized in the raid, and several of the cultists questioned thought there should have been at least one more, perhaps two.

All right, then. The big Fed was ready to believe that someone had two-wheeled his way to freedom while the raid was going down. It could have been Murphy or Bolan, but not, he believed, the two of them together. Dillon Murphy, as the leader of the cult's enforcement arm, wouldn't crave witnesses to his escape, nor would he burden himself with an extra man when speed and stealth were critical.

Brognola rocked forward in his chair, planting his elbows on the desktop, glaring at the telephone connected to his private line.

"Goddammit! Ring, already!"

He willed himself to relax, breathing deeply and slowly, waiting for the knot of tension in his chest to unravel. Another tip from the doctor, and how do you tell an expert that his prescription doesn't work? The only cure for tension that had ever really worked for Brognola was action, and the hell of it was, he could think of nothing to do.

The cult had other hideouts and retreats, including one in Idaho, but a second raiding party had found that compound deserted, stripped clean of all but a few rudimentary furnishings. As for the hideaways Brognola didn't know about, they might as well be on the dark side of the moon, for all the good it did him.

He shot the silent telephone another withering glance. If looks could kill, the damned thing would have melted by now. He picked up the handset and held it to his ear, listening for the dial tone, and felt ridiculous as he dropped the receiver back into its cradle.

So, it worked, he thought. Now what?

But Brognola already knew the answer to that question. There was only one thing he could do, and that was wait until his old friend got in touch somehow, or until they found hard proof that Bolan was dead.

Of course, there was a chance that even in the worst-case scenario, no such proof would ever be forthcoming. That would be the worst of it, he thought: to never really know.

Just wait.

And while he waited, he would have his agents in the field keep pressure on their various informants, digging hard and deep for any piece of information they could find, anything at all to put Brognola back on the trail of the cult.

If Bolan was dead, Brognola vowed to himself, there would be holy hell to pay. And all the spacemen in the universe wouldn't be able to protect The Two or Dillon Murphy from Brognola's wrath.

"You'd better hope he's still alive," he told his absent enemies. "You'd better hope and pray."

BOLAN WAS SICK AND TIRED of loitering around the Flagstaff ranch. It was only his second day with the Peacekeepers Militia, but he felt as if weeks had dragged past, time slowing to a snail's pace while they shopped around for various ingredients and put the bomb together. It was ready to blow, sitting off to one side of the ranch house, in the marginal shade supplied from a tarpaulin strung from poles.

The payload was still relatively stable, but Bolan wouldn't have liked to bet on it two or three days down the road, after the truck had baked in the Arizona desert heat. It shouldn't detonate without the timer and the blasting cap, but you could never really tell for sure.

The sun was going down, heat waves shimmering on the horizon, and he smelled hash cooking in the kitchen. If an army fought with its stomach, as one military leader had said, Bolan suspected that the militia had to be well-equipped for gas warfare.

"Hash again," Canis said, coming up beside him in the dusk. "I'm sick of hash."

"That's two of us." Glancing at the younger man, Bolan still couldn't decide if Canis had been serious when they were talking UFOs and alien visitation earlier in the day. Canis looked and sounded sincere, but that could be acting. On the other hand, if he was telling the truth—what he *perceived* to be the truth—what did it mean?

The "ship" would be a relatively simple gimmick, Bolan thought. A smoke-and-mirrors job would do it, most particularly if the audience had been conditioned to accept a visitation from beyond earth's atmosphere. As for the visitors themselves, that was a bit more complicated. Men in costumes would have been one way to go, but it was crude and easily exposed, perhaps by accident, if anything went wrong. Beyond the physical, there was hypnosis, maybe drugs.

He simply didn't know. And for the purposes of Bolan's mission, here and now, he didn't care. The issue of intelligence on other worlds was totally irrelevant. Assuming that The Path was right about its Ancients, and the men from space *were* coming back, it still didn't provide cult members with a free pass to annihilate their fellow men.

Bolan would make up his mind on the flying saucer question if and when he saw one. When it came to terrorism, though, his mind had long since been decided.

As long as he was able to go on, he would respond to human predators in the only language they seemed to understand: brute force.

The ranch dinner bell was a rusty piece of scrap iron similar to that which they had used to pack the truck bomb, this piece dangling from a corner of the porch roof on a length of faded nylon rope. The cook, a stocky redneck with a port-colored birthmark covering the left side of his face, emerged and smacked the bell several times with the blade of a large butcher's knife, producing a series of desultory clanking sounds.

"I guess there's no escaping it," Canis said with a rueful smile, and started toward the house with Bolan on his heels.

The ranch-house dining room was fairly spacious, but it hadn't been designed to seat a dozen grown men comfortably. Even as they split up, dividing their number between two oaken tables, Bolan felt a hint of claustrophobia, rubbing shoulders and elbows with the enemy. He followed Canis through the serving line with an aluminum food tray in hand, pausing at each of four stations to help himself. The selection included corned beef hash, red beans and creamed corn, with two loaves of sliced white bread at the final stop.

Bolan wondered if anyone in the militia had ever heard of green vegetables. The more he thought about it, the more he came to believe that diet could be responsible for some of the oddities he noted among the group's members: bad or missing teeth, murky complexions and flabby midsections. Even the lean younger members had a fair start on beer bellies and "love handles" that would turn them into replicas of chunky Vern Packer by the time they hit middle age.

As per the militia leader's demand, Bolan and Canis took seats at the table nearest the serving line, where Packer sat with three more of his men. The brains behind the movement was pushing beans around with a folded slice of bread when they arrived, sopping up juice and stuffing the bread into his mouth, even as he greeted them. The result was grotesque, but Bolan nodded and took his seat, ignoring the bean juice that dribbled from Packer's chin.

"I guess you boys been wondering about the target,'' Packer said, when he had swallowed and could speak coherently again.

''It crossed my mind,'' Bolan acknowledged.

''Yeah, I bet it did.'' Packer grinned at his subordinates, dragging it out. He seemed disappointed when Bolan focused on his meal, instead of begging details.

''Well,'' Packer said at last with a curious frown, ''I guess it can't do no harm if I tell you now. You fellas spent much time up in Nevada? Maybe on vacation, like?''

''I've been there,'' Bolan said. ''It's been a while.''

''I drove through once,'' Canis stated. ''That was north of Reno, but we only stopped for gas.''

''Well, boys, I got a nice surprise for you. You're going to Las Vegas.''

Packer beamed at them, lips drawn back in a grin that would have let them know what he was eating, even if they couldn't see the plate in front of him.

''Las Vegas,'' Bolan repeated.

''Damn right, Las Vegas,'' the militia leader said. ''Temples of Mammon everywhere you look. It's time America woke up and saw that she is on the road to hell.''

''I thought the target was supposed to be a federal building,'' Canis said.

''What difference does it make?'' Packer asked, reaching for another slice of bread. ''The body count's what matters, right? The body count and the publicity. Eat up there, boys. Your food is getting cold.''

CHAPTER FIVE

Vern Packer was an early riser, up and ready at the crack of dawn. That morning he was even earlier than usual, already dressed and finishing his second cup of coffee by the time his soldiers and the two men from the flying saucer cult showed up for breakfast, shortly after five o'clock. He waited at his table, watching them pile trays with scrambled eggs, hash browns, limp bacon and toast that was closer to black than golden brown.

There was none of the usual banter, each man occupied with his own thoughts, speaking only when necessary to retrieve the salt or pepper, maybe reach the open jar of jam. Without the chatter, they were done in something close to record time.

The sun had barely risen, and another hour or two would pass before it started burning off the night chill, heating up the desert floor again. By that time, Packer thought, his little love note to the Zionist Occupational Government would be well on its way. It would require a miracle to stop him, and how could that be, when the Lord was firmly on his side?

Packer had hedged his bets and taken some precautions all the same. The final plan called for two soldiers in the truck, and four more in a second vehicle to track the payload and insure its safety on the road. All six were armed and under orders to let nothing keep them from their target. Packer had reminded them to watch the posted speed limits, the chase car hanging back so that a casual observer—or a traffic cop—would think the two vehicles were together.

One of Packer's men would drive, and the cultist known as Canis would ride shotgun on the load. His sidekick, Nimrod, would ride the chase car, with three more of Packer's men. He didn't trust the two of them entirely, even though their boss had given him ten grand, no questions asked, and the militia leader didn't want them talking, maybe plotting something, on the drive to Vegas.

Speaking of the oddballs, Packer saw them standing off to one side, talking quietly while his four soldiers finished checking out the car and stolen truck. He frowned, then shrugged off the apprehension. What could they do once they were on the road? And why was he suspicious of them in the first place, other than the fact that they were both outsiders. Packer couldn't think of any solid reason, and he tried to let it go.

If anything went wrong en route, his own men had the strangers covered, two to one, with orders fresh in mind to watch the new men all the way, give them no opportunity to screw things up. The first wrong move that either of the cultists made would end with two more bodies in the desert, which had swallowed countless others in the past.

Feeling good, except for the unavoidable apprehension, Packer crossed the yard to shake hands with the members of the strike team, Canis and Nimrod included. He looked each man directly in the eye, searching for anything that might set off alarm bells in his mind, and came up empty.

Good.

He had been waiting long enough to strike this blow against the enemy. The last thing Packer needed was a case of nerves at the eleventh hour, prompting him to call the whole thing off.

He headed back toward the ranch house and was standing on the porch when the two drivers revved their respective engines, the truck backing out of its makeshift shelter, lurching through a three-point turn before its nose was pointed toward the highway. Packer waved at the driver and watched the truck pass, the chase car hanging back to give its mark a fair head start.

No turning back, Packer thought, and felt a little shiver of excitement as he realized his fate was sealed. Whatever happened next, before the sun went down, could mean the difference between victory and defeat, between freedom and prison, between life and death. Whichever way it went, Packer was ready.

Hell, he had been waiting for this moment all his life.

THE DRIVE to Las Vegas would take them eastward from Flagstaff on Interstate 40, to Kingman, Arizona, where they would pick up U.S. Highway 93, rolling northwestward, crossing the border over

Boulder Dam, and on from there to Sin City. The total distance was around two hundred miles, and if they really watched the speed limits, with one stop for food and fuel, the trip should take somewhere between four and five hours.

Bolan had that long to come up with a plan, devise some way to stop the bombing without either blowing his cover or getting himself killed.

One way to go would be a tip to Hal Brognola, but that meant a telephone call, and *that* meant he would have to find a public phone at their one scheduled rest stop, somehow avoiding scrutiny from the five other men on his team.

And failing that, he would be forced to do the job alone.

If only he knew how.

The basic odds didn't intimidate him. Five on one was nothing special for the Executioner, but he couldn't afford to take a win for granted, either. It would take only one lucky shot to bring him down, and Bolan knew the four militia men were all familiar with their weapons. Whether any one of them had ever killed a man before was an entirely different matter; Bolan knew Canis had not, but every killer had a first time, and a bullet didn't know who fired it. A novice could sometimes do the job as effectively as a pro—even more so if the pro let himself become complacent, cocky, overconfident.

Killing five men, however, would be only part of Bolan's problem, if he had to go it alone. The real test would be killing them, and then disposing of the truck bomb in some manner that would let him walk away unscathed, and with a good excuse for his own survival and escape.

And that, Bolan knew, would be the really tricky part.

"So, man," one of the gunmen in the back seat said, "you ever met E.T.?"

The others laughed at their companion's joke, while Bolan forced a smile. "I haven't had the privilege," he replied.

"I thought y'all went up on that whatcha call it—mutha ship—and flew all over hell and back," the joker said, eliciting more laughs.

"Not me."

"You still believe in little spacemen, though," the joker pressed. "That right?"

Bolan half turned to face him, taking in the crooked, gap-toothed smile, the boozer's mottled nose. "What is it *you* believe in?" he inquired.

The joker blinked at that, considered it and answered, "I believe in Jesus."

"Have you ever seen him?" Bolan asked.

"Don't have to see him," the militia goon replied, sounding defensive now, less self-assured. "I know he's there."

"Where's 'there'?" Bolan asked. "And *how* do you know?"

"He's up in heaven," the joker said. "And I know it 'cause the Bible says so."

"Ah. You read it in an old book, then. I see." He faced back toward the highway and ignored the muttering behind him. His mind was already racing ahead, across the mile of open desert, to Las Vegas and the target Packer had selected for his truck bomb.

It wasn't, as Bolan had initially expected, a federal building or other government target. Rather, the titanic charge was meant to detonate outside the Holiday Hotel-Casino on a weekend afternoon, when the establishment was booked to near capacity. Bolan had questioned the selection, only to be told by Packer that his wakeup call to ZOG would send a special message far and wide: corruption sanctioned and encouraged by a government of infidels was ruining America, and it wouldn't be tolerated by loyal patriots.

Of course, the militia didn't plan to take credit for the blast. There would be evidence collected from the wreckage: a bogus driver's license with an Arab's name and photo on it; pamphlets from a Palestinian resistance group that Packer had dreamed up and printed at the ranch on a secondhand mimeograph machine. In case the little clues were lost, the FBI in Vegas would receive a phone call, claiming credit for the bombing in the name of "Red November," with enough pro-Arab and antisemitic remarks thrown in to point a finger at the Middle East.

It was a crude plan, granted, but Bolan wasn't concerned with Packer's script-writing skills at the moment. He had a potential mass murder coming up, and he would have to stop it if he could.

Even if that meant laying down his life.

It might not come to that, of course, but Bolan was always prepared for the worst. That way, if he was disappointed by events, the disappointment always came as a pleasant surprise.

THE TRUCK DRIVER apparently preferred his radio to human company, and that was fine with Canis, as the miles rolled past. It gave him time to think, despite the twangy sounds of country music emanating from the dashboard speaker, untrained voices harsh enough to set his teeth on edge.

The air conditioner was broken on the stolen truck, which meant they had to crank down the windows and let the hot air whip their hair around. Canis guessed the driver didn't care, since he was nearly bald already, with a stringy fringe of blondish hair above his ears and trailing down his neck. His mirrored sunglasses were decorated with a smudged thumbprint across one lens, but if he noticed it, the driver didn't seem to care. He smoked nonstop and pitched his butts through the open window, alternating drags with a pathetic karaoke act. He sang anything that came on the radio, regardless of whether the original artist was male or female.

The weird part, Canis found, was that he somehow made the songs sound alike.

A part of Canis welcomed the distraction, though if asked, he would have said that part of him wasn't his ears. He thought about Las Vegas, the hotel-casino he had never seen, packed with strangers he would never meet or know by name. A part of him recoiled from what they were about to do, but Canis wouldn't yield to weakness after having risked so much and come so far.

He owed a debt, not only to his brothers in The Path, the leaders who had shown him the error of his ways, but to the Ancients. They couldn't return and cleanse the earth of all its ills until the final war of Armageddon had become reality. This bombing—blamed on Arab terrorists who would have done it anyway, if they were smart and brave enough—would strike a spark within the Middle Eastern tinder box. With any luck at all, it would ignite the fuse that brought the final conflict from the realm of prophecy to grim reality.

The victims of the blast would gladly volunteer to sacrifice their lives, if only they could see what lay ahead for humankind. Of course, if they had known what was to come, they would have joined The Path, instead of idling away their final hours in a neon monument to lust and greed.

Canis didn't regard himself as a self-righteous man, much less a zealot or fanatic. He had simply learned the Truth, and would do everything within his power to insure that nothing stopped the Ancients from returning with their blessings for the faithful of the earth. If he was called upon to sacrifice his own life toward that end, so be it.

They were passing through Seligman, another long empty stretch of desert before them until they reached Kingman and their cutoff for U.S. Highway 93 to Las Vegas. Staring out his open window, with the hot wind in his face, Canis couldn't help wondering what changes would be wrought when the Ancients returned. Would the desert bloom beneath their touch, perhaps become a brand-new jungle?

Would the earth shift on its axis? Would the polar ice caps melt? Tall mountains crumble, while a host of new ones rose to take their place?

It struck Canis that he had never given much thought to the nature of the changes that would come once the Ancients returned, nor had his teachers ever been specific on that point. He took for granted that the final conflict would be devastating, probably involving weapons of mass destruction, but The Two assured him that the Ancients had means of coping with any pollution—nuclear fallout included—and restoring the planet to pristine condition. The faithful who had never wavered from their purpose would survive, and would be properly rewarded for performance of their duty in those trying times. Those who were lost would be revived, somehow, and would join their fellows in a world transformed into a veritable paradise.

All Canis had to do was go the distance, do his duty and let nothing sway him from his chosen course. No matter how he felt about Vern Packer's plan, it was endorsed by Ares and The Two. Canis wasn't prepared to pit his will against the minds of those who had been first to learn the secrets of the Ancients and relay them to the chosen few on earth.

Canis was one of those, and he had to do his part without fear or favor.

He wondered about Nimrod, riding in the chase car with three of Packer's men. He wished they were together, for moral support, but the very thought made him feel weak and embarrassed. A soldier of Thor's Hammer needed strength to stand alone against the enemies of truth. If he began to weaken now…

Outside, the sunbaked desert stretched as far as he could see, a wasteland virtually devoid of human life. Canis would live to see it blossom in abundance.

He was sure of it.

EARLY GRANT LOOKED forward to the rest stop, trading places with one of the others, maybe sitting in back where he could stretch his legs a bit. As soon as they hit Kingman, he would find a place to stop, gas up the Ford and get some grub.

Two years with the militia, and this was the biggest operation Grant had been on. Hell, it was the biggest operation any one of them had been on, easily the most ambitious raid Vern Packer had conceived. If this one didn't put them on the map, the Peacekeeper Militia might as well pack up and find another game.

If all went well, of course, their names would never make it to the media. That didn't matter to Grant or any of his fellow soldiers. He knew it was better this way, blame the whole thing on the ragheads overseas and let the State Department take the ball from there. It was enough that members of the inner circle knew what they had done, and they could count on Vern to spread the word around—discreetly, natch—among the other groups that shared their patriotic fervor. Grant simply had to do his job, and do it right.

His folks had named him Early, since he popped out six weeks premature and spent his first three weeks of life inside an incubator at the county hospital. He was the family runt until he turned fifteen and started to grow some. By that time he was out of school and on his own, disgusted with the lush who was his father and the bloated punching bag who was his mom. His siblings were a pack of losers, all of them with rap sheets, male and female. Grant had done time himself, but he was never going back.

The pigs would never take him in alive. Not now, when he had found a cause worth dying for.

A bullet-riddled highway sign told Grant that it was fifty miles to Kingman and the scheduled rest stop. Shifting in his seat, he felt the pins and needles in his buttocks that told him circulation had begun to lag. A mile or so in front of them, the truck was making decent time, still hanging in there with the posted limit, even though they had been lucky with the cops so far, no more than two or three patrol cars spotted since they left Flagstaff.

They could be making better time, he thought, but let it go. They didn't need to rush this job. The casino wasn't going anywhere. In fact the more Grant thought about it, he decided that the crowd of gamblers would be larger if they set off the bomb somewhat later in the day.

He thought about the load the truck was carrying and tried to picture the destruction it would cause on detonation. He had seen the videos from Oklahoma City and New York, but no two blasts were exactly alike. It would have pleased him if they could have hung around a while and watched, at least cruise by and check the damage after, when the smoke cleared.

Never mind.

When they got back to Flagstaff, there would be no end of pictures on the tube, no end to commentary from the left-wing bleeding hearts. It would be worth it all, watching as the FBI and ATF went in the wrong direction, sniffing after Libyans, Iranians, whatever.

If there was a part of this that made him nervous, it was working with a pair of wild cards, the two spacemen from some kind of weird cult. He knew their people had put up the money for the operation, but it still seemed wrong to Grant, that two of them should have to ride along, as if they didn't trust the militia and were looking out for their investment, somehow.

If one of them stepped out of line or tried to screw up the operation in any way, it would be Grant's everlasting pleasure to drop the son of a bitch in his tracks. No warning shots when you were on a mission and your life was hanging in the balance. It was kill or be killed, and anyone who knew that going in could take his chances with the rest.

Kingman was coming up, and Grant started to look for a truck stop, where they wouldn't find themselves downtown, surrounded by the law. He saw one coming, with a sign out front that told him it was Bud's, and saw the truck pull in ahead of him.

"'Bout time," he said to no one in particular, already braking for the turn. There was a semi in the lot, a station wagon at the gas pump and about a dozen Harley choppers lined up at the curb outside the diner that was hooked up to the service station and convenience store.

"Break time, y'all," he told the others, as he parked and killed the engine. "Time to stretch those legs and tap those kidneys. I'll find out if they've got anything to eat that wouldn't gag a maggot."

The others were behind him as he made his way into the diner, smiling as a cool blast from the air conditioner washed over him, drying his sweat on contact, raising goose bumps on his skin.

STRICTLY SPEAKING, it wasn't the worst hamburger he had ever eaten in his life, but Bolan reckoned that he could have lubed a small car with the grease that wound up on his plate. The french fries were a change of pace, burned dark and crisp, so that they crunched between his teeth like stale croutons. The coffee might have been fresh-brewed sometime that day, but not within the past few hours.

The six of them were seated in a corner of the diner, two tables pulled together. He counted fourteen grungy bikers at the counter, washing burgers down with beer. Their colors told him they were Widow Makers out of Tucson, headed somewhere on a weekend run. The other customers included one apparent trucker and a sixty-something couple seated in a nearby booth, the latter gumming chicken noodle soup.

He had the pay phone spotted, mounted on a wall in the direction of the rest rooms, and he knew it would require split-second timing if he was to reach

Brognola without being seen. It would be one time only, all or nothing. If another member of the escort party saw him on the telephone, he would be forced to fight or flee. And if he missed the big Fed now, the next chance he might have to call would be sometime *after* they planted the bomb.

Too late, he thought, and finished off his coffee as the sour-faced militiaman named Early pushed his plate back, belching satisfaction at the meal.

"I need to tap a kidney," Bolan said and shoved his chair back, rising to his feet.

"I got the check," Grant stated, rising at the same time, fishing out the roll of cash he had been given for expenses on the road.

Bolan swallowed a curse and walked back toward the men's room, feeling eyes on his back. As he approached the public telephone, he risked a backward glance and spotted Grant at the cashier's register. It was a straight shot line of sight. One sidelong glance, and Bolan's game was up.

He passed the telephone, entered the men's room and stepped up to a urinal. A long-haired biker wandered in some ninety seconds later, just as Bolan hit the flush handle.

"Hey, bro'," he slurred, and headed for the second urinal.

It was the hallmark of survivors that they recognized an opportunity when it presented itself. This was a long shot, granted. It could blow up in his face or simply fizzle out, without effect, but in that instant, Bolan thought it had a better chance than would ever stand of reaching Hal Brognola on the telephone outside.

If he couldn't get help from one quarter, perhaps another, unexpected ally would oblige.

"Is that you?" Bolan asked the biker.

"Huh?" The younger man had swilled enough beer to be a bit confused, but he was steady on his feet, frowning at Bolan as he half turned from his business at the urinal.

"That smell, for Christ's sake," Bolan said. "You ever hear of soap?"

"Hey, fuck y—"

The right cross wiped his sneer away and spun him like a top, spraying urine over everything within a three-foot radius. Bolan stepped back to miss the shower by a clear six inches. He was ready when the biker caught himself, one hand outflung against the stucco wall, shaking his head.

"You fucked up, man," he said, his blood-flecked lips drawn back from his teeth. "You gonna bleed for that."

Instead of charging Bolan, though, he took another moment to arrange himself, still tugging on the zipper of his faded jeans when another right exploded in his face. Bolan restrained himself, applied no killing force, but it was still enough to give the biker's nose an angle it hadn't possessed when he walked in. Blood spurted from both nostrils, dribbling down the young man's naked chest and etching dark spots on his colors.

He was tough, though, staying on his feet, still conscious, furious enough to rush his unknown adversary. Bolan waited for him, took the hairy arm that he was offered in a roundhouse swing and used the biker's own momentum as a tool against him, rolling him across the fulcrum of one hip and slamming him against the nearest urinal.

It knocked the wind out of him, but the guy still had some fight left in him as he hit the floor, immediately struggling to his hands and knees. A glance at Bolan's watch showed him that he was running dangerously short of time. He had to end it quickly, now, before somebody else walked in and ruined everything.

He slammed a kick into the biker's ribs, half lifting him, then bent and grabbed a handful of that greasy hair, before the young man could collapse. He leaned in close and slapped the biker twice across the face, watching his eyes swim into focus.

"I was right," he told the groggy biker.

"Huh?"

"You bikers *are* pussies," Bolan said, and snapped a short left hook into the bloody face.

It was enough to put the youngster down, if not exactly out. Bolan had no desire to leave him comatose, but neither did he want the punk raising an alarm before they had some lead time on the highway.

Just enough, he thought, to make the game a sporting chase.

The driver, Early Grant, was waiting for him at the exit, as he left the men's room. There was no sign of the others, Bolan guessing that they were already with the vehicles.

"Thought you fell in or somethin'," the militiaman remarked.

"All done," the Executioner replied. "Let's hit the road."

CHAPTER SIX

Stroker was mad enough to crush a cue ball into powder with his bare hands, furious enough that he was seeing crimson spots before his eyes, but part of leadership was staying frosty in a crunch, letting the brothers see that you were always in control.

The skinny, bleach-blond waitress had been all for calling the police, maybe an ambulance, but Stroker bluffed her out of it, insisting Weed was fit enough to ride. It took more than a little thumping to derail a Widow Maker and prevent him from obtaining personal revenge.

It had been Freebie who found Weed sprawled in the crapper, barely conscious, bleeding from the nose and mouth. After confirming that his fellow Widow Maker was alive, Freebie had run for Stroker and the others, sounding the alarm that was the first step toward a rousing round of payback.

Weed took several moments to regain coherence—or, at least, as much coherence as he ever had—and tell them what had happened in the men's room. All he knew for sure was that some citizen had sucker-punched him, with no provocation, just some lip before the lights went out. Weed could remember what the stranger said in parting, though.

"You bikers are pussies." Meaning Widow Makers, even if the sneaky bastard didn't call the club by name.

It was a double insult, then. This fucking citizen had kicked a brother's ass, then stuck around to smear the club in general. That kind of crazy shit could get you killed. *Would* get him killed, Stroker decided, just as soon as they could find out who and where the bastard was.

Weed couldn't tell them much about the guy, except that he was big and old—which could mean anything from six feet on and over thirty years of age. Weed didn't have to say that he was white, since Stroker would have noticed any other shades of skin the minute he walked in.

Good luck for them, Juicer had noticed someone coming out of the men's room a couple minutes after Weed went in. He couldn't offer much of a description, either, but he didn't have to. He had seen the guy leave with that bunch who had occupied two tables in the corner. Juicer saw them splitting up outside, four getting into a sedan, two others leaving in some kind of funky-looking truck.

Which way?

Easy supplied a guess that they were headed for the ramp to U.S. 93. He could be wrong, of course, but the alternative to picking one direction from the hat was splitting up and prowling local roads, most likely finding no one, while the sneaky bastard rolled up an unbeatable head start. If they went hunting for him out on Highway 93 and came up empty, they could always find a look-alike, some other citizen to take lumps in the asshole's place.

But Stroker had a feeling about this one. He was smelling blood.

"Let's ride," he said, and gunned his Harley chopper into life.

"ANOTHER FORTY MINUTES, give or take, before we cross the dam," Early Grant said. Nobody answered him, and that was perfectly all right. He wasn't sure why he had spoken in the first place, and regretted it almost before the words were out. The last thing he desired was any kind of running conversation, as their tires ate up the miles.

He had decided not to pass the keys on, after all. The pit stop was enough to let him work the kinks out, get the feeling back into his buttocks. It was better this way, he decided. If he drove the whole damn way from Flagstaff into Vegas, he would feel like he was really doing something for the mission, not just baby-sitting Joe Bob and the spaceman in the truck ahead of them.

He shot a quick glance at the rearview mirror, noticed something there and brought his eyes back for a longer look. It was too small to be another car, he thought, and yet...what *was* it spreading out that way?

A moment later, it came to him. A group of motorcycles was coming up behind them, pouring on the gas and fanning out across both lanes. Where had he seen that many cycles recently?

It clicked. "Looks like those losers from the rest stop must be headed our way," Grant stated.

Beside him, silent Nimrod checked the mirror on his side and shifted slightly in his seat. Was that a frown? Maybe the spaceman didn't care for bikers, Grant thought. Not that he cared much for the so-called outlaw kind himself, with all the drugs they sold and snorted, raping little girls and all. They were like rattlesnakes, in Grant's mind. He wouldn't cross the street to help one out of trouble, but he was content to let them pass by without a fuss, if they were so inclined.

The bikers came on fast, at least a dozen of them closing the gap, and the militiaman estimated that they had to be doing close to eighty miles an hour on their hogs. They all wore sunglasses, so Grant couldn't tell what they were looking at, exactly, but he saw the point man turn his head, shout something to the nearest rider on his left. That one, in turn, held up a gloved, clenched fist and swung it twice around his head, some kind of signal to the pack.

Whatever. Grant kept a light touch on the Ford's accelerator, holding it rock-steady at a speed of sixty miles per hour, waiting for the grungy bikers to whip past him and be gone.

The point man was alongside, now. He turned to stare at Grant and the others in the Ford sedan, as if examining their faces. He was in the wrong lane, but they were clear for miles, with no oncoming traffic anywhere in sight.

Now, what was—

Before the thought could finish taking shape, a

second biker pulled up on the leader's flank, the first bike in between his Harley and the Ford. This one looked like someone had whipped him with the ugly stick, a rusty-colored dry-blood smear around his nose, discoloration like a fresh bruise on one cheek.

The point man turned to face his flanker, might have said something, but Grant couldn't see his face. The battered-looking biker never seemed to take his eyes off Nimrod, in the shotgun seat, as he was nodding, thin lips moving as he spoke.

The leader of the pack was turning back toward Grant and the others, now, his right hand on the Harley's throttle, while the left one whipped around in the direction of the Ford. A shiny chain flashed in the sunlight, Grant barely recognizing it for what it was, before it struck the windshield on the starboard side and left a spiderweb of cracks.

One of the soldiers in the back seat blurted, "What the hell's he doin'?" but Grant had no time for conversation. He would think about the why of it some other time, after he finished dealing with the threat.

He tapped the Ford's brakes, heard the chain glance off a fender as the point man for the biker gang missed his second swipe at the windshield. Something solid struck the trunk lid as he lost momentum, and Grant glanced at the rearview just in time to see another biker draw back with some kind of wrench to take another swing.

Grant stood on the accelerator, whipped the steering wheel hard right and grinned in satisfaction as he heard and felt the Ford sideswipe one of the hogs.

Its rider squealed in pain before he laid down the bike in the middle of the highway, trailing shredded denim, skin and sparks behind him in a skid that carried him another hundred feet or so. Before he came to rest, another Harley tangled with the wreckage, standing on its nose and vaulting forward, while the driver catapulted from the saddle like a human cannonball.

Two down, and that left—what? Another ten or more to deal with? Grant was inclined to think that he could run them all right off the road, and never mind the four-door's paint job, but he changed his mind immediately as a pistol slug crashed through the broad rear window, whispered past his face and took a bite out of the plastic steering wheel.

That put a whole new face on things, and no mistake.

"Heads up, you men!" Grant snapped, already swerving toward the gravel shoulder of the road. "And watch your asses when you hit the deck!"

BOLAN DREW his Beretta as the Ford rocked to a halt, dust swirling up around him as he popped the door and bailed out in a fighting crouch. A glance to his left showed him the tailgate of the truck, still rolling northbound, and he wondered if the yokel at the wheel had even noticed the attack in progress on the chase car.

Dammit! This would all have been for nothing if the truck bomb slipped away from him while they were fighting with the bikers. It was too late to consider that just now, however, as the Harley choppers roared around them, like a raiding party of high-tech Apaches, circling a stranded wagon on the arid plains.

Most of the Widow Makers brandished pistols, but they were clearly not expecting any kind of armed resistance from the four men in the Ford. It took them by surprise when one of the militiamen—a chunky redneck who had introduced himself as Skeeter Ellis—cleared one Harley's saddle with a sawed-off shotgun blast.

"Yeah, boy!" the grinning shooter crowed. "C'mon and get some more, you sons of bitches!"

Ellis had the shotgun at his shoulder, lining up another shot, when he was staggered by a bullet ripping through his side. He lost his footing, went down on one knee, his second shot wasted on empty air.

The wounded gunner wasn't out of action yet, Bolan discovered, but there was a pained expression on his face as Ellis pumped the shotgun's slide to chamber another round. Blood was already soaking through his flannel shirt, deep red against the faded plaid design. It might have been a lung shot, Bolan couldn't tell from where he was, but it would clearly take some time to knock the shooter down and out.

Bolan was watching, waiting for a target in the midst of chaos, engines roaring, gunshots echoing around him. Early Grant was showing off his broad vocabulary of obscenities, while popping up from time to time, returning the incoming fire with what appeared to be a nickel-plated .45. On his third shot, a biker spilled, the Harley racing on without him for another fifty feet or so before it went down with a crash.

Bolan was ruefully aware that he hadn't improved his odds; quite the reverse, if anything. Instead of five to one, if he had faced the other members of the hit team on his own, he had approximately tripled that, by bringing in another dozen hostile guns. It was a calculated risk, of course, and Bolan still hoped he could pull it off. If everything worked out, he ought to have a cover story even Dillon Murphy couldn't fault.

"Goddamn that Joe Bob!" Grant was raving. "Very least the sun of a bitch ought to do is come back here and help us out!"

Bolan was craning for a fresh glimpse of the truck, when yet another bullet struck the windowsill mere inches from his face and ricocheted with a sound like a giant guitar string snapping. The Executioner ducked and pressed his back against the Ford's rear door, hoping that none of the bikers were carrying Magnum revolvers, or firing Teflon-coated armor-piercing rounds that would penetrate the four-door's bodywork. It took only one shot to do the job, he knew. A shooter didn't even have to aim. Dumb luck could—

Bolan heard a cycle engine roaring louder than the rest, coming around his left side, and he turned in that direction, almost bumping into Skeeter Ellis, who was slouched, half-conscious, in the shadow of the car. Before he had a chance to check on the militiaman, a chopper swung around the rear end of the car, off-road, the fat tires trailing dust, its rider leveling a pistol in his left hand, while his right cranked the throttle.

Bolan had no time to aim. He simply pointed the Beretta, trusting to experience and skill, his finger tightening around the trigger, squeezing off a solid double-tap. Both rounds struck roughly in the center of his target zone—the biker's naked chest—and punched the young man backward, sprawling from his charger, as the Harley vaulted through a clumsy somersault and came to rest, wheels to the sky, the engine snarling once before it died.

That left him thirteen shots, and two spare magazines. It was enough to do the job, but not if he started wasting ammunition. Bolan needed every shot to count, go just exactly where he wanted it to go, and do the job that it was meant to do.

Beside him, Ellis coughed and spit a glob of crimson to the dust, between his legs, and struggled to his knees, using the shotgun as a crutch. He glanced at Bolan, watching him, and grinned with bloody teeth.

"This ain't no time to get a suntan, boy!" he said. "C'mon and help me finish off these piss-ants, so that we can get back on the road."

"SAY, WHAT THE HELL...?"

Joe Bob was staring at the mirror on the driver's side, and Canis checked the mirror on his side to see what the distraction was. At first he didn't grasp what he was seeing, then he felt as if a fist had slammed into his gut and driven all the air out of his lungs.

The chase car had pulled over on the shoulder of the road, its passengers unloading on the driver's side, while motorcycles—Canis guessed there must have been at least a dozen, maybe more—roared up and down the highway, back and forth, the riders firing pistols at the car. As Canis watched, one of the bikers took a hit and laid down his chopper across both lanes, the others swerving to avoid him, then the view was lost as Joe Bob cranked the steering wheel and swung the loaded truck around.

"What are you doing?" Canis asked him.

"Goin' back," the driver snapped. "What the hell you think I'm doin'?"

It made perfect sense, of course. They couldn't just abandon their companions to a mob of two-wheeled savages, but at the same time, Canis heard alarm bells going off inside his head. The truck was loaded with explosives, and he was moved to wonder if a bullet, maybe more than one, would set the damned thing off.

Too late to worry, now that they were headed back the way that they had come, toward Kingman and the swirl of motorcycles in the middle of the highway. There was no way out for Canis, now, unless he took a chance and leaped out of the cab, but they were rapidly accelerating, and he didn't like his chances as an unskilled acrobat. Besides, what would he say in self-defense when it was over, if they all survived, and he alone had shown a yellow streak?

He drew the Browning semiautomatic pistol that he wore beneath his nylon windbreaker, thumbed back the hammer, kept his index finger well outside the trigger guard, as they had taught him when he took his firearms training with Thor's Hammer.

All right.

He wondered who the bikers were, and why they would attack the Ford. There had been bikers at the rest stop outside Kingman, and he wondered whether these could be the same ones. You heard stories all the time of psychos on the highway—"road rage" they were calling it in the media. But the punks were in for a surprise this time if they had come expecting easy pickings from a helpless group of travelers.

"Hang on, boy!" Joe Bob shouted, as he aimed the truck directly for the circling pack of motorcycles, like some kind of redneck kamikaze.

Canis braced himself, saw first one bike and then another veer away from impact, drivers shouting curses as they swept past, one firing a shot that struck the window post beside him, ricocheted and whined into space.

The third punk wasn't quick enough to save himself. He saw the truck too late, his full attention focused on the Ford, a shiny automatic bucking in his hand before he glanced up just in time to scream. The stolen truck met him head-on and brought the Harley to a jolting stop, its rider pitched across the gooseneck handlebars, lips drawn back in a scream that never came. His face punched through the windshield, spraying blood, recoiling just as Joe Bob hit the brakes. Reverse momentum tossed the flaccid body backward, and the biker's head popped off as neatly as you please, dropping between Joe Bob and

Canis, wobbling out of sight between the driver's feet.

"Don't lose your head, boy!" Joe Bob shouted at the dead man, as his body slithered off the hood and underneath their wheels. The grisly joke seemed to delight him, Joe Bob cackling like a madman, with his head thrown back, eyes narrowed to glinting slits.

The bullet caught him that way, zipping through the shattered windshield, in between his lips and teeth, exploding from the back of Joe Bob's skull in crimson tatters. He was dead before his foot slipped off the accelerator, hands still locked around the steering wheel as they began to lose momentum, slowly coasting to a halt.

The hogs were all around them now, and Canis heard more bullets peppering the truck from every side. How long until one struck a spark in back, and set off the fertilizer charges? One thing Canis was certain of: He dared not sit and wait to find the answer in a searing, white-hot blast.

And that meant bailing out.

He found the inside handle of his door and wrenched it open with his left hand, timing it to slam a passing biker in the face. The man spilled backward, while his bike kept going. Canis swung out of the cab, in time to find the biker struggling to his feet, and fired a point-blank shot into his adversary's chest.

That's how it's done, he told himself, and swallowed hard to keep his greasy burger down.

Before he could take another step, a stray round drilled through his temple.

THE SLIDE ON GRANT'S .45 locked open on an empty chamber, and he ducked back under cover. Cursing more from habit than for any other reason, he dropped the empty magazine and rummaged in his pockets for another, snapped it home and thumbed the slide release to prime the heavy pistol. That left one more magazine—a maximum of fourteen rounds—before he had to scrounge to find himself another weapon.

He still had no idea what had possessed the bikers to attack them, and he didn't care. When you were in the middle of a shitstorm, you could either shovel or go under, but you didn't stop to scratch your head and wonder why the wind was blowing.

Early Grant could think about that later, if he lived.

The bastards had already finished Skeeter Ellis. Glancing briefly to his right, he saw his old friend slumped against the Ford, staring at nothing, glassy-eyed, blood soaking through his shirt as if he had been drenched in crimson poster paint. He wasn't moving, and he never would again, until they dragged his carcass out of there.

Duke Reeves was favoring what seemed to be a shoulder wound, while Nimrod was apparently unscathed. Damned lucky spaceman, that one, Grant thought. The car was taking constant hits, as well, with two tires flat that he was sure of, and he didn't have a clue how any of them were supposed to drive away from there when they were finished with the bikers. If they finished with the bikers, right.

It had occurred to Grant that they might lose, that

this might be his dying day. He had been pissed, at first, to see the truck with Joe Bob and the other spaceman in it, speeding on its way, but then he felt a flush of something like relief, thinking the bomb would be delivered to its target and would do its job. The soldiers in the chase car were supposed to keep it safe, and they had done exactly that.

At least, he thought they had, until he saw the damned thing coming back. Grant was flooded with a rush of mixed emotions, then: anger at Joe Bob for returning and endangering the cargo; pride that one of his men had the guts to double back and help his comrades; sweet relief, together with a rush of giddy optimism for the outcome of the fight—and fear. One lucky bullet through the sidewall of the truck, he knew, and they could all be blown to kingdom come.

He came up shooting as the truck scattered a number of the outlaw bikers, smashing one head-on and slamming him into the middle of next week. The massive four-wheeled bomb was grinding to a halt, a Harley-Davidson mashed underneath the two front tires, as bikers started to circle it and pump bullets through the cab. Grant caught one of the bastards with his back turned, slammed home a .45 slug between his shoulder blades and watched a lifeless rag doll topple from the Harley's seat.

It was crazy, any way you sliced it, but he realized that he was actually having fun. He had grown sick of talk about the coming revolution, how the Jews and liberals would face a reckoning at some point down the line. A man of action—even though you wouldn't guess it, looking at his gut—he had been aching for a chance to crack some heads and spill some blood.

He was sighting on another biker, elbows braced against the hood of the sedan, when three things happened, more or less at once. The first was that the second spaceman, in the truck cab, swung his door wide open, sweeping Grant's target from the saddle. Next, the spaceman scrambled clear and shot the fallen biker dead before the punk could scramble to his feet. And third, a bullet drilled through Grant's neck, with entry on the left, explosive exit on the right.

The impact staggered him and took him down. He dropped the .45 and tried to catch himself, both hands thrown out against the Ford for balance, but it didn't help. He tried to call for help, unmanly as it made him feel, but the only sound he could seem to produce was a hideous gargling. His ears felt plugged, the way they got sometimes when he was driving through the mountains and forgot to chew a stick of gum.

Grant's hands slipped off the car, and he toppled forward, barely feeling it as his forehead thumped the hot steel. His body twisted, sagging, and his cheek slid down the driver's door. One eye was closed, now, and he couldn't seem to get it open, but the other was enough to see the pavement rushing up to meet his face.

And then he died.

THE LAST THREE BIKERS had more guts than brains. They had surveyed the carnage from a distance, saw the odds were even now, their ammunition running low, and still they lined up side by side, revved up their bikes, and charged.

Bolan was on his feet, behind the Ford, with Duke Reeves tottering beside him, both men pointing their pistols toward the three onrushing Harley-Davidsons.

They opened up as one and met the bikers with a lethal screen of fire that cleared three saddles almost simultaneously. Two of the Harleys collided, went down in a heap, while the third kept its balance, racing forward until it met the truck's bumper with a rending crash.

Almost done.

Bolan scanned the asphalt battleground, saw no more bikers moving anywhere, and knew exactly what he had to do. There was really no choice.

Duke Reeves turned toward Bolan with a crooked grin, his gun down at his side, when the Executioner shot him in the heart.

Reloading as he came around the car, Bolan assessed the damage to the Ford. Both starboard tires were flat, and radiator fluid pooled beneath the front end of the car, where sundry hoses had been ripped by bullets. At the rear, a stench of gasoline told Bolan that the fuel tank had been ventilated, too.

The Ford was finished. It wouldn't be taking him anywhere.

He made a circuit of the killing ground and chose a Harley that appeared to be intact, despite some superficial damage to the chrome and paint job on one side, where it had scraped across the pavement going down. The bike was heavy, straining Bolan's muscles as he grappled with it, but at last he braced it upright, walking it some fifty yards beyond the truck before he put the kickstand down and left it there.

The truck's tailgate was padlocked, and he didn't bother searching corpses for the key. Bolan was very much aware of passing time, concerned that he might be surprised by an approaching motorist—perhaps a roving patrol car—before he could finish what he still had to do.

Bolan stepped back and off to one side, aiming carefully, aware that any ricochet that pierced the tailgate of the truck could end his life in fire and thunder. As it was, he needed two shots to destroy the padlock, then he rolled the tailgate up and back, out of his way, and climbed inside.

The detonator was in place, harmless until he gave the kitchen timer's calibrated knob a sharp twist to the right, then back again, until he had one minute on the clock and counting down. A short drop to the pavement, and he jogged back to the waiting motorcycle, wishing he had tried the starter first, before he primed the giant bomb.

Too late.

The hog responded instantly, and Bolan aimed it north, cranking the throttle as he shifted through the gears. He gunned it, covering three-quarters of a mile before the clock ran down and smoky thunder rocked the highway at his back. He managed to outrun the shock wave, didn't bother glancing at his mirror to survey the scene of devastation. Bolan knew what such a bomb could do, but there were only dead men to absorb the frightful impact of the blast.

Riding with hot wind in his face, he was already working on the fine points of the story he would tell Dillon Murphy, when he called in to report the failure of their mission.

If his luck held, it might even save his life.

CHAPTER SEVEN

Hal Brognola heard about the massacre on television. It was bizarre enough to interrupt the normal song and dance from Wonderland—trade treaties, Jesse Helms denouncing homosexuals, more speculation on the latest budget bill. Brognola didn't know, at first, that it had anything to do with him, but he was interested enough to stop and listen, anyway.

At first the Arizona State Police believed it was the latest outbreak in a biker war that had been sputtering across the dry southwest for several years. The basic order of battle was Mongols versus Widow Makers, but other cycle gangs joined in as the spirit moved them: Hell's Angels, Bandidos, Gypsy Jokers. There had been several dozen deaths so far, scattered across the arid landscape, one or two, sometimes three at a time. This day's events were vastly different, though: a broad-daylight massacre and titanic explosion with seventeen dead, corpses and parts of corpses strewed across the bloody asphalt of U.S. Highway 93, northwest of Kingman. Authorities professed themselves aghast at the violence, promising a crackdown on bikers across the state.

Forty minutes later, there was a new twist to the

story. CNN reported that several of the dead had been identified as members of a right-wing paramilitary group, the Peacekeepers Militia, suspected in various acts of harassment aimed at federal agents and ethnic minorities in Arizona and New Mexico. Speculation was rampant: Had the militia gone to war against outlaw bikers? Were the two groups, perhaps, considering a merger before it fell apart? How did the prevalence of Nazi regalia among Widow Makers relate to the militia's known ties with groups like the Aryan Bastion?

Brognola was no more than a distracted spectator, following the early reports with a fraction of his conscious mind, when his private telephone line rang. Snatching the receiver on the second ring, he brought it to his ear.

"Hello?" No names on this line, just in case it was a rare wrong number—or worse, someone who shouldn't know the line existed, much less who was on the other end.

"You have your TV on?" the caller asked.

Brognola felt a bubble of relief burst somewhere in his chest. "I'm watching," he told Bolan, controlling the sound of his voice with an effort. "You wouldn't be in the Grand Canyon State, by any chance?"

"I was," the Executioner replied. "I'm in Las Vegas at the moment."

"That was quite a fireworks show."

"It was supposed to play right here, downtown," Bolan replied.

Brognola blinked at that, but held his train of thought. "That sounds like a militia show," he said.

"It was," Bolan confirmed. "Our other friends came in on financing and sent a couple of their men along to watchdog."

Bolan didn't have to say that he was one of them. That much was plainly obvious to Brognola, from the result. Now that he thought about it in the proper connection, there was no mistaking the impact of what the big Fed had once called "the Bolan effect."

"What was the target?" he inquired, expecting something on the order of the federal courthouse or a local office of the IRS.

"The Holiday Hotel-Casino," Bolan said, taking Brognola by surprise.

"Say what?"

"You heard me right. I'm calling from the lobby," Bolan said. "I wasn't clear about the choice myself until I got here."

"And?"

"They've got two conventions in this weekend," Bolan said. "One is an international arms show. All kinds of shoppers from Europe and the Third World, checking out everything from pistols to stealth fighters."

That would be a hook for the militia, Brognola thought, but Bolan had mentioned *two* conventions at the Holiday. "And the other?"

"The National UFO Research Team," Bolan said. "That's NUFORT to the faithful."

"Let me guess. The other guys don't like them?"

"That's the understatement of the week," Bolan

replied. "NUFORT consists primarily of skeptics who dispute the notion of alien sightings and contacts. Some of the members still believe in life on other worlds, of course. They just don't think ETs are dropping in to visit us, or that they ever will."

"Which would explain The Path's decision to participate in the militia plan," Brognola said.

"And then some. The conventions are announced months in advance—sometimes a year or more. Both sides had ample time to pick their targets and prepared themselves."

"What happened with the bikers?"

"I had to improvise. They were handy."

"Well, you picked some winners," the big Fed informed him. "From the bulletins I've heard so far, all twelve had records for assorted felonies—narcotics, rape, manslaughter, take your pick. At least four of them had outstanding warrants—two on murder charges—and I wouldn't be surprised to see those numbers take a jump before the day's out. Half of them have tested positive for coke or methamphetamines. Between them and the new heat coming down on the militia as we speak, I'd say you did the state of Arizona one huge favor."

"Maybe so," Bolan replied, "but I'm back out there on a limb with Murphy and the rest."

"Have you checked in?"

"Just now, before I called you. They've got me headed for a ranch outside Barstow."

"You want backup? I can field a team in half an hour, out of San Diego or Los Angeles."

"Not yet," Bolan replied. "I want to wait, see how it plays."

"Okay. Your call." But he could feel the old, familiar knot begin to tighten in his gut once more.

"I'd better hit the road," Bolan said.

"Right. Stay frosty, guy."

"The only way to go," Bolan replied, and the line went dead.

Brognola cradled the receiver and rocked back in his chair, unconscious of the frown that etched deep furrows in his face. The play was Bolan's call, all right, but that didn't mean Brognola was happy with his old friend's choice. It meant they would be out of contact once again, and he had no idea when he would hear from the warrior again.

Dammit!

Short of yanking Bolan's chain, thus jeopardizing his life, there was nothing left for Brognola to do except wait.

California

BACK IN THE DAYS when he was known as Galen Locke, Hermes had learned that visible reactions to bad news were a serious weakness. Friends and allies witnessed the reaction and lost faith in your ability to rise above a problem, while your enemies took heart and were delighted by the fact that they could cause you pain.

When Hermes learned about the massacre in Arizona, therefore, he took care to keep his face deadpan, serene, as if the news had been about a boring garden party, rather than the demolition of another treasured dream. He didn't care about the dead, of course. Among the seventeen, he understood that only one was his, and that a minor loss. The second of his people had survived, somehow, and that, ironically, caused Hermes more concern than if both had died. As for the Widow Makers and the members of the militia who were killed, they meant no more to Hermes than a line of ants crushed underfoot when he went walking in the garden.

They were nothing in the universal scheme of things. He had already paved the way for the Ancients' return, but there was much more to be done before that great day came at last.

He had to smile, remembering the looks that he had got in the old days, when he first proclaimed his message to the world at large. Of course, he still got those looks, with the sneering media reports, but word was spreading. Slowly, surely, he was gathering disciples to the fold, proof positive to Hermes that the Final Days were coming, when a chosen few would recognize the truth and thereby save themselves.

If only the psychiatrists who had reviewed his case could see him now! The mocking bastards would sing a different tune, these days. No more poking and prodding him, as if he were some kind of laboratory specimen. The time would come—and soon, he was convinced—when they would kneel before him, beg his pardon, offer everything they had to gain his blessing and assure themselves a place in paradise.

And it would be his everlasting joy to turn them down.

Hermes had written and memorized a speech for the occasion, making sure he got it exactly right. He would be calm and reasonable to a fault, first asking them if they remembered when he was a patient in their charge and they so casually dismissed his prophecies as the pathetic ravings of a madman. That would doubtless bring another round of groveling apologies, while Hermes smiled benevolently, nodding, giving them a taste of hope...before he dashed it to the ground. He would recite chapter and verse the reasons why their sins against him were unpardonable, why they couldn't share his fellowship with the returning Ancients and had to be destroyed, instead.

Sometimes he dreamed about that day, knowing that it would be among the brightest of his life.

"What shall we do?"

The question came from Circe, seated on the plush divan immediately to his left. Before them, through the tinted picture window facing westward, giant redwood trees obscured the northern California coast.

It pleased him that she still asked his opinion, after all these years. They had been equals from the start, none of the chauvinistic bullshit that had been one of terrestrial society's most glaring flaws. The Ancients spoke to Circe as they did to him—sometimes, in fact, he thought they told her more—and yet, she never failed to seek his counsel on various matters, ranging from trivial to the most critical.

Like now.

"We shall go on," he told her, briefly savoring her face, before he turned back to the panoramic view outside. "It's a minor inconvenience, nothing more. They cannot stop us, now. We've come too far. The Ancients are already on their way."

Circe knew that, of course, but she didn't rebuke him for belaboring the obvious. Instead, she smiled, seeming to draw a kind of reassurance from his repetition of a fundamental truth. Circe could hardly wait until the mother ship arrived, to usher in the last tumultuous hours of Old Earth.

"Can Ares handle this?" she asked.

He thought about the question for a moment, felt a frown begin to tug the corners of his mouth downward and mastered it. Even with Circe—or, perhaps, especially with Circe—he was careful not to lose control. If she lost faith in him, in his ability to cope with every situation that arose, what would the others think?

"What happened with the truck isn't his fault," Hermes said. "No one could predict those unwashed savages would interfere. I wouldn't be surprised to learn that Packer and his private army brought this trouble upon themselves."

"There's still Missouri," she reminded him.

"A calculated risk, my dear. We counted on the FBI to stall for time, negotiate. They would have put our message on the air, I'm sure of it. Such a small price to pay for all those lives. No one could have predicted that a trigger-happy local officer would ruin everything."

"Of course not," Circe said, and there was nothing in her tone to even hint at mockery. "Next time, my love."

Next time.

It was already in the works, and he could only hope that Ares would be more successful than in his two most recent outings. It would be more difficult, of course, now that authorities were tracking them. The Boulder raid was proof of that, and Hermes wondered how much longer Big Sur would be safe for them. None of those arrested in the Colorado crackdown knew about this safehouse; otherwise, he would be standing at some other window, looking at some other view. The government had ways, though. Even with the handicap of earthbound logic and inferior intelligence, they still made some surprising scores.

He would speak to Ares soon, remind him of how critical it was for them to preserve their schedule. The Ancients wouldn't delay their return because of human blunders, and a failure to properly prepare the way could still be disastrous. Prophecy was immutable, Hermes knew, but there were always twists and turns along the way.

The Ancients would return whether Hermes and company helped them or not; that much was inevitable, carved in granite. If the chosen people failed to keep their end of the covenant, however, they would be forgotten, cast aside with the rest of humanity and denied their place in the eternal kingdom. It was a high price to pay for negligence, but punishment would be a fair one, if it came to pass.

Slackers deserved no consideration. They would reap what they sowed.

Yes, he would speak to Ares again, and if The Path's enforcer took offense, what of it? He wasn't a child, after all. One thing kept Hermes from placing the call immediately: he wanted to hear what the survivor of the Arizona ambush had to say. Ares was going to debrief him sometime in the next few hours, and the man's report might shed some light upon the latest setback. If it seemed to Hermes that his military leader was attempting to deceive him, well, then it would be time for a change. Ares was expendable in the cosmic plan.

But he could wait awhile.

The Ancients still had far to travel on their way to Earth. A day or two would ultimately make no difference, and he, Hermes, would still prepare the way for them, cleansing the planet with a firestorm that would sear away the taint of fragile man, clearing the way for something better.

Something eternal.

It was his destiny, and Hermes didn't mean to fail.

CROSSING THE OPEN DESERT in another rented car, Bolan experienced a nagging sense of déjà vu. It wasn't simply Arizona and the recent bloodletting that took him back. Bolan had passed this way before, along this very road, when he was hell-bent on his one-man war against the Mafia, commuting from Las Vegas to Los Angeles in search of targets.

That seemed long ago and far away, somehow. The highway had been widened and repaved since then—not merely once, but several times. Bolan had worn a different face in those days, too, but it had been the same commitment that compelled him to go on.

That much, at least, would never change as long as he was still alive.

Barstow was large, for a backwater California desert town. It was essentially a crossroad, westbound Interstate 40 dead-ending into Interstate 75, emerging on the other side as State Highway 58. The town proper boasted some 17,000 inhabitants, mostly employed in service occupations—restaurants and motels, gas stations and garages, convenience stores and gift shops. The range of local art was limited—postcards depicting "jackelopes"—rabbits with antlers; T-shirts demanding to know Where the Hell Is Barstow?—but few people actually traveled *to* Barstow. Like Bolan, the vast majority were simply passing through.

His destination was another ranch, northeast of town on a narrow track that ultimately made its way into the Fort Irwin military reservation, beyond which point Bolan's map proclaimed the blacktop Closed to Public. He wouldn't be going that far, though.

In fact the last leg of his trip was barely four miles long. He found the turnoff he had been advised to watch for, swung the rental car onto a gravel road and drove due west until he reached the smallish stucco house that was his destination. There was nothing in the way of crops or livestock to complete the image of a working farm, but he hadn't expected any.

Stepping from the car, he saw two young men armed with shotguns waiting for him on the porch. He moved to join them, raised his arms to let them pat him down and offered no resistance when they took away his pistol. He said nothing as they led him to the parlor, where Dillon Murphy waited for him in a wooden rocking chair that looked to be antique.

"I don't know whether I should think you're blessed, or cursed," the leader of Thor's Hammer said.

"I caught a break, is all," the Executioner replied.

"Two breaks," Murphy corrected him. "That's twice you beat the odds. Fact is, you're the only one who beat the odds, both times."

"You're still concerned about Missouri?" Bolan asked him, refusing to let himself be placed on the defensive. "If you felt that way, why the hell did you send me with Canis?"

"It's my job to be concerned," Murphy reminded him. "Why don't you have a seat?"

Bolan bypassed the sagging couch and sat down in a straight-backed wooden chair that creaked beneath his weight. He settled into it and waited, face impassive.

"So, if it's not too much to ask, Nimrod, exactly what went wrong this time?"

"You've seen the news, right? Bikers jumped us on the road."

"Uh-huh. The thing is, I was hoping for a bit more

in the way of a specific explanation, if you get my drift."

"You're asking why they jumped us?"

"That would be the question, yes." Murphy was still in firm control, but he was sounding strained.

"And how would I know that, exactly?" Bolan asked.

"Well, you were there, Nimrod. I mean, you are the only one who walked away from it, correct?"

"It looks that way."

"All right. I'm listening."

"There's not much I can tell you," Bolan said. "We stopped for lunch and gas in Kingman. There were bikers at the rest stop, but I didn't pay attention to their faces. Maybe they're the ones who jumped us, maybe not."

"Let's stick to why," Murphy suggested.

"Still can't help you," Bolan said, deliberately omitting any hint of military courtesy. "From what I hear on radio, it was an Arizona bike gang. Your militia buddies were from Arizona, too, if I remember right. Outfits like that, I wouldn't be surprised if this crowd had a history, some kind of weapons deal, who knows? Those bikers hold a grudge forever. Payback is a bitch."

Murphy considered it, a grim frown on his face. He plainly didn't want to let it go. "You're telling me that no one said a word? They just attacked you?"

"That's a fact," Bolan replied. "We're rolling down the highway, maybe sixty miles an hour, and they come up on our six at eighty, eighty-five. The point man pulled up on my side and started smashing in the windshield with a chain. Next thing I know, we're off the road and everybody's shooting."

"What about the truck?" Murphy asked.

"They were up ahead of us," Bolan said, "with a decent lead. I didn't have a chance to see if there were any bikers after them, but Joe Bob must have turned around."

"Joe who?"

"Joe Bob. The driver," Bolan said. "I didn't catch his last name."

"And the truck just blew. That's it?"

"What can I tell you? It was taking hits all over," Bolan said. "One of them must have set the detonator off."

"And everyone went up with it, except for you."

"Hell, no." Bolan allowed a hint of indignation to invade his tone. "Canis was shot, some of the others, too. You know that, if you're keeping up with the reports."

"Then you just grabbed yourself a hog and hit the road?"

"It made more sense than walking," Bolan said. "Or, then again, I could have stuck around to greet the cops."

"You've got an answer for everything, right?"

"It always helps to tell the truth," Bolan replied.

"I need to think about this for a while. You could use a shower, I imagine."

"That's affirmative. What about the next job?"

"That's one thing I need to think about," Murphy replied. "You may be lucky when it comes to dancing in between the raindrops, but the good luck doesn't seem to spread itself around. I've lost a dozen men, the last two jobs."

Bolan put on a scowl. "You're blaming me for that? If that's some kind of accusation, spell it out."

"I'm not accusing anyone of anything," Murphy replied. "Not yet."

"Well, let me know what you decide," Bolan said, rising from his chair. "I'll be on pins and needles. In the meantime, where's that shower?"

ARES TOOK A WALK around the property to let himself cool off. The sun was going down, which helped. He took off his shades, and was struck, as always, by the contradiction of such beauty in a desert wasteland that was redolent of death. This kind of country had at least two hundred different ways to kill a man, but it was still a favorite subject for innumerable artists and photographers. He knew the desert well enough to fear it, but he saw its beauty, too.

Just now, his mind was fixed on Nimrod and the twisted luck that seemed to dog him: good for Nimrod, bad for anybody else around him. It could be a bizarre coincidence, of course—Ares had heard of people who survived a string of airline crashes, for example—but the notion strained credulity.

There were at least two problems with the story, Ares realized. The first—that both missions involving Nimrod had gone sour in the space of less than two weeks—could maybe be explained by factors outside his control: the edgy SWAT cops in Missouri; some old feud between the Widow Makers and the militia. Nimrod's "lucky" escape from two consecutive traps was more difficult to credit, first evading lawmen, then outwitting trigger-happy bikers *and* avoiding injury when the militia's bomb went off.

Impossible? he asked himself. Not quite. But it was damned unlikely. Still, he couldn't put his finger on a single point of evidence that proved Nimrod was dirty, that he had betrayed his duty to The Path.

Ares didn't need proof, of course. He could order Nimrod's execution on a whim, and no one but the triggerman would ever know the difference. Better yet, he could do the job himself, leave Nimrod in the desert in another day or two when they leave this run-down place forever.

But he would wait. If Nimrod's story was legitimate, then killing him would be a shameful waste of manpower. And if the ex-Ranger *was* dirty, well, they still had time. He wasn't going anywhere. Ares could keep an eye on him, and take him out at leisure, once he knew for sure.

He took the cellular phone from his pocket, snapped it open with a flick of his wrist and drew the antenna out to full extension. He tapped out Star's number from memory and listened to a muffled trilling on the other end, three rings before she picked up.

"Hello." Star never made a question of it, like so many people do.

"It's me," he said unnecessarily. She always recognized his voice.

"Bad business, that," she said. There was no need to ask which business. "Everything all right?"

"I hope so," Ares said. "I need some help, though."

"Name it."

That was Star. She never argued, never told him anything was difficult, much less impossible. If there was anything that could be done with a computer, Star knew how to do it, and a damn sight faster than most anybody else around.

"I want another check on Nimrod," he informed her. "Real name, Mike—"

"Belasko," Star broke in to finish for him. "I remember. I already gave you everything there is, though."

"I was thinking you might try another angle of attack," he said.

"Such as?"

"I'm looking for connections, this time. Any kind of operation that's specifically directed at The Path. If you find anything, backtrack from there and see if anybody—I mean *anybody*—on the other team matches our boy's description."

"You'd be talking federal, am I right?" she asked.

"It's gotta be," he said. "Missouri, Colorado, Arizona—no one but the Feds can hop across state lines like that."

"I'll start with Justice, see what's cooking there," she said, "and then spread out as necessary. ATF's with Treasury, of course."

"I'll leave you to it, then," he said, aware that Star was talking to herself.

"Okay." She beat him to it, even then, and cradled the receiver on her end, breaking the link. He hung up on the buzzing dial tone and returned the small phone to his pocket.

And heard someone calling to him from the house.

He turned in that direction, saw one of his soldiers waving to him from the porch and started back. What now, for God's sake? If it wasn't one thing, Ares thought, it was another. Always something that demanded his attention *now,* without a moment's rest.

Still, what else could he expect from the Final Days? It was a race to finish, and the chosen few couldn't afford to break stride now, when they were so close to the finish line.

"What is it, Corvus?" he demanded of the young man, as he reached the porch.

"You've got a phone call, sir," the soldier said. "Inside."

"Anonymous?" he asked impatiently.

"No, sir."

"Well, tell me who it is!" Ares snapped.

"Well, um, sir...he said his name is Pluto."

Ares blinked twice, rapidly, and pushed passed Corvus toward the open doorway, to accept a phone call from beyond the grave.

CHAPTER EIGHT

Bolan turned off the shower and reached around the corner for a towel. It had a vaguely sour smell, as if it had been used a few times previously without laundering. He managed to ignore the odor as he dried himself and hung the towel, now damp, back on the rack.

His clothes were waiting where Bolan had left them, neatly folded on a wooden chair outside the bathroom door, shoes on the floor beside the chair. A new addition was the pistol that now lay atop the pile—his gun apparently returned by one of those who had relieved him of it on the porch.

He checked the weapon quickly. First the magazine, confirming it was loaded; then a short draw on the slide, revealing that a round was still inside the chamber. Short of fieldstripping the pistol, it was all that he could do. If anyone had tampered with it—with the firing pin, for instance—he would find out only when he pulled the trigger next.

Was the returning of his side arm meant to be a sign of trust? He would have thought so, under other circumstances, but the present set was still too close to call. If Dillon Murphy had a joker up his sleeve, the gun could be a trick, something designed to make Bolan relax, let down his guard.

No chance of that, he told himself, and finished dressing in a hurry, right down to the pistol in its shoulder rig. An afterthought made Bolan check the two spare magazines in pouches underneath his right arm, and he found that both of them appeared to be untouched.

Back in the spacious parlor, he found Murphy waiting for him, this time in a chair beside the window, with a mug of coffee in his hand. He smiled and raised the mug as Bolan entered.

"Want some?"

"Might as well," Bolan replied.

"We've got a fresh pot in the kitchen."

He found it on his own, the two young shooters who had met him on the porch lounging around a table in the kitchen, both regarding him with looks that stopped a hair short of suspicion. Bolan took a clean mug from the sideboard, filled it nearly to the brim and left the kitchen, feeling eyes upon him all the way.

He didn't know these men, and chalked up their demeanor as, perhaps, the usual reaction to a stranger. Were they picking up on Murphy's vibe, or was there something else?

Back in the parlor, Bolan sat across from Murphy, perched on one end of a sofa that had seen much better days. He sipped the coffee slowly, careful not to burn his tongue, and waited for his nominal superior to speak. Murphy sat staring out the window for another moment. When he spoke at last, his voice and attitude were casual, almost as if the first, suspicious interview had never taken place.

"We may be here a few more days," he said. "Feds are already checking out the known retreats, hoping to find The Two, questioning anybody they can find."

Bolan refrained from asking where the leaders of The Path were hiding out. If Murphy already suspected him, it could be seen as evidence of Bolan's spying on the cult, attempting to betray The Two, deliver them to federal agents. It could be enough to get him killed, if Murphy wanted an excuse. And if the cult enforcer was inclined to buy his story of the Arizona massacre, one question out of place could tip him back the other way, revive suspicion where it had been laid to rest.

The safest thing to say was nothing. Bolan sat hunched forward, forearms resting on his knees to keep from slumping backward on the worn-out cushions of the couch, and sipped his coffee.

Waiting.

"Now the trouble is," Murphy resumed, after another lull, "we didn't have a chance to stock properly before we holed up here. It's only been two days, and we're already running short of food. We need supplies."

"There's Barstow," Bolan said. "It's what, five miles away?"

"I can't go in, myself," Murphy replied. "The Feds have paper on me now. You would have missed it, but we made *America's Most Wanted* last weekend. They talked about Missouri, put up pictures of yours truly and The Two.''

"So, what about the Bobbsey twins?'' Bolan asked, nodding toward the kitchen, where the two young guns were killing time.

"They're green. Just between the two of us, I'm worried that they might screw up, let something slip and bring the law right down on top of us. That's all we need right now.''

Bolan pretended to accept the explanation, though it sounded lame. He had a hunch where Murphy's rap was leading, but he couldn't bring himself to help the other man along. If Murphy wanted something from him, whether it turned out to be some kind of setup or a simple favor, he would have to spell it out himself.

"So, I was thinking,'' Murphy said, as if he hadn't paused for something like a minute, "maybe you could make the run. You didn't stop in Barstow, did you? I mean, coming in?''

"I didn't stop,'' Bolan confirmed.

"Then there's no reason anyone should recognize you, is there?''

"None at all,'' Bolan replied.

"Okay, then. You can pick up the supplies.''

"Alone?'' Bolan asked, trying not to sound surprised.

"Why not?'' Murphy's expression was entirely neutral, like a poker face rehearsed with mirrors to the point that he could put it on at will.

Bolan decided it was time to push his luck, if only by a fraction of an inch. He shrugged and said, "No reason, I suppose. It just occurred to me you might not trust me on my own right now."

"Forget about it," Murphy said. His smile impressed Bolan as being no more honest than his poker face. "We took two beatings in a row, and it's been working on my nerves. I know it's not your fault, Nimrod. How could it be? The questions needed asking, though. You see that, don't you?"

"Absolutely," Bolan said, and glanced at his wristwatch. "Give me a list of those supplies, and I'll get on it. If I leave right now, I should be back within two hours, give or take."

"Relax," Murphy said, waving off the suggestion. "Tomorrow will be soon enough, and you can take your time. There's no rush getting back, as long as we have what we need by suppertime."

"Suits me either way."

"You may as well rest up tonight," the leader of Thor's Hammer said. "It's not like you've been sitting on your ass and twiddling your thumbs the past two weeks."

Murphy's solicitous demeanor lifted the short hairs on Bolan's neck. He might be playing straight, but then again...

"I think I'll crash," Murphy said, rising from his chair and yawning like a man already half asleep. "Long day tomorrow. touching bases, finding out who's still around and who the Feds have grabbed."

"I'm not tired yet."

"Suit yourself. I'll get that shopping list drawn up for you tomorrow, after breakfast."

After he was gone, Bolan got up and stood before

the window, staring at the desert waste outside, where stars and a three-quarter moon provided all the light nocturnal hunters needed to pursue their prey. He glanced down at the windowsill, near Murphy's chair, and saw the compact telephone that Murphy had apparently forgotten.

Was it worth the risk?

Bolan made his decision in a flash, picked up the lightweight instrument and made his way outside, into the night.

JACK KEHOE FELT as if he had been resurrected from the dead. By all accounts, he should have *been* dead after the disaster in Missouri, but his training and a certain natural resilience had enabled him to squeak by, while nearly a dozen of his comrades bought the farm. Some might have given Lady Luck the credit for survival, but Jack Kehoe was convinced that each man made his own luck—with a little help from Fate, perhaps.

He had survived, in short, because he still had work to do, a mission to complete. If it came down to simple payback, then so be it. Kehoe lived to serve the cause, and nothing short of death would stop him now.

His comrades of The Path didn't refer to Kehoe by his given name, of course. Indeed, if asked, most could have honestly replied that they had never heard of Jack Kehoe. He had been Pluto to the cult from his induction to the present day, and if his earthly time ran out before the Ancients came again, he would be known as Pluto at his death.

In fact most of the fellow members he had known believed that he was dead already. Some of them had mourned his passing, privately; the rest would simply take for granted that his spirit, Pluto's essence, would return to join them in some other form, once Earth was cleansed of unbelievers and the Ancients reigned in global peace.

But they were wrong, of course.

It was an understandable mistake, all things considered. Pluto had been one of twelve commandos from Thor's Hammer who were sent to a St. Louis suburb less than two weeks earlier, to strike a blow on behalf of their exalted cause. The first phase of the plan had gone like clockwork, when they occupied the Mormon temple in suburban Town and Country, herding staffers into the chapel before their team leader demanded access to the public media. He had a message to deliver, on behalf of the returning Ancients. Once that message had been broadcast, it would be his pleasure to release the hostages. There would be no demands for cash, jet planes or helicopters. No pathetic pleas for amnesty.

It was assumed, in fact, that once the message was delivered, it would have such impact on the global audience that no negotiations for a free pass out of jail would be required. The truth was strong enough to topple governments, change minds and hearts. It could remake the world.

Of course, things hadn't quite worked out as they were planned. Instead of gabbing with an FBI negotiator, as anticipated, they had run head-on into a trigger-happy SWAT team leader from St. Louis, who precipitated an assault. The whole game went to hell from there, with ten of Pluto's friends gunned down like common thugs.

There should have been twelve dead, but two had managed to escape the trap. Pluto was one of them, but he wasn't the first to slip away. Nimrod had shown the way, although he seemed to think that he was unobserved, his traitorous escape unknown to anyone who might report it back to Ares or The Two.

Pluto had never fully trusted Nimrod, from the moment of the new man's first appearance at the Boulder compound. He could never put his finger on a clear-cut reason for mistrusting Nimrod, but he felt it, all the same. He had been watching the man, hoping for an opportunity to bring him down, expose him, when the two of them were chosen as participants in the Missouri raid. Once they were on the site, Pluto had made a point of shadowing his target, worried—so he told himself—that Nimrod might attempt to foil the mission. As it happened, the police had made their move instead, but Pluto had been on the spot when Nimrod slipped away, instead of standing fast and fighting like the rest.

Abandoning his comrades in the temple ranked as one of the most difficult decisions Pluto had ever been forced to make. Too late to stop Nimrod's escape, Pluto was forced to choose between remaining with the others—following his orders, as it were—or trying to pursue the man he now knew as a proved enemy to stop him, or at least to warn the leaders of The Path against a traitor in their midst. In the split second that was granted to him, Pluto chose to live.

Escaping from the temple had been no great challenge, looking back on it—at least, once he had seen how Nimrod pulled it off. An exit from the basement, coupled with the all-white garb affected by the temple staff, and he was out of there in the confusion, while police were busy pumping gas and bullets through the entrances of which they were aware. He had escaped in the confusion, but Nimrod had been too far ahead of him for Pluto to engage in hot pursuit.

From that point on, it had become a deadly game of hide-and-seek. It had been several hours after slipping through the net, before he found a public telephone that he deemed safe to use. By that time, the several emergency numbers that Pluto had memorized in advance of the raid were all disconnected, no alternate numbers available.

Pluto had gone to ground at a motel near Warrensburg, some fifty miles due east of Kansas City. There, holed up in his shabby room, he had watched televised reports of the temple massacre, soon followed by bulletins of a federal raid on the Boulder retreat. The FBI and ATF had linked the action in Missouri to Thor's Hammer and The Path, it seemed, and they were mopping up the sect wherever remnants could be found. According to the televised reports, at least four hundred members were detained from coast to coast, though most of them were soon released for lack of evidence connecting them to any criminal activity. As for the members of Thor's Hammer caught with weapons, several had been killed or wounded battling with the Feds, while others were held without bond, pending grand-jury action or preliminary court hearings.

Uncertain what to do without a contact number, Pluto had continued westward, living on junk food and driving by night, holing up in the cheapest motels he could find during daylight, desperately hoping that an answer would somehow present itself. He was outside Conejos, Colorado, when the news came through about a massacre in Arizona, members of the Peacekeeper Militia and the Widow Makers motorcycle gang battling to the death on a stretch of desert highway north of Kingman. Some kind of massive truck bomb was involved, with seventeen reported dead.

It all meant squat to Pluto, but he listened anyway, as a lieutenant with the Arizona State Police began to name a handful of the dead. Among presumed militia members, ID'd via fingerprints, had been one Herbert Walker Stone.

It rang a bell with Pluto, who had known the dead man by another name. Within The Path, he had been known as Canis. It was sheer coincidence that they had joined around the same time, and that Pluto still recalled his fellow rookie's given name.

That told him that The Path had somehow been involved with the explosive incident, though Pluto took for granted that the scheme hadn't been hatched in order to destroy some outlaw bikers on a sunbaked stretch of desert road. It had to be that the scheme had gone awry somehow, as in Missouri—and that thought, in turn, had instantly renewed the urgency of his desire to get in touch with Ares, warn his chief about Nimrod, the danger of betrayal by a wolf within the fold.

But how to get in touch, when all the contact numbers he had memorized were canceled, and the sect was nowhere listed in a telephone directory?

As soon as he had phrased the question, Pluto knew the answer, furious with himself that he hadn't devised it sooner. It was true enough, of course: there was no listing for The Path, per se. But there were several routes to any given destination, and in this case, there was one which still remained overt and—so he hoped—intact.

Stargate, Incorporated, was the sect's commercial arm, involved in varied aspects of computer programming and software sales. The office was in Denver. Pluto turned his stolen Chevy north and drove until he reached the outskirts of the Mile-High City, where he found a roadside booth and placed his call. He had to settle for a message left on Ingrid Walsh's voice mail—she whom he knew first as Star, The Path's computer brain and overseer of Stargate, Inc. He left a cryptic message—Mr. Pluto calling, with some news about the sales force in Missouri—and supplied the number for the public telephone. That done, there had been nothing else to do but sit and wait, the best part of two hours, until one of Star's subordinates had called him back.

The rest was history.

He had been placed in touch with Ares, out in California, and had spilled his guts, praying the line hadn't been tapped. When he was finished talking, Ares had supplied him with the name and number for a credit card, instructing him to book a reservation on the next flight out of Denver, bound for San Bernardino. Other members of the sect would meet him at the airport, and it was an easy hour's drive to Barstow through the desert.

As he cradled the receiver and prepared to make his final call, Pluto felt better than he had in days. He had a job to do, mixing business with pleasure, and he found that he could hardly wait.

This time tomorrow, he would feel like a new man.

This time tomorrow, Nimrod would be dead.

IT WAS PUSHING midnight when they reached the Desert Palms Motel on Barstow's outskirts, but Celeste Bouchet was wide awake. The hasty flight had keyed her up, and she hadn't relaxed while they were motoring across the moonlit desert, even though they mostly drove in silence, headlights boring tunnels through the dark.

Now, there they were, Andy Morrell inside the office, booking separate rooms, and still she doubted whether she would get to sleep this night. With so much happening, the turmoil that she felt inside, how could she even dare to close her eyes?

The call from Washington had come as a surprise, albeit welcome. Hal Brognola had at last been contacted by Michael Blake, he told Celeste. Blake wasn't dead, as she had feared, nor had he been discovered as a traitor and confined by agents of The Path. A former member of the cult herself, Celeste—once known as Virgo to her fellow members of The

Path—knew how the sect could discipline its own, if they were found in violation of its laws. Should Blake's betrayal be discovered, there could only be one fitting punishment.

And that was death.

But now she knew he was alive and well, if not exactly safe. He had rejoined the cult somehow after the bloodshed in Missouri, and while she had learned no details from Brognola's call, at least she knew where Blake was. Sometime tomorrow, if her luck held, she would see him once again.

In Barstow.

There had been no way to arrange the meeting, but the town wasn't so large that she believed Blake could avoid her if he made the rounds of stores on the main drag. She simply had to watch and wait, unless—

Andy Morrell distracted her, emerging from the motel office with a pair of keys in hand. He slid behind the rented Buick's steering wheel and twisted the ignition key, backed out and made a U-turn in the parking lot, to find an empty space between the doors of their adjoining rooms. They had one suitcase each, and Morrell fetched them both out of the Buick's trunk.

Bouchet took room 19, while Andy stowed his bag next door in number twenty, and returned briefly to see if there was anything she needed prior to turning in.

"I don't know about turning in," she said. "I feel like I could stay awake for days."

"Nerves talking," Morrell said. "You won't be

any good to Blake or to yourself tomorrow if you're half asleep."

"You don't suppose—" She caught herself and stopped before the thought took solid shape as words.

"What's on your mind?" the former G-man asked. "Come on, now. Spit it out."

"I can't help thinking he's in trouble," she replied.

"Who, Blake?" As soon as Morrell asked the question, he lowered his eyes and blushed, knowing how foolish it sounded. When he met her gaze again, he said, "I'd guess you're right."

"That's reassuring," she replied, but when she tried to force a smile, it felt lopsided, awkward on her face.

"I could have lied to you," he said, "but what's the point? We both knew he'd be playing with a rough crowd. So did he. It's what he does, Celeste. The man's a pro."

"Pros still get hurt," she said, and felt her voice begin to break. "They still get...killed."

"Don't sell Blake short. I have a feeling that he's tougher than you give him credit for."

"I hope so." She could think of nothing else to say.

"You really ought to try to get some sleep," he said. "I've got a wakeup call for half-past five o'clock."

"Give me a buzz when you get up?" she asked.

"I will. Good night, Celeste."

"I'll see you, Andy."

After she had double-locked the door behind him, she undressed, debating whether she should shower now or in the morning, and decided it could wait. She pulled on a baggy T-shirt and got in bed, fluffing up the pillows before she leaned against them, with her shoulders pressed against the headboard's thin veneer. She switched on the television with its remote control and channel-surfed until she found a monster movie she had seen about a hundred times, muting the volume so that she wasn't required to hear the snarls and screams.

The room was small and plain, the walls constructed of cinder blocks that had been painted gray by someone with a small budget and even more limited imagination. Sitting up in bed with the lights off, bathed in flickering colors from the silent TV set, she felt cut off from the world outside, and wished that she could stay that way forever, freezing time dead in its tracks. Outside, in her imaginary universe, there was no threat to anyone, including Michael Blake, and wouldn't be again unless she broke the spell and stepped outside.

The next morning she would meet Andy for a hasty breakfast in the coffee shop before they started staking out the streets. She could decide to stand him up, of course, renege on her part of the deal, stay exactly where she was until her cash ran out and the motel owners evicted her by force, but what good would that do?

Outside her little room, the world was going about its business. Nothing that she fantasized in here would make the slightest bit of difference to anyone.

Indeed, she thought, if Ares and the others knew that she was here, nothing but nervous fear would stop them breaking down the door to carry her away, or kill her in her bed.

So much for fantasy.

She tried to concentrate on what she *hoped* would happen in the morning. The ideal scenario, she thought, would be an early rendezvous with Blake, no tails or spies to interfere. They would have time to talk, and she would…what? Convince him to give up the mission, break off contact with the cult and save himself? How could she even broach that subject, when it had been her demands for help that sent him to The Path in the beginning?

She was nothing but a coward and a hypocrite, Bouchet decided. She had taken on a monster she could never hope to beat, not even with the help of Michael Blake or Andy. For all their efforts in the past few weeks, in spite of any superficial damage that the cult had suffered, Ares and The Two were still at large, no doubt still scheming toward the fiery end of all humankind aside from their disciples.

She had never really thought they could achieve that goal. It was too much, too grandiose—too horrible. It was like something from a James Bond movie; even thinking of it seriously made her want to laugh out loud. And yet…

There *had* been acts of terrorism, deaths, destruction. Granted, it was on a modest scale so far, but everything was relative. For those already killed, the Final Days *had* come and gone.

Might any of them be alive, Bouchet asked herself, if she had simply kept her mouth shut and allowed the cult's strange plans to run their course? Would she feel better, in that case, because the lives at risk belonged to strangers, men and women she would never know?

"Too late," she told the empty room, and tried to focus on the television screen. A hulking figure in a blood-flecked hockey mask was lumbering across the tarmac of a filling station, toward a blond young woman who was gassing up her car. She seemed oblivious until the final instant, when she spun and hosed him down with gasoline. The nightmare figure hesitated, glanced down at his dripping clothes and lifted a machete overhead. The young blonde palmed a lighter, flicked it once and tossed it at the shambling ghoul, who instantly exploded into flames.

And kept on coming, like a zombie etched from living fire.

The monster never died, a tiny, nagging voice reminded her. Just when you thought it was dead, a hand snaked out and grabbed you.

Just like in real life.

Exhaustion overtook her well before the movie's credits rolled. Bouchet had been so sure she wouldn't sleep that night, but nature pulled a fast one on her. Nodding in the half-light from the TV set, she was pursued by hulking monsters through an endless labyrinth. Somewhere ahead of her, she heard a woman screaming with a voice that sounded like her own.

CHAPTER NINE

It was another case of hurry up and wait. Bolan was up at dawn and ate an early breakfast, only to discover that he was too early for the stores to be open in nearby Barstow. It would be too conspicuous, he realized, if he drove into town and loitered on the street for hours, waiting for the stores to open, so he turned his mind toward killing time around the desert ranch.

He took a walk and thought about his brief talk with Brognola, some ten hours earlier. The big Fed had informed him that he would attempt to get in touch with "somebody," arrange a meeting for that day in Barstow, but the Executioner had no idea if it would happen. Touching base had been the main thing, and returning Murphy's pocket telephone before he noticed it was missing. If the shopping expedition went as planned, with Bolan on his own, he would have ample time to talk with Brognola again, assuming no one was on hand to meet him when he got to town.

Who would it be, assuming there was anyone at all? His thoughts turned naturally to Andy Morrell and Celeste Bouchet, but he couldn't begin to guess where they were at the moment. Were they still in Boulder? Were they even still together? Bolan knew that he would simply have to wait and see.

Bolan took off at half-past seven, tooling slowly down the gravel drive until he reached the highway, turning south from there and picking up the pace as he rolled on toward town. The desert wasn't baking yet, but it was warm enough to give Bolan a preview of the day to come. Another scorcher, when even rattlesnakes and scorpions would need a place to hide from the relentless sun.

Still short of eight o'clock when Bolan got to town, he drove from one end of the main drag to the other, doubled back again and found a handy parking space once he had spotted all the stores that he would need. His shopping list included groceries—most of them staples, canned or dried—along with certain minor items from the hardware store, some new clothes for himself and ten gallons of unleaded gasoline, for which he came prepared with twin five-gallon plastic cans.

Passing the town's handful of tired-looking motels, he scanned them quickly, wondering if Morrell or Bouchet was there, somewhere behind one of those numbered doors. He reckoned he would stop and get another cup of coffee, kill some time, then start his shopping with the hardware items, followed by the pants and shirts, perhaps an early break for lunch, before he hit the grocery store. The gasoline was last on Bolan's list, to keep from leaving it to bake inside the car. Somewhere along the way, he hoped, there would be contact. In the meantime, he could only watch and wait, go on about his business, killing time.

He dawdled over coffee at a place called Jolly's, sitting at the counter, where a sidelong glance showed him the Tool Time hardware store directly opposite. He counted half a dozen cars pulling into the lot before the store opened at eight o'clock, then watched the early shoppers filing in. When they had cleared the lot, he finished his coffee, left two dollars on the countertop beside his cup and left the diner, pausing on the sidewalk in the sun before he crossed the street.

They had the air-conditioning turned up full blast inside the hardware store, and Bolan was a bit surprised to find how much he had perspired, walking the eighty-odd yards from Jolly's diner underneath the washed-out, cloudless desert sky. The first blast of refrigerated air chilled him, drying the sweat on Bolan's neck and forehead. He regretted the light nylon windbreaker, but had no choice if he wanted to hide the Beretta. When he was finished here, Bolan decided, he would have to work on some alternative arrangement to avoid heatstroke.

The hardware items on his shopping list were fairly basic, certain tools for small repairs around the ranch house, to make life more comfortable for Murphy and his men. Bolan had no idea how long Murphy intended to remain in place; he would be told when it was time for him to know. Meanwhile, it was important that he keep up appearances.

He took a plastic shopping basket, wandering around the aisles until he had retrieved a claw hammer and several packs of nails, screwdrivers, a spanner wrench, some putty and an inexpensive metal spatula. Murphy had given him a wad of cash before he left the ranch, three hundred bucks and change, with instructions to cut the best deals he could find.

The tab came to $26.50 plus tax, and Bolan paid with three sawbucks, pocketing the handful of coins he received as change. Bracing himself for the hundred-yard walk to his centrally located car, Bolan found himself perspiring freely again before he had gone fifty feet.

The jacket had to go, he told himself, even if it meant pulling out his shirttail and shoving the Beretta inside his jeans.

He reached the car, unlocked it, placed his bag of tools in back and slipped into the shotgun seat. He had the sidewalk to himself, from all appearances. If he was quick enough about it, he could make the shift without an audience.

It was a relatively simple matter, slipping off the jacket and the shoulder rig, using one to hide the other as he placed both on the driver's seat. He had already sweated through his short-sleeved shirt, but there was nothing to be done about that now. Pulling out the tails, cowboy style, he slipped the black Beretta 92 out of its holster, tucking it in front at an angle, where it was covered by the baggy shirt. It meant that he would have to leave the extra magazines behind, and maybe do the bunny dip if he was forced to pick out any items from a lower shelf while he was shopping, but he reckoned he could live with that. The odds against a shoot-out here, in downtown Barstow, struck him as extreme.

He stepped out of the car, made sure the keys were in his pocket prior to locking up, and was about to make his next stop, when a short, trim figure materialized at his side.

"Is that a pistol in your belt," Celeste Bouchet asked Bolan, grinning, "or are you just glad to see me?"

PLUTO WAS TIRED of waiting, and he didn't give a damn who knew it. He had barely slept at all the night before, between the red-eye from Denver and his greeting at the San Bernardino airport by half a dozen soldiers of The Path, the drive to Barstow, checking into the motel and swilling coffee while they worked on basic plans.

He had six guns at his disposal—lucky seven, with himself—and while Pluto was glad to have the backup, he still planned to make the hit alone. Nimrod was his, a point that he had stressed repeatedly, while they were hunched over a map of Barstow, in his tiny rented room.

There wasn't all that much to map, of course—nor, truth be told, had there been very much to plan, in any strict sense of the word. Ares had told him Nimrod would be going into town to run some errands, but he was unable to predict exactly which stores he would visit, or in what order. The best Pluto and company could do was scatter, staking out strategic points, waiting for contact, when the spotter would alert his comrades and prepare to close the trap.

Of course, Pluto didn't intend to jump his pigeon in the heart of town. He had already seen a sheriff's prowl on the main drag, cruising slowly, while its hefty driver eyeballed vehicles along the curb. There might not be much law in Barstow, and the quality might suffer by comparison to larger, more professional departments, but a clash with any uniforms could bring the head down on his comrades at the ranch, and it would all be Pluto's fault.

Ares had been suspicious on the telephone, while Pluto was explaining his escape from the Missouri SWAT team. He had managed to deflect the heat from that one with his accusations against Nimrod, and the contract on his adversary's life was the reward. Now all he had to do was get it right, the perfect combination of revenge and service to The Path. If Pluto pulled it off in style, left no loose ends, he might even wind up with a promotion on the other end.

Five of the six young guns assigned to help him were new faces. He knew Fornax, vaguely, from a visit to Los Angeles some months before. The others—Altair, Crux, Dorado, Cepheus and Aquila—were strangers to him, but he trusted Ares to select a crew that knew the basics: how to follow orders, cover Pluto's back and leave the final kill to him.

They had come prepared for the job, each man with a pistol or two, a couple of them armed with compact Ingram MAC-10 submachine guns, Fornax with a stubby 12-gauge shotgun. Pluto had lost his

Uzi in Missouri, leaving it behind when he slipped out of the temple basement disguised as a staffer, but he still had his Smith & Wesson Model 1076 autoloader, one of the same .40-caliber handguns carried by FBI agents nationwide.

It would be all the hardware he required to do the job.

They had decided it was best to shadow Nimrod once they spotted him in town, and take him on the road when he was headed back to the ranch. They had two cars, and Pluto calculated they could box him on the highway, force him to the side—or simply blast him where he sat behind the wheel, if it came down to that. He would have liked to make the bastard suffer, but there simply wasn't time. A quick kill on the highway was the best that he could hope for; plant the body in a shallow grave, if there was nothing to prevent them stopping, and discard the car in Yermo, Daggett, Hinkley—one of the surrounding desert towns that made Barstow seem crowded by comparison.

Now they were spread out on the main drag, one man remaining with each of the cars, parked at opposite ends of the half-mile commercial strip, while the others patrolled on foot. Each hunter was equipped with a small walkie-talkie, the cheap toy store variety, but good enough to serve them in the present circumstances. Pluto had his in a plastic shopping bag, switched on, the volume turned low enough that he could hear incoming calls without alerting any passersby.

As it turned out, he didn't need to wait for an

announcement that his quarry had been found. Pluto was dawdling along the north side of the street, trying to window-shop without being mistaken for a shiftless idiot, when the reflection in a gift-shop window caught his eye. There was a car across the street, one of some half a dozen on the block, and Pluto saw a tall man just emerging from it now, rolling his shoulders like an athlete getting ready for a sprint.

Nimrod?

He wasn't sure at first, half turning so that he could eye the man directly without showing his face. The man's face was averted now, but Pluto mouthed a curse when he saw the woman. Strike one, he thought, and was about to shrug it off, continue on his way, when the tall man turned to face the woman, showing him a profile.

It *was* Nimrod! But who in hell was the woman?

Nimrod was turning in Pluto's direction, prompting him to pivot on his heel and take new interest in the gift-shop window. At the same time, he was sidling to his left, or eastward, where a sidewalk phone booth stood some twelve or fifteen feet away. Trying to keep it casual, he reached the booth and stepped inside. He lifted the receiver, held it to his face, the instrument and Pluto's fist obscuring his profile as he turned back toward the street to keep an eye on Nimrod.

While he wasn't looking, Nimrod and the woman had already crossed the street to Pluto's side, but they had turned away from him, retreating toward the east end of the block. Still clutching the telephone receiver to one ear, Pluto now raised the plastic walkie-talkie in his left hand, thumbing down the red transmission switch.

"All ears!" he snapped into the mouthpiece. "I have contact on the north side of the street, passing the Chaparral Gift Shop, eastbound. Two targets sighted. I repeat, two targets."

"Who's number two?" a voice that sounded very much like that of Cepheus came back to him.

"A woman," Pluto told his backup. "No ID, as yet."

"What if she sticks?" another voice came back.

"No change," Pluto replied, thinking fast. "A doubleheader plays the same. Break off and close on me, now. Careful as you go. Out!"

Pluto stashed the little two-way radio, hung up the receiver and prepared to step out of the phone booth. Reaching underneath the flimsy denim vest he wore, Pluto made certain that his Smith & Wesson was secure, just where he needed it to be when he was called upon to draw and fire.

He still intended to dispose of Nimrod on the highway, north of town, but anything could go wrong in the meantime. Nimrod might spot one of Pluto's soldiers, for example, and attempt to make a run for cover.

If the setup started going south, Pluto was ready to discard all caution and eliminate the bastard where he stood, broad daylight, even with a sheriff's deputy parked down the street.

Above all else, he was determined that this traitor to The Path had to die.

BOUCHET WAS ANXIOUS to know everything that Michael Blake had been involved in since she saw him last, but he was more inclined to summarize, cut corners, leaving out some parts that he appeared to think the woman might find disturbing.

"So, you just walked out the back door of the temple? Just like that?" she prodded him, remembering to keep her voice down, with a vaguely pleased expression on her face. They were supposed to be a pair of friends—or, maybe lovers; why not lovers, after all?—out for a day of shopping, on their way to somewhere else.

"It was a basement exit," Blake reminded her. "That's close enough, though."

"And they didn't have it covered? That strikes me as odd."

"You never know," he said. "It could be someone dropped the ball. Stuff happens."

"Or it could have been arranged?" She met Blake's level gaze and said, "Your friend in Washington could do that, couldn't he?"

It seemed to her that something very like a screen dropped into place behind the agent's eyes. "He might be able to," Blake granted her, "if he was in control. From what I understand, though, what went down in Town and Country came on orders from a local SWAT team officer. That doesn't leave much room for play."

"Well, anyway," she said, "the main thing is that you're all right."

"So far," he told her, grinning as he spoke. "It was a little hairy for a while in Arizona."

She went blank for several heartbeats, then it clicked. "My, God!" she blurted out. "You were involved in that? What happened?"

"Short version," Bolan said, "your buddy Ares cut a deal with the militia to go halfsies on a car bomb meant for a convention hotel in Las Vegas. Seems between the two of them, the brass was pissed off at a couple of attending groups."

"But what about the bikers?"

"That's what we call improvisation," Bolan replied. "A bunch of them were handy, and they all had chips the size of footballs on their shoulders. I decided to enlist their help."

He made no effort to elaborate, and she could tell by looking at him that no grilling she attempted would succeed. Instead, she switched her angle of attack.

"What's next?" she asked.

"I'm clueless. Murphy—Ares—makes it look like he's in hiding, but I'd bet my life he's still got something up his sleeve. As far as what it is, or when it's going down, I haven't got a thing."

"You haven't seen The Two, I guess," she said.

"Not even close. Nobody's mentioned them within earshot of me. They could be anywhere."

"I used to know their hideouts, dammit!" Angry with herself, Bouchet slapped one small fist into her other palm. "They've changed so much since I got out. I feel so useless!"

"Why don't you cut yourself some slack?" Bolan advised. "The chances are we wouldn't be on this at all, except for you. You've brought us this far. No one ever said you had to go the whole way on your own."

"And what have we accomplished?" she replied, a note of challenge in her voice. "How many dead so far—three dozen? Four? And all for what?"

"We've blocked them twice so far," he said. "Missouri and Las Vegas. If the Vegas bomb had gone on schedule, you'd be looking at another Oklahoma City, maybe worse."

"It isn't all for nothing, then?" she asked him, craving reassurance now, when they had come so far and there was still no end in sight.

"Not even close," he promised her. "You've paid your dues, and then some."

She came back to the question Bolan had already evaded once before. "I still need to find out what we'll be doing next," she said, "so I can fill in Hal and Andy."

Bolan allowed himself a little smile at that. "It's watch-and-wait time, like I said. When I get my orders, I'll find some way to relay them back to Hal. From there, my guess would be he'll tell you what you need to know."

She found little to say while they were shopping for his clothing, jeans and long-sleeved denim work shirts, briefs and crew socks. Bolan didn't try any of the items on, selecting them by size and style. They walked back to the car and stowed his latest purchase in the back.

"You want a lift?" he asked.

"Where are we going?" she inquired.

"The other end of town for groceries. It's not that

far to walk, of course, but then I'd have to steal a shopping cart for the return trip.''

''Let's drive, by all means, then,'' she said.

He held the door for her, then walked around the front end of the car. She watched him, sharp eyes scanning all directions, and she wondered to herself if this man ever knew a moment's peace. She hoped so, and the thought had barely taken shape before Bouchet was moved to ask herself why she should even care. He was a stranger and a gunman, almost certainly a mercenary or, what might be even worse, some kind of government assassin. Why was she concerned about his comfort now, when he was only helping her because he had been ordered to, by those who paid his salary and pulled his strings?

That's wrong, she told herself, somehow convinced that she was judging Michael Blake too harshly. There was something more than duty in the way he had performed so far, risking his life and taking other lives. What was it that she *did* feel for this man, this not-so-perfect stranger with a pistol in his belt and eyes like chips of flint?

There was no flint in Bolan's gaze, though, as he slid in behind the steering wheel and smiled at her, reaching for the ignition key.

''Away we go,'' he said, and she couldn't help laughing at the Jackie Gleason imitation, even in the present circumstances.

Right, she thought. Away we go.

IT WAS AN OVEN inside the car. Bolan revved the engine, turned on the air conditioner full blast and shifted into gear. He checked his left-hand mirror, and was just about to pull out from the curb when he glimpsed something in the glass that made him hesitate.

Three spaces back, just nosing forward as if it might follow Bolan, was a black Jeep Cherokee. No problem there, he told himself. Four-wheelers were the rule in desert country, and the fact of two cars pulling out at once was mere coincidence, the kind of thing that happened several million times a day in towns and cities all across the continent.

It was the faces in the truck—one of them, anyway—that held his attention. There were three men inside the Cherokee, one darkly shadowed in the back, the driver young and unfamiliar, though his close-cropped haircut struck a chord in Bolan's memory. It was the passenger whose face arrested Bolan, froze him in his seat with one hand on the gearshift and the other on the steering wheel.

Pluto.

He had assumed the other man was dead back in Missouri. Bolan hadn't paid a great deal of attention to the media reports about the Mormon temple raid, except to learn that something like a dozen raiders had been killed by the St. Louis SWAT team. That was close enough for Bolan, since he made it twelve, the one who got away. There was no reason to assume that any other member of the team had made it out.

And if one had, where was he hiding for the past...what? Ten days now? What brought him to

Barstow with a hit team, at the very moment Dillon Murphy had arranged for Bolan to be on his own?

"Get out!" he snapped.

Bouchet blinked at him, taken by surprise. "Excuse me?"

"We've got company," he said. "They didn't come to help me shop, all right? If you get out right now, you just may have a chance to make your break."

"No way," she told him firmly, crossing tanned arms underneath her breasts. "They grabbed me once, remember? I'm not going through all that again."

"These boys aren't after you," he said, "now, for the last time—"

"For the last time, no!" she flared. "You want to drive, or face them here? I'll be right with you, either way."

"Your funeral," the Executioner replied.

He pulled out from the curb, staying cool and casual, as he rolled past a squad car coming from the opposite direction. If Bolan was going to involve the law, he knew that this could be his one and only chance—but to what end? One deputy could hardly be of much assistance to him in the present circumstances, and he was more likely to obstruct whatever play Bolan devised. An SOS would put the officer at risk, at least a fifty-fifty chance that it would get him killed—and more than likely, it would all be a waste.

"I need to take them out of town," Bolan said. "When that light goes red in front of us the next block down, I'm stopping for it. That will be your last chance to get out."

"I told you I was staying, didn't I?"

"I haven't got a piece to loan you," Bolan said.

"A piece of what?" she asked, then understood. "Oh, well, of course. I understand." She smiled at him and slipped a hand into her purse, extracting what appeared to be a Walther semiautomatic, stainless-steel pistol. "I brought my own."

"Do you know how to use that?" Bolan asked, as they approached the intersection, where the traffic light glowed cherry red. He checked the rearview mirror as he spoke, and saw the Cherokee roll up beside them. Still, Pluto and friends made no attempt to rush him. They were waiting, too.

"I'm qualified," she told him, sounding smug.

"You mean on paper targets?"

"Well..."

"How many people have you killed?" he asked her, knowing what the answer had to be.

"I've never..." Hesitating, biting at her lower lip, she finally told him, "None."

"It makes a difference," Bolan told her. "Paper targets don't shoot back. They don't spit blood and scream. When it's for real, for keeps, you can't let any of that slow you down. Out on the target range, you hesitate too long, you lose points and they make you try again. In combat, any hesitation is too long, and it can damn well get you killed."

"I know that!"

"So be ready. These men want me dead, which means they have to mop up any witnesses, whether they've recognized your face or not. They won't think twice before they drop the hammer on you. Keep that thought foremost in mind, and aim for the center of mass when you fire. Do it right the first time, every time, and you just might survive."

Bouchet was grim-faced, sitting with the pistol in her lap, both hands wrapped tight around the grips. "Is that all?" she asked Bolan stiffly.

"No," he told her, glancing at the rearview mirror once again, as they approached the Barstow city limits.

"No? You mean, there's more bad news you haven't shared?"

"We've got a second tail," he said. "It looks like six or seven guns, instead of three."

CHAPTER TEN

Bolan drove westward. He had decided in the moment that he recognized Pluto behind him, that he shouldn't head back in the direction of the ranch. There were two reasons for his choice. The first was that he dared not bring Bouchet to the very doorstep of her enemies. The second, having recognized Pluto with a team of unknown gunners who were doubtless also members of The Path, was that the order for the hit had almost certainly been issued by Dillon Murphy.

That it was supposed to be a hit instead of mere surveillance, Bolan had no doubts at all. If Murphy was intent on watching him, he could have sent along one of the soldiers from the ranch to keep him company. And if he chose a different route, the last person he would assign to watch Bolan would be a soldier Bolan knew by sight.

The curiosity of Pluto's survival, his escape from the Missouri SWAT team, was the least of Bolan's problems at the moment. Obviously Pluto *had* escaped, had touched bases with the leader of Thor's Hammer and had drawn a death card with Bolan's name on it. That meant the game was up.

The plan, so far, amounted to no more than getting out of town, finding a place where he would have some combat stretch without risk of innocent civilians being cut down in the cross fire. It displeased him that Bouchet was in the car, but he was willing to acknowledge that unloading her wouldn't have meant that she was safe, especially with two cars on their tail.

This way, at least, she had a fighting chance.

Ten miles of open road lay between Barstow and Hinkley, the next town to the west, then another twenty-one miles to Four Corners. Bolan didn't plan to go that far—he doubted that his enemies would let him, in the first place—but his choice of roads, avoiding either of the interstates that passed through Barstow, was designed to minimize the risk to other motorists, while simultaneously cutting down the odds of meeting a highway patrolman.

They were barely out of town when Pluto and his driver made their move, coming up fast on Bolan's bumper, while the second chase car closed the gap.

"Fasten your seat belt," Bolan told Bouchet.

"Got it," she said, her comment punctuated by a sharp, metallic snap.

The Jeep kissed his bumper, and Bolan pressed on the accelerator, felt the car respond, surging forward. It was only a moment's respite though, the Cherokee filling his rearview mirror, Pluto's lips writhing silently, giving orders to the wheelman.

Bolan doubted that he could outrun the two pursuit vehicles, and he had no plans to try. His best choice, in the circumstances, was to pick the place where he would turn and make his stand.

If they would only let him.

Glancing at his rearview mirror, Bolan saw the Cherokee swing wide, out to his left, trying to pass him on the driver's side. He gave the wheel a nudge in that direction, drifting, closing the window of opportunity.

"They want to box us," Bolan told Bouchet. "Be on the lookout for a place where we can stand and fight."

"Can't you just lose them?"

"Not out here," he said. "I make it seven guns. Whatever happens, try to keep your head down."

"I can help," she told him, and he caught a note of irritation underneath the fear.

Bolan didn't respond. He was too busy cranking down his window, grimacing as a rush of hot air stung his face. That done, he shifted hands, so that his left was on the steering wheel, gripping the sleek Beretta in his right.

This time, when Pluto's driver tried to pass, Bolan didn't attempt to cut him off. His eyes were constantly in motion, checking the highway, picking up the Dodge in his rearview, checking the outside mirror on his left to keep track of the Cherokee.

The Jeep was gaining on them, bumper level with his left-rear wheel now, closing fast. Bolan ducked lower, spotting Pluto as the man rolled down his window and stuck out a semiauto pistol. Not firing yet, the shooter was content to bide his time, seek target acquisition for the kill.

Bolan was there ahead of him, checking the open highway one more time for traffic, then returning his attention to the outside mirror. He wouldn't expose himself by leaning out the window as he fired. Only the Executioner's hand and pistol were visible, the weapon's muzzle pointed toward the Cherokee.

The soldier was good, but he didn't pretend to be a trick-shot artist. Squeezing off two rounds, and then two more, he saw one of them punch a shiny divot in the Cherokee's door, a foot or so below Pluto's extended arm, while another cracked the windshield. Any noise of impact blew away, lost in their slipstream, and he heard only the echo of his shots. Bouchet bit off a startled cry and ducked her head, slumped lower in her seat.

The Cherokee fell back, swung in behind him, cutting off the Dodge. Bolan's rearview mirror showed him no further signs of damage to the Jeep, and it was clear that he had scored no hits on any of the occupants. It would have been too much to hope for in the circumstances.

Pluto chose that moment to unload a burst of semiautomatic fire, more rage than planning to it, but he still scored several hits. Two rounds struck Bolan's trunk with the explosive force of hammer blows and wrung another cry out of his passenger.

"Sorry," she said a heartbeat later, angry color rising in her cheeks.

"No sweat," he told her, concentrating on the road ahead of him, the enemies behind.

Another slug glanced off the roof somewhere above his head and slightly to the rear. Bouchet was half turned in her seat, watching the Jeep, her pistol pressed into the cushion.

"Careful with that thing," he cautioned her.

"The safety's on," she told him, yelping sharply as another slug glanced off the fender on her side. "What if they hit the gas tank?"

"We run out of gas," he told her.

"Oh."

There was no reason to discuss the possibility of an explosion, far more likely in a Hollywood production than real life. It was the fumes of gasoline that burned, and some kind of a spark was normally required. Most times, a bullet in the tank, though hot enough to burn your skin on contact, failed to start a fire.

Most times.

The broad rear window shattered, spilling pebbled safety glass on Bolan's purchases in the back seat. This time, although she squealed again, Bouchet seemed more angry than frightened. Bolan saw her aim her pistol through the open windowframe, arms braced against her seat, and squeeze off three quick shots. The Cherokee swerved wide, fell back a few yards, then came back on point.

"Bastards!"

"Don't waste your ammo," Bolan said. "We'll need it when we stop."

"So, when—"

"Hang on!" he snapped, and swung the steering wheel hard left, fishtailing as he made the turnoff on a narrow access road. Bouchet let out a little squeal, but braced herself against the dashboard with her left hand, clinging to the pistol with her right.

The access road was paved, after a fashion, but poor maintenance had given Mother Nature a fair start on reclamation, weeds sprouting up through cracks in the asphalt, potholes deep enough to bounce the car as he raced over them.

Another thousand yards or so, he told himself. He had to keep up the lead, then find a place to stop and come out firing.

Right.

Now all he had to do was stay alive that long, so he could give his enemies another, better chance to cut him down.

CELESTE BOUCHET had never cared much for carnival rides, and she didn't like this one at all. The jolting, rocking car was bad enough without the threat of bullets zipping through a window, drilling through her skull.

The hostile fire had slacked off since they left the highway, granted, but she still kept well down in her seat. That wouldn't save her, either, but it was the best that she could do. She had thought of scrunching down below the dashboard, but she was embarrassed to display such fear in front of Michael Blake.

How was that for stupid? asked a little voice inside her head. To which she had no answer.

All the same, she knew that any seeming show of bravery on her part wouldn't be entirely for Blake's benefit. She had been hiding from the cult for two years now, and she was sick of it. If this turned out to be her final hour, then by God, at least she would do everything she could to take a couple of the bastards with her.

If they didn't kill her first.

She heard another pistol shot behind them, but it seemed to miss the car entirely. Turning in her seat, she peered around the headrest, feeling rather like a small child at a drive-in movie, only this time with the action leaping off the screen. She craved an intermission, but the men pursuing them would never rest until they made the kill—or were themselves wiped out.

The Path bred true fanatics; she had to give them that. Bouchet had no doubt that the men behind them were convinced their hunting party had some vital part in bringing back the Ancients, moving up the schedule of the Final Days. They would regard themselves as heroes—or, at least, as faithful worker bees—and they would give their all, risk anything, to finish the job.

The desert stretched away on every side as far as she could see. Blake had switched off the air conditioner to give the car more power, and the hot air rushing through his open window brought a sheen of perspiration to her forehead. Rivaling the clammy sweat beneath her arms, she felt a sudden need to urinate, inspired by fear. *Not now!* she told herself, and tried to put the thought out of her mind.

She had to give Blake credit, looking at him from her hunched position in the passenger's seat. He seemed nearly as calm as if they had been driving to a Sunday picnic, instead of fleeing for their lives, pursued by homicidal religious fanatics. She supposed it had to be something he was used to, living as he did. Not long ago, when he had stepped into her life the first time, in Los Angeles, she had observed the same expression on his face after he killed four other gunmen from The Path. It had to be second nature to him, but she couldn't help wondering how it had to feel to take another human life.

Brief moments earlier, she had been in that mood herself, but firing at the car behind them, coupled with Blake's warning to conserve her ammunition for the final showdown, had been like a slap in the face. At the moment she fired, Bouchet had been raging, infuriated by years of hiding like a fugitive from justice, being hunted by fanatics who were once her "brothers," finally determined to strike back, sell her life dearly, if she could. The recoil of the weapon in her fist had shocked her, somehow, even after all the practice she had put in on the target range in California, reminding her how fragile life could be.

She wished them dead, all the same. She was afraid, no doubt about it, but she had enough self-confidence to think she wouldn't freeze when Blake had found a place to stop the car, to stand and fight. Bouchet believed that it was likely they would lose, forfeit their lives, and while the prospect terrified her, she wouldn't allow that fear to leave her paralyzed, unwilling or unable to defend herself.

Another bullet struck the car, resounding like the impact of a brick thrown at close range. She winced, ducked lower in the seat, but it didn't appear to penetrate the bodywork. That was pure dumb luck, she realized, but at the moment, she would take what she could get.

"Looks like a fair place up ahead," Bolan told her, speaking in a level tone, as if reporting that it looked like rain.

She raised her head to peer across the dashboard, trying to pick out what he had seen. It all looked like the same wasteland to her, with Joshua trees and cactus, gravel on both shoulders of the road, nothing except the blacktop ribbon underneath them to suggest that other men had ever passed that way. She couldn't see the "fair place" Blake had spotted, but she trusted him enough to follow any play he called.

"I'll need to swing the car around," he told her. "You'll be on the far side from the shooters. When I tell you, bail out on your side, and I'll be right behind you. Clear?"

"I'm there," she told him, reaching with her left hand for the inside handle of her door, keeping the pistol steady in her right.

"Once we're outside," Bolan instructed, "stay under cover all you can. Don't give them any targets, all right?"

"Okay." Her voice was a whisper, barely audible.

She didn't know about that part of it, however, couldn't see herself hiding without a fight, no matter how much she might wish to do exactly that. Thor's Hammer had been haunting her for too long. If she could pay them back in some degree for all the sleepless nights that she had suffered, all the months of watching for strangers on the street, suspecting anyone who made a passing comment to her, she was bound to take the chance.

And if she didn't, then what? If she left this man to fight the predators alone, and he was killed, she would be lost in any case.

"Get ready," Bolan cautioned. "Another fifty yards. Right...*now!*"

She braced herself with stiffened legs, as he stamped on the brake and cranked the steering wheel hard left, swinging the rear end of the car around and screeching to a halt, half off the pavement.

"Go!" he snapped, and she was bailing out of there, a dust cloud swirling in her face, making her gag, her vision obscured. She cleared the open door and scooted to her right, Blake lunging out behind her, kicking back to slam the door when he was clear. It seemed to her the echo of their squealing brakes went on and on, until she realized that she was listening to their pursuers, swerving to a halt and trying to avoid collision with the vehicle that blocked their path.

She held the pistol in both hands as she duck-walked toward the rear end of the car. If only she could get one decent shot, drop one of them and know that he was dead before they cut her down. Just one.

Behind her, Blake was firing, and that fire was soon returned, the car absorbing hits. Bouchet was trembling, but she didn't let it stop her. This was probably her last chance to repay the cult for all that she had suffered, and she meant to make it count.

Beginning now.

PLUTO HAD WASTED half a magazine of ammunition firing at the car, scoring a few chance hits that never even slowed his targets. On top of that, he had come close to being hit himself, not once, but twice. The first time, Nimrod had surprised him, firing through the driver's window, one slug thumping solidly into the door beneath his elbow, while another cracked the windshield. Moments later, when the woman opened fire, one round had struck the Jeep's hood, ricocheted and drilled the windshield, shearing the right side of the rearview mirror.

Pluto had tried to keep his head down after that, the hot wind rushing through his open window, whipping his hair into determined tangles that would cost no end of pain, untangling them with a comb. His grooming was the least of Pluto's problems at the moment, though. Before he started cleaning up, he had to do the job that he had begged for: finish the mission Ares had assigned him as a test of Pluto's ultimate fidelity.

He had to kill Nimrod, and while he still believed the moment when he pulled it off would be a pleasure, Nimrod had already shown him that it would be no easy task.

This wasn't Pluto's first attempt to smoke the man he—for reasons even he couldn't define—distrusted and despised on sight. It *was* the first time he had tried to kill Nimrod with sanction from The Path, however, and he meant to make the most of it.

There was no further shooting from the lead car, and while Pluto squeezed off two or three more rounds, he did it more for show, to demonstrate that he hadn't been frightened into immobility, than out of any hope that he would score a lucky hit and stop the car.

Their target did that for him, after they had lurched and bounced along the rugged access road for something like a mile, by Pluto's estimate. He had been praying Nimrod would be stricken by a flat, swerve off the road—most anything, in fact, to stop him short—and still, when his intended victim hit the brakes and swung the car around to block three-quarters of the narrow road, the move took Pluto absolutely by surprise.

His driver was surprised, as well, but saved it with a lead foot on the brake pedal and some deft handling of the steering wheel. The Dodge behind them swerved to miss colliding with the Cherokee and wound up off-road in the sand. Its right-rear tire spun uselessly for several seconds, raising clouds of dust before the driver gave it up and bailed out of his seat, the Dodge already taking hits.

Pluto wasn't concerned about the other car. His Cherokee was fitted with a winch, and they could always haul the Dodge back onto solid pavement once the job was done. Just now, though, Nimrod was alive and well, and fighting back with everything he had.

How much was that? the hit team leader asked himself. So far, all they had seen or heard from Nimrod's side had been one pistol, maybe two. On Pluto's crew, Altair and Crux were packing Ingrams, Fornax had his shotguns and the rest all had their side arms—Cepheus with two, a pair of twin Glock

17s. What worried Pluto was the thought of Nimrod holding something in reserve—an automatic weapon, say, or hand grenades—to use in case they rushed him.

Bullshit! he told himself. If Nimrod had an edge, he would be using it by then.

The hunters were returning fire, not spraying wildly, but conserving ammunition, as they had been taught. Pluto admired their discipline, but he wouldn't allow himself to think in terms of a protracted siege. It made no difference that they were a fair stretch from the highway and unlikely to be seen by passing motorists. Gunfire was loud out here, and seemed to carry on the dry, hot wind for miles. And speaking of the heat, sweat streaming down his face reminded Pluto that they had no shade, no water—nothing but the white-hot, unrelenting sun above.

It had the makings of a long, hot day; the kind of desert heat that dried you out, produced hallucinations, that would kill you if you didn't watch your step and take precautions—all of which had been ignored by Pluto in his haste to bag the enemy.

He worked his way around the rear end of the Cherokee, still sheltered from incoming fire, to the position where a glance around the right-rear fender showed him part of Nimrod's vehicle. It was a Chevrolet, he realized, for all the good that did him. All along the driver's side, facing toward Pluto, there were ragged lines of shiny spots where bullets had punched through and flaked off the paint in near-perfect circles.

All in vain, so far, from what he saw. Nimrod

popped from cover and squeezed off two quick shots across the Chevy's hood. Another shot, meanwhile, was fired from somewhere near the rear end of the car, the bullet thumping into steel a foot or so from Pluto's head.

Two pistols, then, at least. He wondered briefly who the woman was, but didn't let the problem sidetrack him. Whoever this bitch was, she would be dead before much longer. They could always check the body for ID, and if they never found out who she was, what difference would it make?

Pluto edged back the way he came and nearly stumbled over Altair, stretched out on the ground behind the Cherokee. A lucky shot had drilled through his left eye socket and taken out a fist-sized chunk of skull in back—a crimson halo glistening around his head. Pluto scooped up the Ingram SMG the man had dropped, pulling the magazine to check its load, discovering that there were still some fifteen rounds in place.

They wouldn't last long, with the Ingram's awesome cyclic rate of fire—1,200 rounds per minute, on average—and he balked at pawing through the corpse's pockets for spare magazines. Still, he felt better with the little submachine gun in his hand.

"Get over here!" he snapped at Fornax and Aquila. Hunched below the line of fire, they waddled over to him, faithful trolls, and waited for their orders, shooting little glances at Altair, sprawled out on the pavement.

"We're fucked up if we just sit here, plinking back and forth," he told them. "It's already cost us one man, and he may as well have gone out doing something helpful.''

''Helpful?'' Fornax echoed, looking doubtful.

''Look, we've got them three to one,'' Pluto said. ''Those are standard odds for an assault in any book on strategy you want to name.''

''Assault?'' Fornax sounded gravely skeptical and didn't seem to care who knew it.

''Right.'' Pluto glared at him, brooking no defiance. ''We were sent here with a job to do, and we can't do it sitting here.''

''So what's the plan?'' Fornax asked.

''We divide our force and rush them,'' Pluto stated, ignoring solemn frowns from both of his subordinates. ''The three of us will break around the north end of the car, while they—'' he nodded toward the Dodge and the three men crouched behind it ''—take the south end. Fornax, you slip over there and tell them to be ready on my signal, then get back here.''

''I was wondering—''

''I mean right now, soldier!'' There was a cutting edge to Pluto's voice, and Fornax bobbed his head, crept back along the full length of the Cherokee, until he reached the right-rear fender. Hesitating for another moment, waiting for a heartbeat's respite in the cross fire, he crossed fifty feet of open ground with loping strides, dropping and sliding for the last few feet, much like a baseball player stealing home.

Pluto watched Fornax and the others arguing, his runner nodding toward the Jeep from time to time, once cocking a thumb toward their leader. Pluto briefly feared that he would be confronted with a mutiny, but he got lucky, with Dorado and the others nodding their acceptance of the order, even as they scowled and grumbled.

Moments later, Fornax made a dash back to the Cherokee, with spotty cover from his friends behind the Dodge. The soldiers spent another moment checking weapons, topping off their magazines, until the team was ready, all eyes fixed on Pluto.

He raised an empty hand. No spoken signal to alert Nimrod, no fleeting moment for the bastard to prepare himself. Pluto was conscious of the muscles cramping, aching in his thighs, but he would run because he had to, charge because there was no other choice.

Right...now!

His arm slashed downward, and Pluto was on his feet and running even as he gave the signal, panicked for an instant by the thought that no one else would follow him. Too late to check, he fired a short burst from his liberated SMG and watched the Chevy's windshield sprout a maze of cracks.

Someone was roaring with a harsh, almost inhuman voice. Pluto had covered nearly half the distance to the other car before he realized that voice was his.

THE RUSH DIDN'T TAKE Bolan by surprise—his enemies were down to certain basic choices: charge, or sit and wait—but knowing it could happen didn't mean that he was perfectly prepared. An automatic weapon would have served him well, but he was down to the Beretta 92, while Celeste covered the rear end of the Chevy with her Walther.

"Watch yourself," he called to her, and then all hell broke loose.

He counted six men rushing at them from behind the Jeep and Dodge, three to a side, all of them firing as they came. The plan was obvious—to keep their heads down while the shock troops closed the gap and finished it—but Bolan had defended worse positions in his time, against much larger forces, better trained and better armed. He stood his ground, with bullets snapping past his face on either side, swung his weapon toward the three men charging on his side.

His first round caught a gunner who was blasting at the Chevy with an Ingram MAC-10 submachine gun, punching through his rib cage, spinning him. He went down firing, finger frozen on the Ingram's trigger as he fell, spraying the cloudless sky, the Jeep behind him—anything and everything, in fact, except the target of his choice.

The fallen shooter might still be alive, but Bolan had no time to think about it. Shifting inches to his right, he brought a second target under fire, this one a young man with what appeared to be Glock semi-auto pistols in both hands. The guns were accurate, well-made, but they made no allowances for jumpy, nervous handlers, and his slugs were snapping over Bolan's head.

He shot the two-gun adversary twice, aiming a foot or so above the belt buckle, sighting on center of mass. It would be wasted effort if his target wore a Kevlar vest, but jolting impacts rocked the shooter backward on his heels, blood spurting from the wounds that took him down.

One remained on Bolan's side, and the enemy sent a bullet from his handgun close enough that the Executioner felt it snag his sleeve. Dead on at twenty yards, he drilled a single Parabellum mangler through the cultist's forehead, slamming his assailant into a clumsy backward somersault. No points for style, but plenty for enthusiasm, as the dead man hit the pavement in a crumpled heap.

Bouchet was blasting with her Walther as he spun in that direction, moving back to help her. Bolan stuck his head up, peering through the Chevy's right-rear window, out the back, in time to see two gunners closing from the north. He couldn't see the third man, didn't know if he was hit or simply hiding, but he had to deal with the adversaries he could see before he went in search of the invisible.

As Bolan reached her side, Bouchet squeezed off a final shot. The slide locked open on her pistol's empty chamber, and she cursed, ducking below the fender. Seeing Bolan close to her, she made a sour face and told him, "I don't have another clip."

"Stay back," he cautioned, moving past her, rising up to meet the two attackers as they closed the gap to thirty feet or less.

One of them had a shotgun, while the other plinked at Bolan with a shiny pistol. The Executioner took the scattergunner first, because he was more dangerous, a double-tap above the solar plexus dropping him, with what appeared to be a dazed expression on his face.

The *pistolero* hesitated when his friend went down, broke stride and glanced in the direction of the fallen man. It was a fleeting lapse, but all the Executioner required to put a bullet through his temple, blowing him away.

And that left...who?

Bolan rose cautiously, scanning the battleground in search of living enemies. He was about to step from cover, when a sudden movement at the corner of his eye brought him around, his pistol following the turn.

"You bastard!" Pluto shouted at him, lurching to his feet, some forty feet beyond the car that sheltered Bolan. "Traitor!"

He was sighting down the short length of an Ingram SMG when Bolan shot him in the chest and throat, instinctive rounds that found their target more by feel than any conscious planning, pitching him backward on legs that turned to rubber as he fell. The Ingram fired a short burst, emptying its magazine, but none of the projectiles came within a yard of Bolan, drilling empty air.

He checked around the killing field, found number seven lying dead behind the Cherokee and called out to Bouchet that it was safe. The Chevy had absorbed its share of hits in the exchange, but when he checked beneath the hood, he found the engine, with its wires and hoses, still intact. It came to life at once when Bolan twisted the ignition key, and he experienced a mighty feeling of relief.

"What now?" Bouchet inquired, when she was seated in the car beside him, voice and manner notably subdued.

"Now you go back to town and get the word to Hal," he told her. "I can drop you off before I go."

"Go where?" she asked him pointedly.

It was a question he had asked himself already, and despite the risks involved, the answer Bolan got turned out to be the same each time.

"I'm going back to keep a date with Murphy," Bolan told her, "at the ranch."

CHAPTER ELEVEN

It was a gamble going back, with stakes of life and death, but so was every other move he made when dealing with The Path. Bolan had weighed the odds against him, insofar as that was possible, and he had picked the better of his choices—or the lesser of assorted evils—where the outcome of his mission was concerned.

If Dillon Murphy was the author of the contract on his life—and Bolan failed to see how Pluto could have drawn his orders, much less backup troops, from any other source—then Murphy would expect him to be dead by now. By the same token, if he had survived, Murphy would have to calculate that Bolan had to have recognized Pluto among the triggermen. With that in mind, it stood to reason that the last thing Bolan would attempt, if he survived the hit and knew himself to be a guilty traitor, would be a reunion with the very group he had betrayed. In doubling back directly to the ranch, Bolan had hopes—however slim—of making Murphy doubt his fatal judgment, question whatever he may have heard from Pluto prior to setting up the hit, and think twice about having Bolan killed.

Of course, it could be a colossal waste of time, and one that would result in Bolan's death the moment that he showed himself to Murphy's bodyguards. He understood the risk and had prepared himself as much as possible, considering the fact that he would be alone with Murphy and at least two other guns—perhaps, by now, considerably more.

He dropped Celeste Bouchet at her motel in Barstow and got out of town as rapidly as the speed limit would allow, relieved to meet no prowling squad cars on the way. In terms of preparation, Bolan had reloaded his Beretta, donned the shoulder rig once more and slipped on his nylon jacket despite the midday heat. The empty seat beside him had become a mobile arsenal: two liberated Ingram submachine guns, freshly loaded; three spare magazines to feed the stutter guns; the stubby 12-gauge shotgun lifted from another fallen adversary and a dozen extra buckshot rounds.

If it came down to killing at the ranch, at least Bolan was confident that he could give his enemies a rude surprise before they took him down.

He took his time, nursing the shot-up car along, wind moaning through the many bullet holes when he topped forty miles per hour on the highway. He imagined what the lookouts at the ranch would think when he pulled in, whether they knew about the Barstow trap or not, and grinned at the mental image of it, rolling up the gravel drive, across the yard before the ranch house in a car that resembled a prop from *Bonnie and Clyde*.

With any luck at all, he thought, the very shock

of it might be enough to put the soldiers off their guard. But how much luck was left to Bolan, after Pluto had turned up from out of nowhere, and apparently convinced Dillon Murphy that the new man was a traitor to the cause?

Pluto was correct, of course, but that wasn't the point. How had he known? It went back to the temple in Missouri; that much was as clear to Bolan as the hot wind blowing in his face. He could have witnessed Bolan slipping out, perhaps, but would that be enough to bring a death sentence from Murphy? Had the field commander of Thor's Hammer cleared his action with The Two?

If he hadn't, it could turn out to be another weakness—or a strength, from Bolan's point of view—but it would make no difference either way if Murphy had him shot on sight. That was the greatest risk he faced, a danger that he might not get the chance to speak before the guns went off, that there would be no time for him to plead his case.

Forget about it, Bolan told himself. He had assumed the risk, and he would stand—or fall—by his decision. At the very least, he knew that his arrival would confuse the young guards at the ranch. Murphy wouldn't have issued standing orders for him to be shot on sight, since he wouldn't have been expecting Bolan to return, alive or dead. If Murphy's bodyguards had been informed of Bolan's death sentence, they would be startled by the sight of him, a brief but critical delay that would—if nothing else—permit him to respond in kind, when they reached for their guns. Conversely, if the guards knew nothing of the Barstow ambush, they would have no reason to be gunning for him. Murphy would be on his own, compelled to do the dirty work himself, or else to issue orders that could only be pronounced in Bolan's presence, thereby giving him a chance to strike before the guards were clear what was happening.

It didn't sound so bad that way, but Bolan knew that he was headed into mortal danger. It was old, familiar territory for the Executioner, but you could never take success for granted, even when the odds were "simply" one-to-one. Complacency could get a soldier killed as quickly, and as surely, as a lapse in training, faulty gear or any other problem that confronted warriors on the battlefield.

He made the turnoff, following the rutted gravel track until he saw the ranch house ahead. There was nobody on the porch at first, but by the time he pulled into the yard and switched off the Chevy's engine, both of the guards in residence were waiting for him there. Their guns were slung, with muzzles down, but Bolan checked the windows for any subtle movement that would tip him to a sniper hiding in the shadows. He couldn't be absolutely sure, of course, but there was no more time to waste.

He stepped out of the car, deciding not to take an Ingram with him, hoping he could dive back in and arm himself if someone opened fire. The young guns stood there, staring at him, at the bullet-riddled car, but neither of them made a move to raise a weapon.

"What happened there?" one of them asked.

"Damned potholes," Bolan told him. "Can I see the boss, or what?"

BROGNOLA LISTENED GRIMLY to the brief report. Andy Morrell had spent enough years in the FBI to learn that good reports were simple and concise: get in, say what you had to say without a lot of adjectives, get out. If anyone upstairs desired a personal opinion, he or she would ask for it.

"That's all I have," Morrell said, wrapping up. They had been on the telephone no more than ninety seconds, by Brognola's wall clock.

"No one was hurt, then?" Brognola inquired. He felt a bit embarrassed by the question, like a mother seeking reassurance that her children were all right, but having spoken, he couldn't withdraw the words.

"No one on our side." Morrell had described the violent death of seven men in sketchy terms, but no specifics were required. Brognola had seen countless corpses in his time, a fair proportion of them Bolan kills. He didn't need a file of crime-scene photographs to know what Bolan's enemies had looked like when he finished with them, lying stretched in the desert sand.

When you got right down to the bottom line, dead men were all the same.

"And he was going back there, to the ranch?" It was the question that filled Brognola with dread, because he knew the answer in advance. Morrell had already explained it once, and when he thought about it, going back to face the dragon in its lair was just exactly what he would expect from Bolan.

Not that it was logical, in any normal sense. Your average man or woman, once having escaped a brutal killing situation, would have made tracks in the opposite direction. In that sense—as so many others the big Fed could think of—the Executioner was anything but normal.

Bolan's way of coping with a threat had always been to seize it by the throat and shake the life out of it, leave it broken and lifeless on the ground. So far, the head-on method had worked well enough, but Brognola couldn't help thinking it was bound to fail sometime. No one had that much luck and skill that he could beat the odds forever.

Sometime, someday, the warrior would run out of time.

But not today, Brognola thought. Please, God.

There had been a time—and it didn't seem all that long ago to the Justice man—when he had been preoccupied, even obsessed, with Bolan. That had been another lifetime, back when Brognola was hunting Bolan as a fugitive from murder charges and a host of other felony indictments. Now that they were allies, things were different. He sometimes went for hours at a time without thinking of Bolan, allowing himself to become immersed in other matters.

"Are you still there, Bouchet?" he asked.

"I'm here." Her voice on the extension sounded small and distant. Trying to imagine what she looked like, he came up with something like a mental mug shot, nothing in the face to match the fear he picked up in her tone.

"You know this outfit best," he said. "How are they likely to react?"

"I wish I knew," she replied, "but nothing like this ever happened in the cult while I was there. If

Ares—Murphy—ordered the attack, he may have acted under orders from The Two."

"May have?" Brognola didn't have to fake the vague note of confusion in his voice.

"He wouldn't need their order. As leader of Thor's Hammer, he could take that kind of action on his own, as long as he could justify it later. That's all hypothetical, you understand. I never heard of anything like this. With a defector, well, like me, they mount surveillance sometimes, bluff and threaten sometimes, but until that morning in L.A., they never really made a move. It's getting so much worse."

"What I was hoping you could tell me," Brognola broke it, "was what we might expect."

"In theory, if there was no order from The Two, then Murphy has a choice to make. One way to go, would be to bury Blake. Of course, that leaves him seven dead men to explain. He didn't have a chance to make them disappear, which means they'll make the news. Seven dead on top of what happened in Arizona, it will probably go national. Film at eleven, you know?"

"Which means?"

"The smart way, if he's thinking straight, would be for Murphy to break the news first, try to explain himself before The Two find out by other means and get angry. It would be up to them, in that case, what comes next. Some kind of hearing, theoretically. A trial, of sorts. Murphy could be required to prove his actions justified."

"And if he failed?" Brognola asked.

"I can't begin to guess," she said. "He's never been accused of anything before, as far as I know."

"You're talking, now, about a situation where there was no order from the top," he said.

"That's right."

"Suppose there *was* an order for the hit," Brognola said. "What happens then?"

"If Blake presents himself to Murphy with an execution order pending," she replied, "that order would be carried out on sight. He'd be as good as dead."

"I see." It was the answer that Brognola had expected. "So, we need to hope this Murphy character was acting on his own initiative. Is that the bottom line?"

"It seems to be the lesser of two evils," she replied.

"If there's a so-called trial," Brognola said, "how would the play go down?"

"Presumably Murphy would have a chance to show The Two whatever proof or evidence he had that Blake deserves to be eliminated. I'm just guessing, now, but he would have a stronger case if it was something detrimental to the cult. If Murphy knew that he was working for the government..."

She let it trail away, no need to finish. There were four people on the planet who knew about Bolan's assignment, and three of them were on the telephone. Brognola knew that he had leaked no information, nor did he suspect the others. How could Murphy know, unless...what?

And again, he came up empty.

"Okay," he said at last, "you've given me some things to think about. I'll be in touch as soon as I hear anything at all. Same number?"

"Right," Andy Morrell replied. "We're staying here until we find out something...one way or the other."

"So, I'll be in touch," Brognola said. "Take care."

He cradled the receiver, leaned back in his chair, wishing for a cigar. Everyone died, sooner or later, and Bolan had had a longer, more exciting run than most in his martial profession.

Brognola just hoped it wouldn't happen this day.

THE SAFEHOUSE in Big Sur was small compared to the quarters normally occupied by Hermes and Circe, but no expense had been spared on renovations and furnishings. The deed was held by a paper subsidiary of Stargate Incorporated, several times removed, with no familiar names in black and white to tip off the authorities.

Hermes wasn't uncomfortable in the house, which is to say that he lacked for nothing in terms of creature comforts. Still, his mind and heart weren't at ease. As long as he was forced to hide, frustrated in his need to move among the people in these Final Days and spread the holy word, he couldn't rest.

Now here was Ares on the line again, undoubtedly with more bad news. Hermes had put him on the speaker phone, insisting that the caller speak to him and Circe as a couple.

After all, they were The Two.

"Now, Ares, first things first," Hermes said, as he settled into his easy chair. "This line. Is it secure?"

"I've checked it twice," Ares replied.

"Proceed," Hermes stated.

"I've run into trouble here," Ares began. "The new man—"

"New man?" Hermes interrupted him.

"Nimrod. He joined us after that unpleasant business in Las Vegas, where the crowd went after Circe."

"I remember him," she said, speaking for the first time.

"Yes, ma'am. Well, it turns out that he's disloyal," Ares declared. "I have good reason to believe he may be working for the Feds."

"What reason?" Hermes asked.

"It goes back to Missouri, sir, if you—"

"Remember?" Hermes interrupted. "I'm not likely to forget it, am I?"

"No." Ares was flustered by the interruptions, but he carried on. "It turns out that Nimrod wasn't the only one who got out alive. The other man was missing, but he called me yesterday, and—"

"Yesterday?" There was a brittle razor's edge to Circe's voice.

"Last night," Ares replied. "He told me about Nimrod slipping out, just when the trouble started. He was under orders to remain and fight."

"And did those orders," Hermes asked, "apply to everyone?"

"Yes, sir."

"I see. So you had *two* men slip away."

"The second felt, um, that it was his duty to find out why Nimrod left, and—"

"Saw a chance to save himself in the bargain," Circe said. "Is there a point to this, Ares?"

"There is," the sect's enforcer said. "From talking to the second man—Pluto—I came to an executive decision that Nimrod should be removed."

"*You* gave the order?" Hermes probed.

"That's correct."

"And was it carried out?" Circe asked.

"There's been...a problem."

"Explain." The tone of Hermes's voice left no room for evasion.

"I sent half a dozen men with Pluto. It should have been more than enough."

"Indeed it should have," Hermes said. "So what went wrong?"

"Nimrod got lucky. He took them all."

"Meaning they're dead," Circe said.

"Right."

Hermes frowned, closed his eyes for a moment, trying to ignore the sudden churning in his stomach. "So, now you've lost another seven men?"

Ares didn't respond at first, but after Hermes cleared his throat, the cult enforcer said, "Yes, sir."

"May we assume, at least, that you were able to retrieve the bodies?" Circe asked. Her face had gone a trifle pale behind the perfect sun-lamp tan she cultivated.

"They weren't here," Ares replied. "That is, they were supposed to take him in the desert, off the ranch. They were discovered by some motorist before I had a chance to clean things up.''

Which meant there would be more bad news on television, more pressure from the authorities. Hermes was furious. He felt like picking up the speaker phone and hurling it across the room. If it had been within his power to reach across the miles and throttle Ares, he would have done so cheerfully. Still, despite the rage that nearly overwhelmed him, he maintained a calm exterior. He had learned that trick in the mental institution, under constant scrutiny from men and women who presumed to look inside his mind and judge what they found hiding there.

''Is there the slightest hope,'' he asked, ''that you can still locate this Nimrod?''

''He's right here,'' Ares said.

''What?'' His voice lashed out at Ares like a whip before he caught himself.

''He, uh, came back here afterward.''

''Back to you?'' Circe asked.

''Right.'' It clearly pained Ares to say it.

''Hardly the behavior of a guilty man,'' Circe replied.

''He claims he didn't know who jumped him. By the time he recognized Pluto, it was too late. He calls it self-defense.''

''Under the circumstances,'' Hermes said, ''his explanation does not sound unreasonable.''

''But—''

''You have some proof, I take it, that this Nimrod had betrayed The Path?''

''Pluto—''

"Is dead," Circe reminded him. "A witness who, at best, was questionable from the start, and who cannot be called upon to testify, in any case."

"I still believe—"

"You disappoint us, Ares," Hermes said. "It seems that you have acted...shall we say, in haste, and brought more trouble down upon us in the process."

"It was my judgment—"

"Your hasty judgment," Circe interrupted him again. "Your rash judgment."

"Which now has cost us six good men, at least, and untold difficulties with the law," Hermes put in. "I would have thought we had enough trouble in that regard, without your help."

"What should I do?" This time when Ares spoke, his voice was stiff, not humble yet, but waiting for his orders.

"We must find a way of judging who is right in this," Circe declared.

It came to Hermes then, a revelation, tugging the corners of his thin mouth into a smile. He knew the answer now.

"Bring Nimrod here," he said at last.

"To you?" This time when Ares spoke, there was no hiding his surprise.

"For trial," he said. "The two of you together."

"Trial?"

"Make haste," Circe commanded. "But take care to leave no trail. You have made quite enough mistakes for one lifetime."

"I'm on my way," the sect's enforcer said, and broke the connection.

Hermes touched a button on the speaker phone to still the buzzing dial tone. As he sat back in his chair, he glanced toward Circe, found her watching him, a question in her eyes.

"I don't know, yet," he said, in answer to her silent query. "We shall have to wait, my love, and see what we shall see."

"HE SHOULDN'T HAVE gone back."

"You tried to talk him out of it," Andy Morrell replied.

"It didn't help." There was bitterness in Celeste Bouchet's tone. If asked, she couldn't have said for sure if she was angrier with Michael Blake, or with herself.

"The man knows what he's doing," Morrell said. "He's done this kind of thing before."

"You still don't get it, do you?" she challenged. "These people are crazy. Andy, they don't know what they're going to do five minutes from now, understand? They're taking orders from spacemen, for Christ's sake. How can Blake second-guess a bunch of lunatics?"

"He's done all right so far," Morrell reminded her.

"He's nearly gotten killed three times in the past two weeks," she said. "There's close to forty other people who *are* dead. This whole thing is going to hell in a handbasket, Andy. They're onto him! Don't you get it?"

"That's exactly why he went back to the ranch," Morrell replied. "He could have gone the other way and split, but what would that have done, except drive them deeper underground? This way, at least he's got a shot...and we've still got a man inside."

"You think they'd trust him after this?" Bouchet shook her head in weary disbelief. "What planet are *you* on?"

"Just think about it for a second," he replied. "Could Murphy bury this, now, even if he tried?"

She thought about it, remembering the early news flash on television, promising details to come. Inevitably it would get back to Hermes and Circe, no matter where they were hiding.

"He could still kill Blake and try to lay the whole thing off," she said, hoping that she was wrong.

"It doesn't scan. All they have to do, as far as verifying names and numbers for the latest hit, is turn the TV on or read a newspaper. That's seven dead, not eight. If Murphy does the job on Blake himself, he'll still have to explain why Blake came back to take his medicine after he whacked seven other members of the cult. Now, *that's* crazy."

He could be right, she thought. But could be was a country mile away from certainty, and she was still afraid of Murphy, still afraid *for* Michael Blake.

"Suppose you're right," she said. "Then what?"

"You tell me. You had the inside track there, once upon a time."

She thought about it for a moment, frowning to herself. "If Murphy kicks it back upstairs," she said, "The Two will have to make the call. It could go either way, from there. Jesus, they might decide to flip a coin. Heads, Michael dies, tails, Murphy takes the fall.''

Too late, she realized that she had called Blake by his first name, getting personal. She glanced at Morrell, checking him to see if he had caught it, but he either didn't notice, or he didn't care.

''What would they do if they were playing by the rules?'' he asked.

''Set up some kind of trial,'' she said.

''You mean, like with a jury?''

''Not quite. The Path is no democracy, remember. Everything finally comes down to Hermes and Circe. They could always listen to both sides and make the call.''

''But you don't think so.''

''No,'' she admitted. ''Something that you have to understand about The Two—for all the sci-fi trappings, part of them—a major part—is still... Geez, what word am I looking for...? Romantic. As in days of yore, with knights and ladies, chivalry, the whole nine yards. We had some arguments when I was still inside the cult, and they were often settled by some kind of contest, like a show of strength.''

''As in the saying, 'Might makes right'?''

''More or less. Call it a trial by ordeal, if you like. It's all the same.''

''Meaning they send Murphy and Blake into the ring?'' he asked.

''Something like that. The trial could take on many different forms,'' she said.

''And if it goes that way, the winner walks?''

"In essence, yes."

"How good is Murphy?" Morrell asked.

"I understand he was some kind of soldier once," she said. "That's all I know."

"I guess we'd better hope Blake's better, then."

Bouchet leaned backward in her chair and closed her eyes, but she could find no comfort in the darkness, so she opened them again. Morrell was watching her, not frowning, but there was compassion in his eyes.

"I'm sorry," he said simply.

"Yeah," Bouchet replied. "Me, too."

CHAPTER TWELVE

The first leg of the trip had been a flight from Redlands Municipal Airport to Monterey. A car and driver waited for them at Monterey Peninsula Airport for the drive along the coast on Highway 1, through Carmel Heights, beyond Point Sur, turning off on a narrow side road a mile above Big Sur itself.

The trip—two hundred miles by air, another twenty-some by car—was made in silence, for the most part. Murphy had hardly spoken to Bolan since they left the ranch, having informed him that, "The Two request the pleasure of your company."

There had to be more to it than that, however, Bolan realized. If he was merely being sent to die in California, why would Murphy tag along? Murphy had told him they were headed for a trial, and while Bolan initially assumed that Murphy would be prosecuting, he was slowly coming to accept a different theory.

Bolan had been more or less straightforward in describing the attack to Murphy, leaving out Bouchet, but otherwise relating the events as they had happened. He admitted recognizing Pluto after it was over, when he lay among the dead, and sketched an outline of the personal antagonism that had grown between them at the Boulder compound. As for Pluto's tale that Nimrod was a traitor, based on his escape from the Missouri temple, Bolan did his best to turn around the charge, asking why *he* was treated with suspicion for surviving, while Pluto was not. Instead of answering, Murphy had placed a call, returning with the news that they were bound for California.

The road was serpentine, winding through redwood forest, gaining altitude. The driver didn't speak once they were in the minivan, which came equipped with four-wheel drive. He concentrated on the mountain road, ignoring Murphy in the shotgun seat and Bolan in the back with fine impartiality. Unarmed, Bolan volunteered to ride in back, not wanting anyone behind him, for an easy head shot. This way, if Dillon Murphy or the driver pulled a gun, the shooter would be forced to swivel in his seat, face backward, giving Bolan fleeting time to strike.

But they wouldn't do that, he was convinced. Murphy might hate him, probably was wishing Bolan dead that very moment, but the Executioner believed that he had told the truth about one thing: some kind of trial before The Two was planned. And something told him that he wouldn't stand alone before the bar.

The prospect of a hearing, rather than a summary conviction and elimination, was enough to raise his spirits slightly, but he knew the odds were still stacked heavily against him. If and when the two of them were called upon to tell their stories, Murphy would enjoy a huge home-team advantage, based on long association with The Two, common beliefs, a legacy of trust. Bolan, by contrast, was the new kid on the team, with nothing but his unsupported word—a lie, at that—to balance out a string of incidents, including three ‘‘impossible’’ escapes—the temple in Missouri, followed by the Boulder compound and the highway slaughter north of Flagstaff—and, now, the massacre of seven fellow cultists in the California desert.

There was no reason for them to buy it, but he would have to sell it anyway, if he intended to survive. The first thing Bolan had to do, though, was to bide his time, find out exactly what The Two had on their minds before he tried to formulate a final plan of action. Once he knew for sure which way the wind was blowing, he could better plan the moves required to save himself.

Failing all else, he thought, if he could only reach The Two before they dropped him, there was still a chance he could deal the cult a mortal blow.

He was unarmed, of course—Murphy had seen to that—but if he just got close enough, was quick enough to strike before their bodyguards could intervene—

He stopped himself at that. Before he started laying any plans to sacrifice himself, he had to judge the situation from inside. It called for patience, something he had learned firsthand in Southeast Asia and refined in all his private wars since then.

The waiting game.

The road began to level out, and Bolan saw a

house in front of them. It was an A-frame, built from logs, with wooden shingles on the sloping roof. Based on its size, he guessed that it would easily sleep a dozen people, and half that number had come out to greet the minivan, all of them armed.

Their driver parked and killed the engine, stepping out without a word or backward glance. Murphy turned in his seat and smiled at Bolan, the expression seeming forced.

"Let's go," he said. "They're waiting for us."

As THE ACCUSER, Ares was entitled to speak first, lay out the charges, while The Two sat side by side on matching wicker thrones and listened to his spiel. Despite the curt reception given to his statement on the telephone some hours earlier, he had expected better than the cool gaze that they turned upon him now. Neutrality was one thing, but he thought The Two were taking it a bit too far.

He hit the high points: Nimrod slipping out of the Missouri temple, shadowed by a loyal member of the team; his dereliction of duty at the Boulder compound, fleeing when he should have stayed to fight; the strange coincidence of the attack by outlaw bikers in Arizona, with Nimrod once again the only member of the strike team to survive; his massacre of seven loyal Path members in the desert north of Barstow. Winding up, he even ventured to suggest that it was something more than luck that he had been on hand to rescue Circe from a hostile audience on the occasion of his introduction to The Path—a situation more extreme than any speaker for the sect had previously faced.

When he was finished, Circe was the first to speak. "You seem to think the incident in which Nimrod assisted us was staged. What is the phrase—a 'put-up deal'? Do you have any proof of that?"

Ares took pains to keep his posture ramrod straight as he replied. "No, ma'am, I don't," he said. "But as I've already explained, in order to accept the strange series of coincidences that follow this man—"

"Coincidence," Hermes interrupted him, "or Fate?"

"Excuse me, sir?" Ares felt angry color rising to his cheeks, but did his best to keep the cutting edge of it from his voice.

"Might not the Ancients lend a hand from time to time?" the founding father of The Path inquired. "Our faith presumes contact throughout the ages, even to the present day. I trust you've not forgotten that?"

"Of course not, but—"

"We'll hear from Nimrod now," Circe informed him, silencing his answer.

Bolan had been standing on the sidelines, watching silently while Ares did his best to get him killed. As he stepped forward now, he didn't strike a military pose before The Two, but faced them squarely, seeming to ignore Ares.

"There's only so much I can tell you," he began. "The first time I saw Circe, I was looking for a way to kill some time. Now, Ares claims I set the whole thing up—the riot at the auditorium—but he still hasn't told you how I got it done. How could I? I was new in town, and Ares must have checked my military background, right?"

Instead of waiting for an answer, Bolan forged ahead. "As far as how I came to join the path, I'm sure Circe recalls that it was Leo who invited me to tag along that night."

"Leo's no longer with us," Circe said.

"I'm well aware of that, ma'am, but it doesn't change the facts. He took me to the Boulder compound, set the whole thing up. I didn't show up on my own and ask about a job. The fact is, *he* recruited me. I wasn't looking for a cause to follow. It just happened."

"Serendipity?" Hermes asked.

Bolan shrugged. "Whatever. Pluto had an attitude the first time that I met him at the compound. There was no love lost between us. I'm the first one to admit it. The first day Ares set me up to run a training exercise, Pluto got frosty with me, called me out. I kicked his ass. My guess would be, he was the kind to nurse a grudge."

"You fled the temple in Missouri," Hermes said.

"That's right," Bolan replied. "I found a way out, and I took it, *after* I discovered that the plan had gone to hell. If Ares wants to say I mobilized the SWAT team and sidelined the FBI negotiators we were hoping for, he needs to show how I could do something like that. He hasn't shown you anything, so far, except how much he wants me dead."

"Pluto observed your flight," Hermes said.

"So I'm told. If he had shown himself, instead of hanging back and spying," Bolan said, "he could have gone with me."

"Tell us about the Boulder raid," Circe directed him.

"There isn't much to tell. I didn't have the watch that night, so I was in my quarters, sleeping, when the fireworks started going off. The Feds were close enough to drop a flash-bang in the camp itself before I got outside. The place was being overrun. I would have stayed, regardless, but I saw him—" Bolan cocked a thumb at Ares "—take off on a dirt bike through the woods. I figured, what the hell, why stick around and die for nothing, when I couldn't save the camp?"

Ares was conscious of The Two observing him, but kept his eyes on Nimrod, hoping that his poker face would hold. He yearned to grab the new man by his throat and squeeze the life out of him, watch his face turn blue before he died.

"Can you explain the Arizona business?" Circe asked.

"From what I hear, nobody can," Bolan replied. "All I can tell you is that we were tooling down the highway, and this bunch came up behind us. One starts flailing with a chain across the windshield. Packer's man pulled over, and it turned into a shooting match."

"Which you survived, again," Hermes reminded him.

"The first thing I was taught, back when I joined the Rangers, was that soldiers who get shot are no damned use to anybody. I know how to keep my head down when I have to.''

''Still,'' Hermes broke in, ''this business with your brothers, in the desert...''

''Self-defense,'' Bolan said without batting an eye. ''Ares sent me on a run to get supplies. Today, I know it was a set-up. At the time, I had no choice but to react. I didn't recognize Pluto until the fight was nearly over. When I saw him, I assumed the hit was personal. I had no way of knowing Ares had decided to run games behind my back.''

''Damn you!'' Ares snapped. ''It's my job—''

''Enough,'' Hermes said, raising one pale hand to halt the flow of angry words. He glanced at Circe, locked eyes with her for a moment. Ares was moved to wonder, as he had on more than one occasion, if The Two were really able to communicate by pure telepathy, without a spoken word. When they faced forward once again, Ares could read nothing in their expressions.

''It is our decision that a test must be applied,'' Hermes announced. ''The test shall be as follows...''

BOLAN STOOD underneath the stinging, ice-cold shower spray and counted thirty seconds more before he turned it off. He used a heavy terry towel to scrub the goosebumps from his skin, and stepped into the next room, where his gear was waiting for him.

Lying folded on a chair, it wasn't much: a set of crisp, new camouflage fatigues, a black T-shirt, brown leather belt, a pair of hiking boots, crew socks, Bolan's own freshly laundered shorts. A long, bone-handled hunting knife, complete with leather sheath, topped the pile.

The Two had ordered that the test required to settle Murphy's claim against Bolan should be a hunt, of sorts, conducted in the woods surrounding the A-frame. The cult owned close to eighty acres, and the nearest neighbor was supposed to live three miles away, to the southwest, so that the risk of an intrusion by third parties had been minimized. Bolan would have a half hour's head start before Murphy began to track him.

He knew enough about Dillon Murphy's background, which included eight years spent in the U.S. Marines, to know that he would be a cunning adversary. Bolan wasn't worried in the ordinary sense, but there was no doubt in his mind that he would have to watch himself, avoid taking a victory for granted. There was every reason to believe that Murphy might have walked the chosen hunting ground before, might be familiar with its hiding places and potential ambuscades, while Bolan would be fighting for his life on unfamiliar turf.

He wasted no time getting dressed. If it had been his choice, he would have picked fatigues that had been worn and washed a few times, but the new clothes fit him well enough, and they would do their job, as far as aiding his concealment in the forest was concerned. The hiking boots felt good. He wore the knife on his left side and slightly toward the front, for a convenient cross-hand draw.

He had no compass and no map of the terrain, but it wasn't the first time he had gone into a hostile wilderness with nothing but his wits and skill to guide him. He had managed to survive this long, and there was nothing in the present situation, as it stood, to shake his nerve.

Hunting—or being hunted by—one man had pros and cons. The up side was that they were fairly matched in size and weight, with no reinforcements standing by at Murphy's beck and call to help him out. The down side was that one man, if he knew his business, was more difficult to track and trap. A larger force left more signs of their passage in the woods, and any traps prepared were more likely to bag an enemy, if there were several targets in the same vicinity.

He made it fifty-fifty, then, and knew some combination of experience and skill would tip the balance, in the final confrontation.

When he had finished with his preparations, Bolan went outside and found the others waiting for him. Locke and his better half were flanked by half a dozen guards, including those who had come out to meet the van when it arrived. Murphy was standing to one side, tracking Bolan with his eyes, a grim expression on his face.

"Are we all ready, then?" Helen Braun asked.

"Ready," Bolan said, while Murphy nodded.

"Then let the games begin," Locke said. "As we agreed, Nimrod will have a half hour's head start to use as he sees fit. Ares, as the accuser, will pursue him at...what time?" Locke wore no watch, and glanced at one of his young soldiers as he asked the question.

"Thirty minutes from right now," the gunman said, "makes it 5:28."

"So be it," Locke replied, and smiled. "Nimrod, be on your way."

Without a word or backward glance, Bolan struck off due north, jogging away from the A-frame and into the woods. He felt eyes tracking him—some hostile, others merely curious—until the redwoods hid him from their sight.

There was a world of difference between the redwood forest of Northern California and the steaming jungles of Asia, where Bolan had learned woodcraft the hard way, as a Green Beret. He didn't need to hack his way through vines and creepers here, watching for vipers in the undergrowth, while reeking mud sucked at his boots. The ground he jogged across was firm, beneath a layer of fallen leaves, with trees down here and there, presenting minor obstacles.

He used up fifteen of his thirty minutes moving to the north, then turned due west and ran for five more minutes, finally reversing his direction, toward the A-frame. It wasn't part of Bolan's plan to lead his adversary on a long trek through the woods, if he could close to killing distance quickly, and be done with it.

That would depend, of course, upon Dillon Murphy. How much of the skill picked up in the Marine Corps did he still retain? Had he grown soft while serving as the field commander of the cult's private army? How long had it been, indeed, since he had killed another man himself...or had he *ever* taken a human life with his own hands?

Bolan was confident that he would know the answers to those questions soon, perhaps before the sun went down. He was supposed to be the prey in this contest, but he intended to reverse that role as soon as possible, let Murphy find out how it felt to be the hunted, for a change.

There were no troops for him to hide behind out here; no buttons he could push from miles away to order Bolan's death. Whatever Ares might accomplish, he would have to do it on his own.

IT WOULD BE three more hours before the sun went down, but shadows were already growing longer, darker, in the redwood forest that surrounded Ares. It was his intention to dispose of Nimrod quickly, while he still had daylight in his favor, but the first half hour of his hunt hadn't gone well.

Ares had never been much of a tracker, even when he served with Force Recon in the Marines. He knew the ins and outs of how to hide, prepare an ambush, scout a trail for booby traps, but he wasn't a manhunter, per se. There was no trick to spotting footprints in the mud, for instance, but it was a different game entirely when you had to look for broken twigs or dangling leaves. Ares was well aware that he could wander through the woods for hours, even days, and find no trace of Nimrod, if he didn't catch a lucky break.

The question was, exactly how to *find* that break before Nimrod found him.

Ares had no illusions as to Nimrod's skill when it came to killing. He had proved himself in that regard with Pluto and the others when they tried to take him in the desert. He had been outnumbered seven to one in that fight, Pluto at liberty to choose his time and place, but Nimrod had survived without a scratch, while seven adversaries wound up in the morgue.

What would the clever bastard try to do in this scenario?

The one thing Ares was convinced that Nimrod *wouldn't* do was go to ground and hide, avoiding confrontation, dragging out the game. Nimrod struck Ares as a soldier who preferred to take the battle to his enemies, whenever possible, and ram it down their throats. That meant *he* would be stalking Ares, or attempting to.

His mind shut down immediately when he found the trail. It startled him at first, the clear print of a hiking boot dead center in the trail, where soft earth was exposed for several feet, without the scattering of leaves that carpeted a great part of the forest floor. He froze, knelt beside the print, wishing he knew some way to tell how fresh it was. No dead leaves overlay the track, but Ares would have felt more confident if he had known the last time it had rained, how long ago the footprint could have been pressed into fresh mud by the wearer of the boot.

For all he knew, the track could have been made by someone from the A-frame: one of those assigned to guard The Two; perhaps Hermes himself.

He spied a second track, this one a fragment of a heel print, but it matched the other footprint perfectly, except that this foot was the left one, while the first had been a right. Beyond that point, the forest's leafy carpet had obscured the phantom hiker's trail, but Ares knew which way the man was headed now.

Nimrod? he asked himself. And came back with the swift reply: Who else?

The Two would never let their bodyguards go hiking through the woods, he thought. Not now, when they had suffered one setback after another, and the law was breathing down their necks. In other times, perhaps, when they were simply on vacation, no threat in the air, it might have been another story. But the leaders of The Path were justly paranoid these days and kept their soldiers close beside them at all times.

Nimrod.

Ares was smiling as he drew his hunting knife and ran a thumb along the keen edge of its blade. He wasn't home yet by a long shot, but he knew the prey's direction now, and he would make the most of it.

He took it easy, picking up the pace a little, constantly on guard. The forest undergrowth wasn't so thick that it would be an easy thing for Nimrod to surprise him, spring from ambush like a hunting cat, but Ares knew he dared not make it easy for his enemy by bumbling along the trail and making noise. If he could find a middle ground between stealth and speed, he had at least a fighting chance.

Another twenty minutes passed, and Ares had begun to fear that he had lost the bastard's trail when suddenly he saw his target twenty yards or so in front of him. He recognized the camouflage fatigues, identical to those he wore, broad shoulders slumped as Nimrod sat, back braced against a fallen log, head down.

Ares could feel his heart pounding against his ribs, as he ducked hastily behind a giant redwood, letting precious moments slip away until he found the nerve to move again. Ares glanced around the tree trunk first, to verify that Nimrod hadn't moved, then he slipped around the far side of the redwood, creeping forward, with the knife held out in front of him.

Fifteen yards.

Ten.

When he had narrowed it to five, he took a breath and held it, steeled himself for contact, charging out from cover in a headlong rush and launched himself, his gleaming blade, at Nimrod's unprotected back.

TWELVE FEET above the scarecrow he had crafted from his camo shirt and two forked branches, the Executioner watched Murphy make his rush. He waited for the outstretched blade to shear through empty fabric, Murphy sprawling on his face, before he pushed off from the sturdy branch and dropped behind his foe.

The trap had been a gamble, but it had paid off. Bolan had laid a trail which anyone—he hoped—could follow, and decided he would give the stand an hour, more or less, before he gave it up and started hunting Murphy more aggressively. The hour had ten minutes left to go when Murphy came in through the trees, moving northeastward, and attacked the decoy from behind.

Now he was down and cursing, grappling with the sticks and empty shirt, trying to extricate his knife, as Bolan dropped behind him, landing in a crouch. He drew his own knife as he landed, circling to his left as Murphy lurched and scrambled to his feet.

The camo shirt was dangling from his wrist, where Murphy's knife thrust had torn through the fabric, all his weight behind it as he tried to skewer Bolan from behind. He tried to lose it with a sharp flick of his wrist, but merely wound up waving it around in front of him, like some peculiar flag. At last, disgusted, cursing through clenched teeth, he used his free hand, ripping through the shirt to free the arm that held his knife.

"Cute trick," he snarled.

"It worked," the Executioner replied.

"It bought you thirty seconds, asshole. How's it feel to see death coming for you?"

Bolan's voice was steady as he said, "I haven't seen it, yet."

Murphy began to circle counterclockwise, making passes back and forth in front of him with the hunting knife's blade. He had been trained for this work, Bolan saw, but there was still a world of difference between training and application.

Murphy's circling put him on the crest of a declivity, head and shoulders above Bolan, and the new position seemed to give him confidence. Smiling, he seemed about to take another step to his right, then barked some kind of battle cry and leaped toward Bolan, pushing off with both feet against the bank.

Instead of jumping backward, Bolan sidestepped, reaching out with his left hand to clutch a handful of his adversary's shirt. Murphy's momentum, coupled with the tug that Bolan gave him, sent the cultist plunging headlong down the slope. As he flew past, the Executioner's right hand sprang forward, jabbing with the knife. When he pulled back, the shiny blade was streaked with crimson.

Murphy landed on one shoulder, crying out in pain, and wallowed through a crazy somersault before he found his balance, lunging to his feet. Bolan allowed him points for the recovery, but there was no mistaking his discomfort as he pressed a hand to his left side and drew back his fingers blood-slick.

"You bastard! You cut me!" he rasped, sounding surprised.

"This is a knife fight," Bolan said. "Or, did I get that wrong?"

"You got it wrong the day you joined The Path," Murphy replied, coming uphill to meet him.

"That's your story."

"Damn right," Murphy growled, climbing steadily. "And this is where I put an end to it, right... now!"

He lunged to punctuate the threat, charging uphill, his knife held well in front of him. As Murphy was slowed by pain, fatigue and gravity, the move wasn't as quick as he might have hoped—and nowhere near the speed he needed to connect with his adversary and a killing thrust.

At the last moment, Bolan switched his knife to his left hand and used his right to grab for Murphy's leading wrist. He gave a sharp tug forward, throwing in a roundhouse kick with his right leg that whipped around to catch Murphy in the back of the head.

The cult enforcer went down on his face with a grunt, eating dirt, as Bolan spun to straddle his torso, knees digging into the earth. Bolan's right hand cupped Murphy's forehead, drawing his head sharply back, as the hunting knife slid under his chin, biting deep.

The dead man wriggled underneath him for a moment, nearly bucking Bolan off, but it was too little and much too late. The Executioner stayed where he was for just a moment longer, waiting while his adversary's life spilled into the soil, then wiped his knife on Murphy's shirt and stepped away.

Hermes and Circe would be waiting for him.

It was time for him to pick up his reward.

CHAPTER THIRTEEN

"So, where the hell is he?"

Delphinus glowered at Lacerta. "How the hell should I know?"

"You're in charge, for Christ's sake!"

"Ares is in charge," Delphinus angrily reminded him. "Don't be forgetting that."

"I'm not forgetting anything," Lacerta said. "But where the hell is he?"

They stood together in the forest, both men armed with Ingram M-10 submachine guns that were fitted out with foot-long MAC sound suppressors. The giant redwoods towered over them on every side, and there was no sign of their leader, who had whispered orders for the two of them to back him up against Nimrod. Ares had sounded confident that he could make the kill himself, but he had also taken out insurance, just in case. Of course, the soldiers had to find him first, before they could begin to do their job.

"We'd better not be lost," Lacerta groused.

"Goddammit, we're not lost!" Delphinus snapped at him. "How could we be, a hundred yards out from the house?"

"All right," Lacerta said. "So, you tell me—where is he, then?"

"You ask me that once more, and I'll—"

His threat was cut off and forgotten as a cry of mingled pain and anger came to them from somewhere in the forest to the north.

"Shit fire!" Lacerta swore. "Was that Ares? It sounded like his—"

"Follow me," Delphinus said, "and keep your mouth shut!"

Homing on the sound—or where he hoped the sound had come from—Delphinus struck off through the forest, double-timing with Lacerta on his heels, the Ingram held in front of him, ready to fire. He prayed that they would find Ares in time...and that Lacerta wouldn't stumble, accidentally squeezing off a burst into his back.

Delphinus—born Gerald Schaefer, in Chicago, Illinois—had served Thor's Hammer for the past three years, and he had never dropped the ball. So far. This new assignment, even though it seemed to flaunt an order from The Two, had been explained to him as necessary for the welfare of the sect, to keep the Ancients' timetable on track, and failure was a prospect he refused to contemplate.

No matter how it preyed upon his mind.

They seemed to run forever, though he knew that it was only moments, and because there was no repetition of the cry, Delphinus feared he may have led Lacerta in the wrong direction. It wouldn't take much to miss Ares or Nimrod in the forest. Ten feet either way, one massive tree obscuring vision, and it was entirely possible that they would pass by one or both of those they sought.

He was about to stop to catch his breath, rethink his course, when he was suddenly distracted by a breathless cry behind him.

"Over there!" Lacerta gasped, winded from running. "Look!"

Delphinus halted, crouching, with the Ingram tight against his hip. He followed the direction of Lacerta's pointing index finger, squinting in the shadows, and at last picked out what seemed to be a body, sprawled facedown against a sloping earthen bank off to his left.

It *was* a body, he decided, dressed in camouflage fatigues, which could be either of the men who had been sent into the forest by The Two. No movement, but Delphinus took no chances, raising one hand as a signal for Lacerta to keep silent, edging forward with his Ingram leveled at the prostrate figure. Was the other somewhere close, perhaps observing him right now? What difference would it make, if true—a hunting knife against two automatic weapons?

Screw that! Delphinus thought, keeping up his guard. At last, he stood over the body, edged around it on the right until he caught a glimpse of profile.

Ares.

Even with the dirt and blood smeared on his face, there could be no mistake. And he was dead as hell; there could be no mistake about that, either.

"Shit!"

He hadn't meant to speak aloud, and now the curse, though barely whispered, sounded like a shout to Delphinus in the forest's stillness. Feeling naked and exposed, he spun in a complete three-sixty, checking out the shadows, finger tensing on the Ingram's trigger.

"What?" Lacerta asked him, stepping forward, staring at the corpse. "Oh, man! Oh, man!"

"Shut up, goddammit!"

"But—"

"Shut up!" This time it *was* a shout, Lacerta cringing, while Delphinus bit his tongue, letting the pain remind him of his situation.

Which was what, exactly?

Glancing down, Delphinus saw the hunting knife that lay a foot or so away from Ares's outstretched hand. He knew the boss had come into the woods without a gun, as had Nimrod. That meant their adversary still had nothing but a hunting knife, against their SMGs.

"Too late," Lacerta said. "We're too damned late."

"Not yet," Delphinus told him. "You remember what our orders are?"

"Stop Nimrod," his companion said, as if by rote.

"No matter what," Delphinus said. "Stop him no matter what. We've still got work to do."

"But, where—"

"Where else?" Delphinus asked, surprised to feel a grim smile on his face. "The fucker thinks he's done. He's headed back."

"So what?"

"So, we split up and run like hell until one of us

heads him off," Delphinus said. "And then we do our job. Now, move!"

BOLAN WAS HALFWAY to the A-frame when he heard a sound of movement in the woods, away and to his left. He stopped and turned in that direction, caught a glimpse of something man-sized, dodging under cover of a redwood there, then heard the muffled stutter of an automatic weapon fitted with a sound suppressor.

He hit the ground and rolled behind the nearest tree, as bullets started chewing up the trunk, slapping among the dead leaves on the forest floor. The weapon had a rapid cyclic rate of fire—one of the smaller SMGs, he calculated—which was good and bad news, all at once. The good news was that Bolan's enemy, whomever he might be, would burn up ammunition quickly, if he didn't exercise a fair amount of self-control. The bad news was that once he made his move, even a careless spray of bullets from the SMG might score a hit and take him down.

He didn't draw the hunting knife, since it was useless to him at the moment. He would have to be much closer for the blade to do him any good, and that meant leaving cover, closing with the enemy.

But first, he had to find out how many were stalking him. The who and why of it were less important to him, though he could hazard a guess. Somebody from the cult, that much was obvious, and while it could have been some kind of double cross cooked up for Bolan by The Two, his money was on Murphy. Back-shooting from ambush was the late enforcer's style, and Bolan reckoned that the trap was some kind of insurance policy. Whether the shooter had arrived too late, or the attack was scheduled to proceed only if Murphy lost the game—a kind of doomsday payback mechanism—made no difference whatsoever in the present circumstances.

Bolan had to move, and that meant risking everything. Until he knew how many enemies he faced and where they were, he had no realistic chance to save himself. Still, he could use an edge, if there was any way to throw off the gunner...

He hunched forward, scooping up a double handful of dead leaves and crushing them together. Hesitating for another beat, he braced himself, made ready for the move that would reveal his enemy or get him killed. There seemed to be no third choice on the menu.

The Executioner twisted to his right and hurled the mass of leaves out from behind the tree, off to his right, hearing the SMG cut loose with a distinctive sound like canvas ripping. At the same instant, Bolan broke from cover on the left, charging hard toward the next tree that would offer him substantial cover, knowing where it was and trusting to his legs, while sharp eyes swept the woods around him. Searching...searching...

There!

He saw the gunman, even as the other guy saw him and spun to bring the moving target under fire. Too late, a stream of bullets sliced the air behind Bolan, but he had found his sanctuary, hunched behind another redwood's trunk.

Bolan considered trying to communicate with the would-be assassin, telling him his boss was dead, but he abandoned the idea as soon as it took form. There was a fifty-fifty chance the shooter already knew Murphy was dead; if he didn't, the news might just as easily provoke a new resolve to carry out his task.

Elimination was the only course of action that appeared to offer any prospect of success, and even that was marginal. He had to close the distance with his adversary, first, and that would mean exposure to a deadly stream of automatic fire. The shooter didn't strike him as an expert marksman, but the little SMG eliminated any need for great precision. All he really had to do was hold down the trigger and spray.

It was impossible to guess how many rounds his adversary had expended, and it hardly mattered, since reloading could be carried out in seconds flat. The shooter easily could have reloaded half a dozen times by now, although experience told Bolan that he hadn't wasted that much ammo.

What he needed, Bolan thought, was time enough to tag the hunter when he *knew* the gun was empty, and the only way he could accomplish that was rushing toward his enemy, instead of playing ring-around-the-redwood. He would have to draw the shooter's fire deliberately, advancing all the while, and gain sufficient ground that he could strike the very instant that the SMG ran dry.

It was a kamikaze play, but Bolan knew he had no choice.

He drew his knife, turning it around so that the fingers of his right hand gripped the sharp tip of the eight-inch blade. As well prepared as he would ever be, he took a deep breath and broke from cover in a headlong rush.

Before he took three strides, the SMG was sputtering at him, bullets snapping through the air around him. He lunged forward, twisting through a shoulder roll, zigzagging as he bounced back to his feet.

He saw the gunner clearly now, some thirty feet ahead of him, still firing. Bolan ducked, dodged, hit another shoulder roll, keeping his firm grip on the knife. This time when he sprang to his feet, there was no muffled sound of firing, and he saw the shooter fumbling to reload his piece, haste making awkward hands.

The hunting knife wasn't balanced for throwing, but he let it fly anyway, still charging toward his man. Bolan's momentum gave the pitch more force, the bright projectile flipping over once, twice in the air before it found the mark. It sank an inch or two into the gunman's shoulder and staggered him, the submachine gun tumbling from his fingers as he bleated out a cry of pain.

Before he could recover or attempt to reach the pistol on his hip, Bolan slammed into him and took him down. He made no effort to retrieve the knife, closing big hands around the young man's face instead, twisting his neck with brutal force. The snap of vertebrae rewarded him a heartbeat later, and the man went limp in Bolan's grasp.

Rising, he found the Ingram SMG and its spare magazine, reloaded swiftly and chambered a round.

The dead man also had another loaded magazine, and Bolan put it in his pocket. He was ready now.

For what?

For any other gunmen lurking in the woods.

The Executioner moved out, in search of human prey.

LACERTA LIKED THIS JOB less by the minute, creeping through the woods and searching for a glimpse of Nimrod or Delphinus—hell, of anyone at all. Delphinus was so confident that they couldn't get lost when they were this close to the A-frame, but where was he, then?

A muffled rattling sound off to his left, due eastward, froze Lacerta in his tracks. A woodpecker? Lacerta—born George Shelby, in the Bronx—was clueless, but he thought the feathered hammerheads were louder, somehow. Could it be Delphinus, firing at Nimrod?

That settled it, then, for Nimrod. He had lucked out in the fight with Ares, but the bastard wasn't bulletproof. It would have been a feather in Lacerta's cap if he had tagged the traitor, but…

He hesitated, thought of something that had briefly slipped his mind, and couldn't stop the smile that broke across his face. Ares had called the hit on Nimrod on his own initiative, against the wishes of The Two. Delphinus and Lacerta had agreed from force of habit, used to taking orders from the leader of Thor's Hammer. But it struck Lacerta that it may not have been the wisest choice to make. Suppose The Two were angry when they learned of Nimrod's death. They couldn't chastise Ares now that he was dead, which meant the punishment would fall on those responsible for taking out Nimrod. It might be luck after all, Lacerta thought, that he had never spotted Nimrod, never had a chance to use his gun.

He felt a sudden urge to quit the field and rush back to the A-frame, try as best he could to separate himself from any guilt that fell upon Delphinus. There was still a chance that he could pull it off, if he—

The hopeful train of thought was instantly derailed, a new pang of anxiety replacing hope.

What if Delphinus missed Nimrod? What if the tricky bastard who had murdered Ares turned the game around, somehow, and took Delphinus out? What then?

Lacerta realized that he might have a much worse problem on his hands than disapproval from The Two. If Nimrod took Delphinus out, it meant the ambush was exposed, and there was every chance that Nimrod might be hunting *him* right now, instead of hiking back to the A-frame. He had already slaughtered seven members of The Path—eight, if you counted Ares—and another one or two cut down in self-defense would make no difference.

His only chance, Lacerta told himself, was to move out as quickly as he could, track Delphinus and find out exactly what was happening. He needed only one clear shot to finish off Nimrod, and if Delphinus had already fallen, well, perhaps that made it all the better. He could stage the scene to look as if the two men killed each other. That done, he could slip back to the A-frame, hopefully, and take his quiet place among the other guards. There was no reason why The Two should ever know of his involvement in the ambush, no just cause for punishment.

Lacerta moved off in the general direction of the sound, which hadn't been repeated, praying it didn't turn out to be a damned woodpecker after all. He took his time, putting one cautious foot before the other as he traveled through the woods. How could terrain like this seem beautiful and yet oppressive, all at once? The latter feeling came, he knew, from playing games of life and death with an opponent who had shown himself a stone-cold killer, time and time again.

He held the Ingram ready, with the safety off, his finger through the trigger guard. He had two extra magazines, but hoped he wouldn't need them. If he couldn't drop his target with the first thirty-two rounds, he was in deep, deep trouble, and no mistake. Still, it was good to have the backup, just in case.

He drifted through the trees, no longer certain whether he was heading in the right direction, hissing curses through clenched teeth.

The noise he had been hoping for—hoping he wouldn't hear, at the same time—was suddenly repeated. It was louder now, which meant that it was closer. And he knew damned well it was no woodpecker this time. It was Delphinus, blasting with his silenced Ingram.

Lacerta picked up his pace, trying to strike a

happy medium between speed and stealth, discovering that there was no such thing. He made fair time, still hoping that Delphinus would finish the job before he got there, wrap it up and make things simple.

It couldn't be much farther; he was sure of that.

He glimpsed something advancing toward him, through the shadows cast by giant trees. Lacerta sidestepped into deeper shadow, seeking cover, squinting in the semidarkness as he tried to make out features, anything that would identify the figure.

Human, definitely. Taller than Lacerta? Possibly. He saw the Ingram, no mistake on that score. It was only when the figure moved into a shaft of sunlight that he saw the camouflage fatigues. There could be no confusing them with the blue denim that Delphinus wore. Lacerta didn't have to see the face to know that this was Nimrod, and the very fact that he was carrying the Ingram meant Delphinus must be dead.

That recognition spurred him into action, roaring out a challenge as he stepped into full daylight, leveling the Ingram from his hip and holding down the trigger, spewing slugs at Nimrod.

NEVER SECOND-GUESS a gift of fate.

It was the shout that saved him, echoing among the trees before his adversary stepped from cover, squeezing off a wild burst from the silenced Ingram. By the time those bullets started ripping through the air where he had stood, Bolan was facedown on the ground.

Bolan returned the fire one-handed, just a short

burst, half a dozen rounds, to send his adversary scurrying for cover. In another moment, he was on his feet, as well-concealed behind a redwood tree as he could hope for, under the circumstance. Hiding out wasn't enough, though. He would have to take this enemy, as well, before he could return and face The Two.

How many other guns were waiting for him in the woods? Bolan had recognized his first kill as one of Murphy's shooters who had made the trip from Barstow with them. If this was his companion, taking him should be the end of it—always assuming that the trap was Murphy's plan alone, with no collusion from the leaders of the cult.

He risked a glance around the tree and drew fire immediately, but the shots went wide, not even scoring bark. Bolan immediately doubled back, trusting the gunner's shaky nerves to give him breathing room, and sprinted toward the cover of another nearby tree. He made it with a beat to spare, a swarm of angry hornets buzzing after him, and paused to catch his breath.

The move had put him several paces closer to his adversary, closing the gap from thirty-odd yards to something under twenty. One frag grenade could have resolved the situation instantly, but Bolan was compelled to work with what he had. At least this time he found himself on equal footing with his enemy in terms of hardware.

"Is this the way you want to play it?" Bolan called out to his enemy.

The other man said nothing for a moment, then

his voice came back to Bolan. "You killed Ares and Delphinus," he accused.

"Ares set up this game," Bolan replied. "You want to join him?"

Quicker on the uptake this time, Bolan's enemy replied, "I'm not dead yet." And added almost as an afterthought, "I've got a job to do."

"You'd better do it, then."

As Bolan spoke, he stepped from cover in a crouch and fired another short burst toward the point where he had last seen his opponent. He didn't charge directly toward the sniper's nest, but rather ran at a diagonal, toward yet another redwood that would place him within six or seven paces of his enemy.

The cultist tried to tag him, leaning out just far enough to hose the trees with a one-handed burst of automatic fire. The rounds went wild, and Bolan returned fire. While he didn't score a hit on human flesh, his bullets sprayed jagged shards of bark into the gunner's face. The young man staggered backward, triggering another wild burst as he ducked from sight, the slugs passing a yard or more above his target's head.

Bolan hadn't come this far just to hide behind another tree. He clung to cover only for a heartbeat, moving on before his assailant had a chance to wipe the bark and splinters from his eyes. The cultist had to have heard him coming, boot heels crunching into earth. He lurched back to the firing line and rattled off a burst that came within a hair's breadth of decapitating Bolan, as the Executioner made a long dive for cover.

The best that he could do, under the circumstances, was to reach a fallen tree that had been partly overgrown by ferns. It covered him, but barely, leaving Bolan with a sense that he had better move, and quickly, if he meant to stay alive.

A lull in firing told him that his adversary was reloading. The first shooter he had taken out was packing two spare magazines, but that didn't mean that his companion wasn't carrying three, four, even half a dozen spares. Bolan, for his part, had the clip already in his gun—roughly half empty, now—and one more in his pocket. Call it fifty rounds, all told, which the machine pistol could devour in two and a half seconds. There was no selective-fire switch on the Ingram—nothing in the way of selected 3-round bursts, for instance—meaning Bolan would be forced to ration the rounds by feel, trusting experience and discipline.

The first thing he would have to do, if he intended to survive, was to find a better vantage point from which to fight. The longer Bolan waited, the more likely his opponent was to lock on target acquisition, nail him even as he rose to make his move. The longer he delayed, the more he played into the opposition's hands.

For Bolan, after all his years of combat, thought flowed into action with an ease that even many veterans would have found remarkable. He vaulted to a crouch and instantly pitched over backward, left arm thrown out to catch himself, his right hand leveling the Ingram at the spot where his opponent was concealed.

The guns went off together, half a dozen rounds spitting from Bolan's, while his adversary burned up close to half a magazine. Closer this time, but Bolan's luck was holding, and he came out of the backward roll already on his feet, breaking immediately to his left.

The shooter had reloaded, clearly, but he had no sense of fire control in his excitement. Even when he braced the little SMG in both hands, he was troubled by the muzzle climbing, jerking up and to his right. It was an opportunity too good to miss, and Bolan didn't let it slip away.

He went in firing, milking 3- and 4-round bursts out of the Ingram with an artist's touch. He saw the bullets strike their target, denim ripping, spouting crimson as the slugs drilled through and found the flesh beneath. His adversary staggered, reeling, pumping out the last half-dozen rounds from his own weapon as he fell, his lifeless body twitching for another moment, even after he was down.

Bolan reloaded on the move, scooped up the second SMG and stood there for a moment with a gun in each hand, checking the woods around him, ready to respond if there were any more surprises waiting for him in the shadows. When no one showed, he heaved a sigh and turned back toward the A-frame once again.

It was a short walk back from there. Whoever came to fetch the corpses back wouldn't have far to go.

As for the Executioner, the end of his trek through the hellgrounds still wasn't in sight.

CHAPTER FOURTEEN

Hermes dragged deeply on his cigarette, holding his breath a moment afterward, as if it were a joint, letting the nicotine kick in. A smoker since his twelfth birthday, Hermes had quit at least two dozen times before The Change, at which point he discovered his relationship to the immortal Ancients and decided that he was invincible. It didn't save him from such things as shaving nicks and thinning hair, of course, but Hermes was convinced that he would live to see the mother ship return, at which time all believers would forever cheat the reaper. Smoking was the very least of his concerns.

"Smoking," Circe said, wrinkling up her fine patrician nose as she passed Hermes and took a comfy seat directly opposite, where she could peer out through the A-frame's giant picture window at a redwood panorama fading into night.

"It calms me," he told her, with a beatific smile.

"You're nervous?" Circe didn't frown, but he could hear it in her voice. He knew his soul mate inside out, could read her moods precisely by the smallest gesture.

"Concerned," he said, correcting her. "I think we both have ample reason for concern."

"Ares, you mean," she said.

"He's part of it, of course." Hermes had swallowed something very much like fury when he was informed that seven of his men were dead because Ares had put out an unauthorized death warrant on this new man, Nimrod. Coming close upon the heels of the abortive action in Missouri, federal raids against the Boulder compound and other retreats, the massacre in Arizona, it was damned close to the final straw. If he hadn't been buoyed by his faith...

"The government can't hurt us," Circe said, as if reading his mind. "There's nothing they can do to stop the Ancients."

"No, of course not." He knew that much without being told. Still, they could make things damned uncomfortable for members of The Path before the end.

"Should they be finished soon?" she asked him, artfully changing the subject.

"It's impossible to say," Hermes replied. "If they're evenly matched, it may well take all night. On the other hand—"

A knocking on the doorjamb interrupted Hermes, and he turned to find one of his soldiers frowning at him from the open doorway.

"Yes?"

"He's back, sir."

Hermes glanced at Circe, saw her arch one graceful eyebrow. She didn't insult him with a smile.

"Ares," he said.

"No, sir," the bodyguard replied. "The other one."

Hermes was on his feet before he knew that he was moving. Brushing past the startled guard, he heard Circe behind him, almost on his heels. They stepped outside and found Nimrod standing before the house with guards on either side of him. Two automatic weapons lay at Nimrod's feet.

"What's this?" Hermes asked, facing Nimrod as he spoke.

"A couple of your boys decided Ares shouldn't lose," Nimrod replied. "They did their best. It wasn't good enough."

"Where are they now?" Hermes inquired.

"Back there." As Nimrod spoke, he cocked a thumb back toward the woods behind him. "I can show you, if you've got some flashlights."

"Ares?" Circe asked.

"Your boys weren't quick enough to help him out," Nimrod replied.

"We did not send them," Hermes said. "I hope you can believe that, Nimrod."

The survivor shrugged. "Whatever. I was sent to deal with one and wound up facing three."

"They had those weapons?" Circe asked.

"That's right."

"And you…?"

"Took them away," Nimrod said. "They don't need guns anymore."

Three dead, Hermes thought. Three more dead. He had lost count of all the bodies recently. Now, he would have to have his soldiers dig three graves and plant the latest victims where both animals and men would let them rest in peace.

Circe was watching him. Hermes could feel her eyes upon him, and he turned to face her, frowning.

"We sent no one to help Ares," she said, facing toward Nimrod once again. "You have been vindicated. His reward for the false accusation and defiance is death."

"I've taken care of that already," Nimrod said.

"Which leaves us with an opening," Hermes stated. "We have much to talk about, but first, I would imagine you could use a shower and some food? Perhaps a bit of rest?"

"I'm not tired," Nimrod answered, "but I'll take that shower and some food."

"Indeed." A finger snap sent one of the bodyguards back inside ahead of Nimrod to prepare a meal. They had a freezer full of steaks, ribs, anything a hungry soldier might desire.

Nimrod moved past Hermes, vanishing inside the A-frame, leaving The Two on the porch. Circe was frowning now.

"An opening?" she asked.

"Why not? If you really feel that he's been vindicated, who better to replace Ares?"

"Who better?" she repeated, almost dreamily. "Indeed."

Together, they went back inside the house.

BOLAN WAS HOPING that his second shower of the day would help him to relax a bit, but he had no such luck. Hot water eased the nagging pain of bruises he had suffered in the brawl with Murphy and the later contest with his two back-shooters, but it did nothing at all for his peace of mind.

Hermes had spoken of an opening, and while logic would indicate that he was speaking of Dillon Murphy's vacant job as the commander of Thor's Hammer, it could just as easily have been a dodge to make him let down his guard, placing Bolan at the mercy of the next hit team that came for him.

Why fake it, Bolan wondered, when they could as easily have killed him on the spot, there in the yard, and planted his corpse with the others? Did they have some other game in mind, or was the notion of a step-up in the ranks for real?

Fresh linen clothing had been laid out for him, the carbon-copy shirt and slacks that were a standard uniform for members of the cult. Whoever laid them out while he was in the shower knew his size, or guessed it well enough that Bolan had no problems with the fit. When he was dressed, he went back to the parlor, passing by the kitchen, where the smell of grilling steaks made Bolan's mouth water.

Hermes and Circe stood before the A-frame's giant window, hand in hand. Bolan couldn't be sure if they glimpsed his reflection in the glass, or if they heard him coming, but they turned as one to face him, wearing smiles that looked enough alike to have been crafted from a mold.

"No lasting damage, then, I hope," Hermes said.

"I'm all right," Bolan replied. "You had something to tell me, sir?"

"Indeed. As a reward for courage and faithful service—not to mention consolation for the charges made against you by the late Ares—we have decided you should take his place as our chief of security."

"I'm honored, sir." He bobbed his head and tried to look appropriately grateful. "It's an honor."

"Well deserved, from everything I've seen," Hermes said. "And we were hoping that you could assume your duties right away."

"Of course. I'll need a briefing on the different operations that are underway."

"Aside from general security," Circe remarked, "there's only one of any consequence right now."

Bolan suspected it would be the kiss of death for him if he appeared too eager. Nodding once again and putting on a little frown of concentration, he replied, "Which is?"

"Our working partnership with Mr. Packer's Peacekeeper Militia was an effort to, ah, shall we say, maintain a low profile?" This time, the smile that Hermes wore was tinged with irony. "Of course, it didn't quite work out as we had planned. We have a backup, however. Just in case."

"Another bomb?" Bolan asked.

"Not exactly," Hermes said. "Are you familiar with the Japanese Supreme Truth sect?"

"Yes, sir. They sprayed nerve gas around the subway tunnels," Bolan said. He still recalled the videos on CNN, police and ambulance attendants wearing gas masks, hauling shrouded bodies out of subway stations, while survivors sprawled around them, retching, gagging. Something like a dozen victims had been killed, with hundreds suffering from lesser injuries. Authorities had rounded up known members of the cult and put its crazed guru on trial for murder, but the grim example had been set and beamed around the world on satellite TV.

"We have a laboratory in New Mexico," Hermes went on, "outside Roswell. You appreciate the irony, I'm sure."

"Yes, sir." Some irony, he thought, to plant a New Age doomsday lab near the alleged site of a flying-saucer crash from half a century ago. It could have been a halfway decent joke, except that they were talking life and death, perhaps for hundreds, maybe more.

"Our chemist is—or was—well-known in private industry before he found The Path some time ago. The recipe for sarin is not terribly complex, from what I understand."

That much was true. The Aum Supreme Truth cult had brewed its own nerve gas from various ingredients available at any chemical supply house, without special licenses or permits. All that a potential terrorist required were purchase orders that would pass a cursory inspection and appear to issue from some company involved with plastics. Bolan had no doubt that he would find at least one company that fit the bill, if he took time to scan a roster of Stargate's subsidiaries.

"You have a target?" Bolan asked.

"We have no end of targets," Hermes said. "Selection is a mere formality. It won't be long, but you'll have time to visit the facility, familiarize yourself with the program. Since our associates in the militia let us down, we'll do the job ourselves.''

''Discreetly, I assume,'' Bolan added.

''But of course.'' The words were Circe's first since he had joined them in the parlor. ''It would scarcely help advance the timetable for Armageddon if the government knew *we* had lit the fuse, now, would it?''

''No, ma'am.'' Bolan forced a smile, pretending to appreciate the plan. And then he asked, ''Who takes the fall?''

''A group of suitably detestable outsiders,'' Hermes said. ''They are, in fact, participants, although they have no grasp of our true plans. It serves our purpose for them to believe they are in charge, while we simply provide the means of their revenge against America for some imaginary insult. They will proudly take the credit for whatever happens—and absorb the punishment, as well.''

The plan made sense to Bolan. Its simplicity was frightening. He didn't press his luck by asking further questions at the moment. The identity of the outsiders, for example, would reveal itself to him in time. There were enough hate groups and half-baked ''liberation armies'' in the world—left-wing and right, religious, anarchistic, revolutionary and reactionary—that he had no difficulty believing that the plot could work.

Unless he stopped it.

''I'd like to see the lab,'' said Bolan, making it a casual remark.

"My thoughts exactly," Hermes told him. "Can you leave tonight?"

"Tonight, sir?"

"After we have dined, of course. There's no great rush, and you've had quite a tiring day. If you'd prefer to wait until tomorrow..."

"No, sir. I'm fine. Tonight's no problem."

"Excellent," Hermes said, and the smile on Circe's face appeared to be a mirror image of his own. "Those steaks are nearly ready, I imagine. Shall we go?"

CELESTE BOUCHET was drinking root beer with a twist of lemon, wishing she had something stronger, knowing that she didn't dare get wasted now, of all times, when they might be called upon to move at any moment. Not that she had been much help to Michael Blake, so far—no help at all, in fact, as far as she could see. The whole damned mess was basically her fault, and she was sidelined, watching from a distance, lucky if she found out what was happening before it broke on television.

"You should really cut yourself some slack," Andy Morrell remarked, as if reading her mind. "It's really *not* your fault, you know."

"I hear you," she replied.

"You don't believe me though."

It didn't come out sounding like an accusation, just an observation from a friend. They had been working on this project for some time collecting evidence enough to get the Feds involved, force them to act. They had achieved that goal, but what else had she set in motion with her curious, one-woman effort to derail The Path? Would several dozen dead men be alive and well today, if she had chosen not to interfere? Or would the body count be even higher—in the hundreds, maybe—if she hadn't blown the whistle on Hermes and Circe when she did?

There was no answer to that question, and it drove her to distraction. She had done what she believed to be the best thing, still...

"They won't give up, you know," she said.

"How's that?"

"The bombing in Las Vegas," she explained. "He stopped them, but they won't give up. They'll find another target, try some other angle of attack. They're not like anyone you've ever dealt with in the past."

"You'd be surprised," Morrell replied. "I covered lots of ground when I was with the Bureau, and I met a lot of freaks. One guy in Oregon set up a commune, had his followers convinced it was a mortal sin for any one of them—I'm talking male *or* female, young or old—to sleep with anyone but him. He punished so-called sins in ways you can't imagine. If somebody got sick, he prayed for strength to cure them himself. I don't just mean the laying on of hands, you understand. I'm talking surgery, the whole nine yards. No anesthetic, mind you, and his sense of hygiene made the men's room at Grand Central Station look like something out of *Better Homes & Gardens.* If he lost a patient, he was philosophical about it. Nothing went to waste around the farm, but he hung on to souvenirs—a rib, a vertebra, whatever. When we busted him, he had an altar set up in the barn with the bones laid out to form a 'holy power sign.' There's nothing so unique about The Path."

"Except they don't just kill each other," she reminded him. "They're not just threatening their neighbors in some isolated little town, a hundred miles from anywhere. They won't be satisfied until they've shattered civilized society around the world."

"And you believe they have that capability?" Morrell's smile was both gentle and infuriating, all at once.

"I don't know," she responded, nearly snapping at him. "That's the trouble, dammit! With the way things are today, so many countries at each other's throats, so many of them nuclear, it might not take a genius or an army to provoke another war. Look at the Middle East, the Balkans, I mean—"

"Easy, there," he interrupted her, raising one hand, as if he was directing traffic at a busy intersection. "I don't doubt this outfit's zealotry, okay? It strikes me, though, that you may give them too much credit. Even if they'd pulled off the Vegas bombing, for instance, well, it would have been a tragedy, but it's a long, long way from World War III."

"And what about next time?" she asked him pointedly. "We've already agreed Hermes and Circe may have tried to use the Peacekeeper Militia, set them up to take full credit for the Vegas bomb. Suppose next time they use some other group to focus blame outside of the United States. What then? You know about these things, Morrell. How much would be required to constitute an act of war?''

''Depends,'' he said, the gentle smile replaced by something like a thoughtful frown. ''You wouldn't need a massive body count, if the attack was aimed at something critical—the White House, Congress, something along those lines. The proof of an unfriendly power's setting up the hit would have to be airtight, of course. Barring an ICBM strike, the President still needs a vote from Congress first before he goes to war.''

''Like Desert Storm, you mean?'' she asked him, raising one eyebrow. ''Like Vietnam? Korea? Panama? Grenada?''

''Okay,'' he said, ''but none of those touched off the big one. Even Stalin kept his finger off the doomsday button, right?''

''He wasn't crazy,'' Bouchet replied. ''Or maybe he was just too busy getting fat on other people's misery to set the world on fire. That kind of thing derails the gravy train, you know? But think about some of the so-called leaders in the new republics, in the Palestinian commando groups, in Africa—hell, right here in our own backyard. Ask any one of them, they'll tell you they've got nothing much to lose.''

Morrell was silent for a moment, thinking. When he spoke again, his voice had taken on a kind of hollow, haunted sound. There was a grim cast to his usually amiable features. "So," he asked her, "what are you suggesting that we do?"

Bouchet responded with a question of her own. "What *can* we do? It's all in Blake's hands now. That is, if he's alive. We've got no options left, except to sit and wait."

CHAPTER FIFTEEN

New Mexico

The Cessna touched down at Roswell Industrial Air Center at 11:42 p.m. The young man waiting for him at the gate was twenty-something, introduced himself as Hercules, although he didn't look like he could bench press fifty pounds without a spotter. He was deferential to a fault, tacking a ''sir'' onto the end of every sentence as he led Bolan outside. A Chevy C-K 1500 pickup waited for them in the nearly empty parking lot, and Hercules held Bolan's door before he ran around and slid behind the wheel.

They drove northeast from town on Highway 70 until the wheelman found the side road he was looking for and turned off to the right. Another hundred yards and they ran out of pavement, rolling over gravel for the next three-quarters of a mile until they reached a long, low blockhouse type of structure, painted beige to match the desert landscape.

''Here we are, sir.'' Hercules was on his way around to open Bolan's door, but the Executioner beat him to it, stepping out into the high-desert chill. He let the driver take his duffel bag and followed

Hercules across a sandy yard of sorts until they stood before the front door of the blockhouse.

Bolan's escort jabbed his index finger at a button set beside the blank steel door: two shorts, one long, one short. A moment later the door was opened by another young man, this one with an Uzi submachine gun slung across his shoulder. He stepped back to let them pass, then closed the door behind them, slipping three bolts home.

"Your quarters are this way, sir." Hercules led Bolan to the left, along an L-shaped corridor, past several doors, until he stopped and opened one, then stepped aside, allowing Bolan to precede him. There was nothing even vaguely posh about the room. He had seen more luxurious accommodations at a string of military bases stretching from Fort Benning, Georgia, to Da Nang, in Vietnam.

"Is it too late for me to see the lab?" he asked.

"No. I mean, no, sir."

The lab was underground. They had a choice of stairs or service elevator; Bolan chose the latter, checking out the stainless steel interior.

"What is this place?" he asked. "I mean, what was it? It's been well-maintained, but it's not new."

"No, sir," Hercules said. "It used to be some kind of research station for the U.S. Agriculture folks. They had some kind of budget trouble in the eighties, and they had to sell it off. Now here we are."

As if on cue, the elevator stopped, its door slid open and they stepped into a modern laboratory that reminded Bolan of a stage set from a James Bond movie. There were people working even at that hour, wearing white lab coats and plastic safety goggles. Bolan looked around for gas masks, then remembered that they wouldn't help. While sarin could be lethal if inhaled, it killed you just as quickly if you got a tiny droplet on your skin.

One of the three lab coats glanced up and saw them standing by the elevator, tucked a clipboard underneath his arm and came to greet the new arrivals. Hercules was plainly a familiar face. He made the introductions, standing at a fair approximation of attention as he spoke.

"Auriga—Dr. Campbell—this is Nimrod. He's replacing Ares in the Hammer, and he needs a briefing on the setup here."

"Of course," Campbell-Auriga said, while pumping Bolan's hand. His own was just a trifle on the clammy side, but strong. "I'll tell you anything you want to know."

"The basics are enough for now," Bolan replied. "You appear to be in full production here."

"We are indeed. We have enough volume already for the job at hand. As for the future—"

"What exactly is the job at hand?" Bolan asked.

Campbell blinked at him, surprised. "You weren't informed? I thought The Two..."

"Apparently they wanted you to run it down for me."

"Well, yes, of course. Most definitely." Campbell straightened a bit, as if the thought of delegated authority filled him with a new sense of pride. "We have delivery on target scheduled for next week—Monday, to be precise. The team is already in place,

I understand. All they require are the, um, the supplies. The sponsors are expected for a spot inspection, bright and early in the morning. VIPs, sir. You'll be meeting them, I guess, and showing them around."

"No problem," Bolan said. "About that target, though..."

"Yes, sir?" The doctor's smile was stuck somewhere between vague curiosity and eagerness to please.

"What is it?" Bolan asked. "The target."

"Hmm? Oh, yes, of course. Excuse me, sir. The target is Los Angeles."

THERE WAS NO FENCE around the lab facility. As Hercules explained it, back when this was federal land it was decided that an agricultural site devoted to analysis of pesticides and fertilizers needed no particular security precautions. Once the sale was finalized through one of Stargate's paper companies, The Two had calculated that erecting a new fence would only start tongues wagging from Roswell to Santa Fe. They had elected to let things remain the way they were—outside the lab, at least—while trusting in the open desert to provide them with sufficient warning if a raid was organized.

The underground laboratory was already in place. Refitting it to manufacture sarin nerve gas was a relatively simple operation, carried out in stages, so that no particular supplier of equipment, chemicals or incidentals could guess what they were up to at the site. The bills that weren't settled in cash were paid by check through one of three Stargate subsidiaries in California.

Simple.

It was so ridiculously easy, Bolan thought, to lay the groundwork for a nightmare.

Hercules had been opposed to Bolan walking out across the desert on his own, but the Executioner had assured the younger man that he could find his way back safely to the blockhouse. He wasn't afraid of snakes, and while the moon was nearly full, he took along a flashlight just in case. He also carried the Beretta Model 92, tucked into the waistband of his jeans, at the small of his back.

The next morning's visit by the "VIPs" and "sponsors" occupied his mind as he walked out into the desert, warm enough inside his windbreaker, although a chill breeze mussed his hair. Who would they be, these visitors? He reckoned that the VIP label might be a reference to high-ranking members of the cult, but what about the sponsors? Bolan guessed that they wouldn't be members of The Path, but someone else—analogous, perhaps, to Packer's militia in the Vegas operation he had managed to abort.

But who?

He took for granted that the gig with the militia had been small-time, a preliminary. Even if the bomb had been delivered to its target, blamed on the militia, with no mention whatsoever of The Path, it still wouldn't have moved the world appreciably closer to the scorched-earth field of Armageddon. Locke and Braun required some foreign element to make that angle work, but even knowing that did precious little to restrict the field of possible accessories. Few nations on the planet were without at least one group of violent, well-armed dissidents, and many—if not most—of those fanatics seemed to hold America responsible for their reported grievances. It hardly seemed to matter whether they were left- or right-wing groups, religious or political; no matter what their beef, it always seemed that the United States was implicated, somehow, in the plot.

He wasted no time guessing who the visitors might be. That much would be revealed to him when they reached the site. The *real* question was what—if anything—could Bolan do about the plan?

There could be no contact with Hal Brognola from the blockhouse; that was obvious. Having supplanted Ares as the leader of Thor's Hammer, he could make time for himself as needed for the call, but he would still have to be sure that he was undetected, unobserved. His rank wouldn't protect him from a whistle-blower, if his treason was detected by an underling, and Bolan knew The Two could still arrange to have him taken out at any time, if they were so inclined.

But there were ways. He simply had to watch his back, make damned sure that he wasn't being shadowed when he made the call.

And first he needed something to report.

The lab was something, but it wasn't enough. If Bolan had a chance to blow the whistle now, this very moment, what would he achieve? Brognola could have sent a raiding team to close the lab, sweep up the personnel, but what would that accomplish in the long run? None of those employed here would be likely to confess or point a finger at The Two, and Bolan knew there could be other labs in other states, concocting other poisons meant for other targets.

No.

Frustration of the L.A. raid was only part of Bolan's job, and not the major part. Unless the cult itself was broken up, effectively removed from action, there would always be another threat waiting around the corner.

A hint of movement in the moonlight, off to Bolan's left, brought the warrior to a sudden halt. He turned in that direction, narrowing his eyes, and recognized a sidewinder, some eighteen inches long, looping its body rapidly across the sand in the distinctive S-curve common to its species.

Bolan stood and watched the rattlesnake approaching. As the snake was a pit viper, he knew that it could sense body heat, the same method it used when hunting rodents in the desert. Would it shy away from Bolan, when it sensed his presence? Would it strike?

The sidewinder was fairly small. Bolan didn't believe its fangs could penetrate his denim jeans; he knew they couldn't pierce his hiking shoes. With that in mind, he stood and watched the reptile as it closed the gap between them. It was three feet from him when it stopped and drew its slender body into a coil, its rattle whispering a threat.

Bolan had studied snakes when he was in the

Green Berets, the same way he had studied weather, botany and other subjects: with an eye toward survival in the field. He knew, for instance, that a coiled viper could strike roughly one-third of its length—a distance presently beyond the sidewinder's effective range.

He stood and watched the little rattler for another moment, then deliberately scuffed one toe across the sand. Immediately the sidewinder's warning rattle took on new urgency, rising an octave in pitch. The flat, triangular head with its characteristic horn above each eye was slightly elevated, well back from the forward coil, in position to strike. Had it been daylight, Bolan knew, he would have seen the forked tongue, flicking in and out to taste the air.

He wished the hunter well and backed away. The snake had no concept of victory or defeat, pride or embarrassment. There was only survival, which relied as much on bluff as on the reptile's venom glands.

Bolan retreated toward the blockhouse, leaving the sidewinder to its lonely pursuit. He had enough predators to deal with, at the moment, without taking on Mother Nature, to boot.

He needed rest, knew he could sleep despite the problems weighing on his mind, since he had trained himself to relax when and where he could, regardless of surrounding circumstances.

He would sleep, all right. But Bolan hoped he wouldn't dream.

THE FOUR MEN in the Chevy Blazer passed most of the two-hundred-mile trip from Albuquerque in silence. Apollo occupied the driver's seat, in charge of both security and transportation for the visit. To his right sat Icarus, some twenty years his senior, dressed in a sport shirt and slacks, which, somehow, didn't seem to fit properly, although they were clearly the right size. Apollo sensed that Icarus was uncomfortable, nerves on edge, although his rugged face betrayed no more than irritation spawned by the protracted drive.

The two men in the back were likewise silent, but Apollo couldn't read their mood. Both faces had a swarthy, weathered look, one bearded, while the other wore a tired-looking mustache. The desert they had come from could not have resembled this one, since they both spent much time staring out the Blazer's tinted windows, studying the landscape. Cactus, Joshua trees and tumbleweeds were all Apollo saw, and none of it made him nostalgic.

They had started driving south at dawn, after a hasty breakfast at an all-night coffee shop. Four hours later, they were gaining on their destination, and Apollo still imagined he could feel his breakfast, settled like a lump of soggy cardboard in his stomach.

Pigs in a blanket, right, he thought, then recalled the looks his two Muslim companions had worn, watching him wolf down the sausage wrapped in pancakes. It was worth the indigestion, he decided, just to get under their skins.

Apollo knew that he shouldn't have felt so hostile toward his back seat passengers, but old habits died hard. For eight years on his other job, he had been trained, indoctrinated and expected to watch for exactly this type of individual—these very men, in fact—and to take them out on sight. It went against the grain to help them, now, despite the dictates of his faith. A part of him still felt as if he should be driving them to jail, but he was faithful to The Path, and he would do as he was told.

It wasn't always so, of course. There was a time, not all that long ago, when he would certainly have laughed at anybody who believed what he—Apollo—now believed with all his heart. It had required a miracle of sorts to change his mind and heart. He knew that, and he had a debt to pay.

Three years before, he had been driving back to New York City from a small town in Connecticut, not far from Bridgeport, when another car came out of nowhere, sideswiped him and roared away. Instead of giving chase, Apollo had been busy fighting for his life: the four-door he was driving jumped the shoulder, flipped onto its roof and slid downhill a hundred feet or so, flattening brush all the way like some giant toboggan, until it crashed into an ancient tree.

Apollo's shoulder harness may have saved his life, but he was still in no great shape, blood streaming from a head wound, his left shoulder dislocated, two ribs broken, every move he made a trigger for some new and unexpected pain. The strange part, though, had been the way his totaled car had come to rest, its trunk and rear bumper wedged in against the tree that stopped his slide, the front end of the car pointing up-slope, in the direction he had come from. It was a distorted, topsy-turvy view, but he could see out through the windshield.

He could see the sky.

When he attempted to release his seat belt, one hand braced above him, on the ceiling of the passenger compartment to avoid a sharp drop on his head, the latch refused to open. It was one of those things that "could never happen" in a modern, safety-conscious vehicle, and yet, it did. The stubborn harness kept Apollo dangling upside down and staring at the brilliant stars so far beyond his reach.

Until he saw the craft.

The shrinks had tried to talk him out of it after the fact, and he had played along to keep his job. The first light he had seen, so far up in the heavens and performing acrobatics that no manmade craft could ever hope to mimic, was a product of the sharp blow he had suffered to his skull. Indeed, what else could it have been? As for the other light, which had approached the vehicle up close and personal, casting half a dozen stunted figures in stark silhouette, the shrinks had no opinion, since they never heard the story. He had never talked about the little men who pulled him from the car and helped him up the slope, speaking in voices that were only audible inside his skull.

It was entirely natural, the doctors told him, that he would have certain blank spots in his memory. His exit from the car—still unexplained, in that the shoulder harness had been buckled when the car was winched uphill and towed away—could easily have been forgotten in his dazed condition. He had doubtless struggled up the slope himself, to drop where he was found by a passing motorist four hours after leaving Bridgeport.

Case closed.

Apollo kept the crazy details of his story strictly to himself—that was, until the day he had been on assignment in Miami, and he saw an advertisement in the *Herald* for a lecture by The Two. He had attended on a whim, as if drawn to the auditorium by some invisible, compelling force, and what he heard that night had changed his life forever. For the first time since the crash—or years before, when he considered it—Apollo felt at home.

He had been willing to forsake his job and follow his new calling, but The Two had taken him in hand, persuading him that he could better serve The Path by staying where he was, using his skill, experience and contacts in the service of the cause. It had worked out all right, so far, but in his private moments, he couldn't deny a measure of impatience, waiting for the Final Days. If ferrying his latest passengers around New Mexico would help advance the timetable, it was the very least that he could do.

"We're almost there," he said to no one in particular. Nobody answered him, and that was fine. The two behind him craned their necks to see the blockhouse up ahead.

They were expected, and two men came out to meet them as the Blazer pulled up to within a few yards of the door. Apollo killed the engine, pocketing the keys as he stepped out and stretched his legs.

The two-man welcoming committee had no weapons on display, but he could see that both of them were armed, pistols concealed beneath their black, loose-fitting shirts. The taller man took a forward step, extending his hand.

"I'm Nimrod. Welcome."

Apollo shook his hand, resisting the urge to make it a contest of strength. "Apollo. We were, um, expecting Ares," he remarked.

"There's been a change of plans," the stranger said. "You won't be seeing him again.

"I see." In fact Apollo didn't see a frigging thing, but he wasn't about to ask. That's how you got in trouble, when you didn't know the game, much less the rules.

He snapped out of his momentary daze, finished the introductions: Icarus next, then the Arabs, keeping a straight face as he called them Mr. Smith and Mr. Jones.

"Well, if you're ready, then," Bolan said after he had finished shaking hands, "what do you say we get you started on that tour?"

THE MAN CALLED Icarus was fifty-something, Bolan calculated, and his military bearing indicated that he had to have spent substantial time in uniform. There was no foreign accent when he spoke, as far as Bolan could discern, but what did that prove?

At the moment, Bolan had more interest in the others. They were plainly Arabs, maybe Palestinians. They kept their mouths shut, for the most part, and when they addressed each other, it was always in a whisper, leaning close to catch the muttered words, as if afraid of eavesdroppers. What little Bolan overheard sounded Arabic, or was it Farsi?

Either way, he recognized the men for what they were and who they represented. Bolan didn't know the faces, but he knew the type. Killers were drawn from every race and nationality on earth, but there was something in the eyes that marked them, regardless of the clothes they wore, the god they worshiped, or the color of their skin. Killing did something to a man, regardless of the cause or motive. When a man has killed repeatedly, whether it weighs upon his soul or not, it takes something away from him, replacing what he's lost with something else, something that showed up in the eyes.

Bolan knew all about that look.

He saw it in the mirror every day.

Inside the blockhouse, Bolan turned the tour-guide function over to young Hercules. He knew his way around the plant, but he wasn't at home there, yet. Hermes and Circe had supplied the basic details of the plan: a sarin gas attack, downtown Los Angeles, with foreign sponsors taking credit for the raid, and kicking in some very welcome cash, besides. He hadn't been informed of who the sponsors were, and it seemed to make no difference at the time.

Now, Bolan understood that it made all the difference in the world.

If Packer's militia had succeeded with the Vegas bomb, it would have led to crackdowns on assorted right-wing paramilitary groups around the country, heightening the paranoia that was already their stock-in-trade. If foreign agents were involved, however, it increased the stakes. There would be saber-rattling, at the very least; investigations, maybe economic sanctions. If the terrorists were traced to the Middle East, it was conceivable that the Israelis would be granted leave to punish those responsible. Whatever happened, even if it went no further than the long embargo on Iraqi trade, it would increase the hatred of Americans already felt by many radicals in that part of the world. It wouldn't be enough, perhaps, to start an all-out war, but if the action were repeated, even escalated...

Dr. Campbell did the honors in the lab, while Bolan watched him from the sidelines. The man who was called Apollo was security. He stood and watched the other members of his party, watched the lab staff watching them, instead of following the doctor's presentation. It was entirely possible that he already knew the recipe for sarin, how it killed. He concentrated on the other three, stuck close to them, his light windbreaker open, granting easy access to the pistol on his hip.

Icarus was seemingly in charge, although he had little to say for himself, and nothing at all to his swarthy companions. The Arabs, for their part, followed Campbell like a pair of paying tourists in a grand museum, peering closely at each new piece of equipment in turn. They whispered back and forth, occasionally asking Campbell a question in English, frowning and nodding at his replies. Bolan couldn't have said if they understood him or not, but it appeared to make no difference, either way.

The pair, or those they represented back at home—wherever home might be—were sponsoring a terrorist event for which they would presumably claim credit when the time was right. Whether they loosed the gas themselves, or not, was immaterial to Bolan at the moment. He had memorized their faces and would know them next time, whether in a photo lineup or in person. Whether he got a chance to take them out this time or not, the gas had to be his first priority, frustrating what could only be regarded as a plan for mass murder in the heart of America's third largest city.

The lab tour took the best part of an hour, part of that consumed with questions from Icarus, after they had seen all the equipment. He was interested in patterns of dispersion, projected kill radius and decontamination procedures. He almost seemed to know the answers in advance, but Bolan reckoned that he may have simply wanted to show off. On the other hand, he may have wanted to impress the foreign clients that they were getting their money's worth.

When they were finished, and Campbell had shaken hands all around, Hercules brought the quartet back to Bolan. Waiting for the elevator, Bolan asked them if they cared to stay for lunch. Icarus confirmed his first impression of command by speaking for the group without consulting anybody else.

"We're heading back," he said. "We'll pick up something on the road."

"All right, then," Bolan told him. "Suit yourself."

He walked them back out to the porch and

watched them pile into the Blazer, with Apollo at the wheel and Icarus beside him in the shotgun seat. In back, their traveling companions huddled close together, seemingly in conference. As they drove away, young Hercules was smiling to himself, a look of utmost satisfaction on his face.

"What is it?" Bolan asked him.

"Sir? Oh, well, I was just thinking. This is the start of it all, right? I mean, the real beginning of the Final Days. We're making it happen. Before you know it, everything is going to be different."

Bolan looked at him, returned the smile and said, "I wouldn't be a bit surprised."

CHAPTER SIXTEEN

They started on the long drive to Los Angeles at dawn, the second day after the visit from Apollo and the VIPs. Bolan had planned the route himself: Highway 285 northwest from Roswell, picking up Interstate 40 in northern Torrance County, sticking with the interstate across Arizona, through Flagstaff and Kingman, until they entered California for the run to Barstow. There they would find Interstate 15 and follow it to the southwest, until they reached the freeway labyrinth that was L.A.

The trip was close to seven hundred miles. Bolan rode with Hercules in a jet-black GMC Yukon, while three more cultists followed with the sarin in a Ford Econoline van. The four canisters of nerve gas were concealed inside a cooler, cushioned with foam pellets. There was no danger of a premature release unless someone opened the spray nozzles or a canister was accidentally punctured. In which case, Bolan knew, his three subordinates would be the first to die.

But not the last.

Given the nature of the payload this time, Bolan couldn't risk another ambush on the highway, as he had with the militia's truck bomb. There would be no catastrophic blast, if something happened to the canisters. Instead, the nerve gas, once released, would travel on the wind killing along the way until it gradually dissipated over time. Hundreds might die; thousands, if they were in a densely populated area. Bolan himself would be among the victims if he spilled the gas without donning a decontamination suit, with bottled oxygen.

Ideally Bolan hoped to find a way to neutralize the hit team—and the helpers waiting for them in Los Angeles—before the deadly gas could be released. While it was safe inside the canisters, he could deliver it to Brognola, ATF or anybody trained to handle and dispose of it in safety. First, though, he would have to get in touch with the big Fed, tell him what was intended for Los Angeles and see what kind of help his oldest living friend could mobilize.

They drove straight through, some thirteen hours on the road, including lunch in Winslow, Arizona, where they wolfed down hamburgers and French fries, with plenty of coffee to keep them alert on the road. It was pushing eight o'clock before they reached Los Angeles, and would have been full dark outside, except for several million city lights.

They stopped at different motels for the night in Santa Ana, in Orange County. Four of them met for dinner at a coffee shop, midway between the two motels, while number five stayed with the nerve gas, waiting for his meal to come back in a doggy bag.

The conversation over dinner was reserved, generic, steering clear of any reference to their mission in L.A. They were supposed to meet their helpers in the morning, case the target area and make their final preparations. There was nothing to discuss about the job while they were eating, unbelievers all around them who might overhear and drop a coin to the authorities. They didn't even talk about the Ancients or The Path, from fear of letting something slip that would betray them.

Bolan had a steak and baked potato with a salad on the side, and tasted none of it. He didn't need three cups of coffee with the meal to keep his nerves on edge, but he was under scrutiny and drank them, anyway. He joined the younger men in small talk, recycling some anecdotes from boot camp that got them laughing, putting them at ease.

They were already taking orders from him, but he wanted them to trust him fully, to relax as much as possible when they were in his presence. That way, Bolan knew, they would be easier to kill, when it was time.

Bolan and Hercules had separate rooms at the motel. The younger man had asked no questions when the Executioner booked rooms for two, accustomed as he was to following directions from the cult in every aspect of his life. They said good night at Bolan's door, scheduled to meet again at 6:00 a.m.

The door to Bolan's room locked automatically, but he took no chances, locking the dead bolt that was provided for extra security. He turned on the television and killed the other lights, finding sufficient light to work from the TV screen alone. Some kind of cops-and-robbers movie was in progress, badly censored from the big-screen version for its network airing. They had cut so much profanity, for prime time, that the final product reminded Bolan of a poorly dubbed Godzilla flick. The frequent shoot-outs had been whittled to little more than muzzle-flashes, breaking glass and jump cuts that resembled amateurish splicing of a damaged film.

No matter.

Bolan left it on for background noise and sat on the bed, slipped the Beretta from its shoulder rig and laid it beside him as he reached for the telephone. He gave no thought to listening devices, since the choice of lodging had been his, decided on a whim, but there was still an outside chance that someone—Hercules, perhaps somebody else—would try to creep around and eavesdrop on him from outside.

He cranked up the TV's volume another notch and started tapping numbers on the touch-tone phone. It meant disturbing Brognola at home this time, but that was nothing new. The big Fed was used to it, and he could always catch up on his sleep another time.

Los Angeles was on the brink of a catastrophe, and Bolan had no time to spare for common courtesy.

Virginia

AS IN HIS OFFICE, Hal Brognola had two separate phone lines at his home. There had been three lines, once upon a time, before the kids left home, but number three was history. Both numbers were unlisted, but, then again, some telephone numbers were more unlisted than others. His regular number still received nuisance calls from time to time—solicitation from some joker who had dipped into credit records, whatever. The one and only time his very private line had taken such a call, the caller *and* the phone company had been recipients of visits from the FBI next morning, and the problem was never repeated.

When the private line buzzed him at 12:47 a.m., therefore, Brognola came awake instantly, attuned to the muted but insistent sound, so different from the family phone. He lifted the receiver on the second ring, already sitting in bed, but didn't speak.

"Sorry to wake you up," Bolan said.

"Not a problem. Where've you been?"

"I've been around," Bolan replied. "What counts is where I am."

"I'll bite."

"Los Angeles. We've got an action going down tomorrow that you need to be prepared for. Interception may be necessary," Bolan said. "If it goes south, we're in a world of hurt."

"What's going on?"

Bolan told him, speaking plainly, in the knowledge that the phone line was secure. As Brognola sat there and listened in the dark, he felt the short hairs bristling on his nape, the almost-ulcer he had held at bay for years demanding his attention as his stomach twisted into knots. To keep his hands from trembling at the news, he gripped the telephone more tightly in his left and clenched the right into a fist.

Arabs. Nerve gas, for Christ's sake. Brognola felt

sick imagining the kind of hell a sarin discharge could produce downtown at the height of L.A.'s famous rush hour. He pictured bodies lined up on the sidewalk, zipped in rubber bags, while traffic snarled and men in decon suits kept track of the apocalypse, counting the dead.

The Vegas bomb, if it had gone ahead on schedule, could have slaughtered hundreds in the instant of the blast, but that was nothing in the shadow of a nerve gas dump on the teeming anthill of Los Angeles. It wouldn't be a simple matter of a single blast with shock waves, but a creeping pall of death and terror carried on the breeze, wriggling through cracks and under doors to find new victims, maybe claiming thousands on the street, in offices and homes, before it dissipated.

Even as a portion of his mind was screening nightmare images, Brognola listened closely to the disembodied voice of his old friend, absorbing all the details as they were revealed to him. Logging directions to the laboratory in New Mexico, descriptions of the visitors Bolan had met there. It would be impossible to track them from what he had so far, Brognola realized, but he was memorizing everything for future reference.

"What kind of backup do you want?" Brognola asked. He didn't ask about the worst scenario, a sarin spill producing massive loss of life. If that happened, procedures would kick in without his impetus. That much, at least, was carved in stone.

"I've got four people with me," Bolan said. "They shouldn't be a problem. On the other end, I still don't have a fix on how many the other side is sending, or exactly what they plan to do. In theory, it's their job to vent the gas—your basic all-for-Allah martyrdom—but they could just as easily have cards they still aren't showing.''

Once again, Brognola's mind coughed up a stream of graphic images, unbidden and unwanted. He could still recall Lod Airport, Munich, other suicide attacks employing car bombs, automatic weapons, frag grenades, plastic explosives. What if those involved as sponsors of the scheduled gas attack decided they should add some fireworks, just to liven up the game? That put a whole new face on the impending problem, painting it bloodred. He would require not only decontamination teams and medics, in that case, but also shooters who could deal with kamikaze gunmen in the middle of a nerve-gas cloud.

He wondered if the Bureau's Hostage Rescue Team could handle it, or whether he should try the Pentagon. A flying squad of Navy SEALs, perhaps? They were supposed to be prepared for anything the human mind could contemplate, but there had never been a mission quite like this one, and Brognola knew that training—even when it winnowed out some seventy percent of those involved—was never quite the same as the real thing, when lives were riding on the line.

''I'll have the necessary teams in place,'' Brognola said. ''I'll need specifics on the where and when.''

''Downtown, on the subway. They don't want to risk dispersion in the air, topside, and I suspect they've got some kind of sneaking admiration for the bunch that pulled that stunt in Tokyo."

"Terrific." Brognola made no effort to cover his disgust. "The time?"

"High noon," Bolan replied. "They want a body count."

"I guess we'd better give them one."

"I'll see what I can do. Good luck," the soldier said.

"You, too."

Brognola listened to the dial tone for a moment before putting down the receiver. He rose in darkness, navigating more by feel and memory than sight until he cleared the bedroom, softly closed the door and gave himself some light. He kept a file of special numbers in his study under lock and key. The people he was going to disturb within the next two hours wouldn't be amused, but each of them was paid to deal with crises of the down-and-dirty, killing kind. Brognola needed guns, medics and experts from a CBW biohazard team.

But first, he needed *pull.*

Brognola had a fair amount of rank at Justice, but he couldn't sound a national alert, inducting personnel from CDC, the Pentagon and other groups unless he had more weight behind him. Bottom line, he needed all the help that he could get. Which meant that he would have to wake up the attorney general.

Too bad, Brognola thought. If this deal didn't qualify as an emergency, then nothing ever would. If he didn't sleep, he told himself, half smiling at the thought, nobody did.

He was still smiling grimly when he sat at his desk and reached for the telephone.

California

AMAL SAYOOB DIDN'T EXPECT to leave the city of Los Angeles alive. His mission wasn't calculated as an act of holy sacrifice, as certain bombings were, with no advance provision for escape, but it was clear from the beginning that the chances for survival would be marginal at best. The weapon they were using—nerve gas, rather than the usual explosive charges—made the risk much greater, even though Sayoob and other members of his team had come equipped with gas masks. Likewise, the location only made his chances that much worse. This wasn't some kibbutz, or even downtown Tel Aviv, where Sayoob and his men could blend easily into the crowd. Los Angeles was cosmopolitan and ethnically diverse, of course, but not so much that they could hope to carry out a major action on the subway during rush hour and escape unseen.

"All ready," a voice said behind him, and he turned to meet the level gaze of his lieutenant on the mission. Mustafa al-Wadi was two or three years younger than Amal Sayoob, but almost equally experienced at fighting for the freedom of their homeland in the Middle East.

Al-Wadi had the weapons laid out on a bed in the motel room they shared. The seven submachine guns were Swiss Spectres, measuring 350 mm overall, with folded stocks, each fitted with a 30-round box magazine. Sayoob wasn't sure where they came from, and he didn't care. Al-Wadi had test-fired the guns himself, each one of them, and verified that they would function properly. Spare magazines, four to a man, lay stacked beside each gun.

The side arms were a mixed lot: two Berettas, two Brownings, one Colt .45, one P-38, and one Glock 17. Sayoob took one of the Berettas, with its two spare magazines, and watched al-Wadi choose a Browning double-action pistol for himself. They had no holsters, but it wouldn't matter. They could tuck the pistols underneath their belts and wear the submachine guns slung beneath their jackets, bound by leather thongs al-Wadi had obtained from an establishment called the Survival Store in Hollywood.

America was wonderful, Sayoob thought to himself, remembering immediately that the country and its people were his mortal enemies. They had supported Israel's usurpation of Palestine for over half a century, with no end yet in sight, and bankrolled wars between the very Muslim states that should have been cooperating toward destruction of the infidels. America had to suffer for her countless crimes...but he would miss the stores no less for all of that when he was gone.

When he was dead.

It would be no great loss to his country, to the movement, when Sayoob and his six men were gone, but they would be remembered for their contribution to the cause. For every warrior sacrificed, there would be hundreds—maybe thousands—of Americans who paid with their lives for all the crimes their government had perpetrated through the years.

God would have His just revenge for all of it, this day. Amal Sayoob was proud to be His humble instrument, assuming such a contradiction didn't violate the universal laws of logic. Before the sun went down over America this day, people from sea to sea would know the details of the massacre. Sayoob might never be identified—he had already taken pains to hide his phony passport and ID, near certain in his heart that he wouldn't be back to claim the items—but it was enough that God knew and recognized his courage, faithful even unto death.

The guns were for insurance, since all manner of distractions could occur on any job like this. They might be intercepted by police en route to carry out their mission, or an armed civilian would try to intervene, once they were on the subway. Then again, once they released the sarin and had done their job, it might be necessary for the raiders to fight clear of panicked, screaming crowds, while the police were rushing toward the scene.

Sayoob poked through the pile of seven rubber gas masks lying on the pillow of the same bed that had been converted to an arsenal. They weren't small, but they would fit inside the brightly colored canvas shopping bags he had obtained for carrying the nerve gas canisters. The Spectre SMG would fit in there, as well, if anyone decided not to wear a jacket in the noonday heat.

As for Sayoob, he hadn't yet decided whether he would take his gas mask with him, much less wear it when the action started. He wasn't afraid of death—even the drooling, twitching kind produced by sarin—and he had approached this mission from the start in the belief that it might be his last.

One reason he didn't fear death, Sayoob reasoned, was that he had nothing to lose, no one to leave behind. His parents and three sisters had been killed in an Israeli air strike on the Jordan refugee camps twenty years ago next month. The Jewish media informed him that the strike was necessary, a reprisal against terrorists from Jordan who had crossed the river, murdering Israeli children in a school, but all it had meant to ten-year-old Amal Sayoob was loss of home and family, an instant shift to living on the streets, surviving hand-to-mouth.

The movement had recruited him when he was twelve, and while they wouldn't let him fire live ammunition at a man for three more years, they kept him safe and taught him well.

The television had been playing while they double-checked the gear, some movie about counterfeiters and the men who hunted them. There was a lot of shooting on both sides, which seemed appropriate, in light of the commando's brooding thoughts. Ironically even the movie's title was an echo of the Arab's mood.

It was called *To Live and Die in L.A.*

Sayoob noted the use of *and,* instead of *or,* between the verbs. It spoke to him subliminally, confirming his sense of impending martyrdom. He had no wife or lover to shed tears for him when he was gone, but he imagined all the beautiful young women who would weep bitter tears for him back home.

He smiled, imagining the women who would wait on him in paradise.

IT HAD BEEN 3:30 a.m., when Hal Brognola called and roused Andy Morrell from an uneasy sleep disturbed by haunting dreams, which he was pleased that he couldn't recall. Whatever had pursued him through his dreams, Brognola's news was worse.

"Nerve gas?" Celeste Bouchet had nearly shouted it when Morrell told her. "They're dumping nerve gas in Los Angeles?"

"They hope to," Morrell said, trying to calm her, although he still felt far from calm himself. "Remember, though, Blake's with them. Hell, if anyone can stop them—"

"And suppose he can't?"

"Hal has people moving as we speak," Morrell replied. "They'll handle it, Celeste."

"Oh, sure," she muttered, almost as if talking to herself. "They'll handle it. Nerve gas, for Christ's sake. How, exactly, do you handle nerve gas?"

Morrell understood what she was feeling, and he also knew that only part of it was worry over what might happen to a mob of total strangers in L.A. She was afraid for Michael Blake. She felt a bond to him that still eluded Morrell, even though he viewed the somber soldier as a friend and ally.

"They'll have military decontamination teams on hand," he told her, "just in case there's a release of any toxic agents, but my money's still on Blake. He hasn't let us down so far. Besides, he's got an extra edge this time."

Bouchet looked wary when she asked, "What do you mean?"

"He's got a new job since we heard from him," Morrell replied, smiling a little, teasing her.

"A new job? Will you tell me, dammit!"

"Seems like he bumped Dillon Murphy. He's the big dog in Thor's Hammer, now."

Bouchet blinked at the news, frowning as if she still couldn't interpret Morrell's words. "Bumped Ares?" she replied at last, using the cult name that was more familiar to her, from her time inside The Path. "There's only one way that could happen that I know of."

"Murphy made some kind of challenge, what I hear. Could have resulted from the Arizona thing, I guess. Whatever, he's on top."

"Not yet," Bouchet replied, adding, "We can't forget about The Two. They had to put him where he is, and they can take him out again whenever they feel like it. Just the way they did with Ares."

"Even so, he's in a position to observe what happens in Los Angeles and try to head it off."

"And I suppose they've done this kind of thing before?" She sounded skeptical, and Morrell couldn't blame her under the circumstances.

"They've been trained," he said, knowing it didn't qualify as any kind of decent answer. Sitting there, he knew Celeste had to be aware that there had never been a nerve gas incident involving terrorists in the United States. It was a nightmare that cropped up in movies now and then, but as for practical experience, the only ones who had been forced to deal with sarin in a killing situation were the Japanese.

Bouchet's voice interrupted his private thoughts. "When do we leave?"

"I was thinking," he began, but she was way ahead of him, a stern expression on her face.

"Don't even say it, Andy. There's no way you're leaving me behind a second time."

She still hadn't forgiven him for going off alone with Hal Brognola, to the Missouri Mormon temple that Thor's Hammer had invaded, seizing hostages. That time, Brognola had pulled rank on her, inviting Morrell as a former FBI man, while insisting that the scene would be no place for unarmed and untrained civilians. Clearly, though, she didn't mean to let herself be sidelined for a second time.

"Celeste—"

"I know what you're about to say," she told him, leaning closer, placing one hand over his. "I'm not a Fed. Civilians just get in the way. It's all too dangerous."

"You're right, across the board," Morrell replied. "Especially the danger part of it. It's not just shooting, this time, or a truck bomb. With this gas, well, we don't know exactly what could happen if it gets away from us. There's no safe place for anybody in Los Angeles right now."

"You're going," she reminded him.

"That's different," Morrell said. "I'm—"

"A civilian, right? I mean, you *are* retired, as I

recall.'' Her smile stopped short of mockery, but he could see a challenge there. ''This drill won't be an FBI alumni meeting, will it?''

He felt warm color in his cheeks and knew it was embarrassment, not anger. Either way, it put a stern note in his voice as he replied. ''Dammit, I won't allow—''

''Hold on, right there,'' she interrupted him. Her smile had slipped, her full lips tightening. ''You won't *allow?* Since when are you in charge?''

''Since you agreed to let me get in touch with Hal,'' he said. ''It's in official hands now. I—''

''Have no official standing whatsoever, right?'' The smile was coming back, but there was steel behind it, flashing in her eyes.

''Celeste, I don't—'' He caught himself, thought twice about the words caught in his throat, what it would mean to him—to both of them—if he should speak. And if he didn't, then what?

''Andy?'' Her hand tightened on his as she spoke his name softly, and Morrell felt a lump in his throat.

''I just don't want you getting hurt,'' he said. ''I don't...I couldn't...''

Morrell's hands were trembling, and the color in his face now was embarrassment. She squeezed his hand, her own cheeks colored by a blush. ''I'll be all right,'' she said. ''Don't worry, please.''

''Who, me?'' He nearly burst out laughing, then, imagining his own face on the cover of *Mad* magazine, with ''What, Me Worry?'' printed underneath his stupid grin. Was this what it felt like to be hysterical? he wondered.

"I'll be all right," she told him earnestly. "I promise, Andy."

If only that was a promise she could keep, he thought, but kept it to himself.

"I guess you'd better pack then," he suggested, "if we're going to L.A."

CHAPTER SEVENTEEN

Bolan was up and dressed by five o'clock, his hair still damp from the shower. It was cool enough outside that he could hide his shoulder rig beneath the lightweight nylon windbreaker, and yet avoid looking suspicious on the street.

He had to smile at that, asking himself exactly what would be required to draw a second glance from any native of Los Angeles. Perhaps, he thought, if Sasquatch rode a skateboard down Broadway, wearing an emerald top hat and a sandwich board announcing that The End was near, it might raise eyebrows. Then again, it might not, in the town that had for all intents and purposes invented movies, where the outré was routine, and the outrageous barely drew a second glance.

He double-checked the micro-Uzi with its foot-long sound suppressor attached, and slipped the weapon into an Adidas sports bag, along with half a dozen extra magazines, cushioned with spare towels from the motel bathroom, to prevent the hardware clanking every time he made a move. A small gas mask was tucked into one corner of the bag, out of the way. He hoped the SMG wouldn't be needed, but he couldn't say for sure, as yet. The four cult members on his team were one thing, but the Arabs...

Hercules was waiting for him on the sidewalk when he stepped out of the rented room. "We're almost there," the young man said, sounding excited, grinning eagerly.

"Almost, but we're not there yet."

"Is something wrong?" the cultist asked. "If it's the strangers—"

"Nothing I can put my finger on," Bolan said, glad for any chance to put the other man's nerves on edge. "But help me watch them, will you? Just in case."

"Yes, sir." The smile had vanished now, young Hercules considering his new assignment. "I'll stay right on top of them. One false move and you'll know about it, sir."

"Don't make them *too* suspicious," Bolan cautioned him. "Remember that they're paranoid already."

"Right. I know just how to do it, sir."

They had a six-o'clock breakfast date at a Denny's restaurant with the other members of their crew. Hercules drove the Jimmy, pulling into the all-night restaurant's parking lot with ten minutes to spare. The Econoline van pulled in five minutes later, two men visible in front, the third concealed in back seated beside the cooler that contained the sarin canisters. The shotgun rider saw them in the Jimmy and raised a hand in greeting. They met up on the sidewalk, near the double doors.

"I'll stay out with the cargo, if you want, sir," a young cultist known as Grus told Bolan. "I'm not all that hungry, anyway."

"It should be fine," Bolan said. "We can get a table near the window, over there, and keep an eye on the van."

A smiling hostess met them just inside the door and led them to the table they had chosen. Bolan waited until coffee had been poured and their orders taken by a waitress before he spoke to the assembled troops.

"We've got three hours before we meet the sponsors," Bolan said. "I still don't know how many men they're sending, or exactly how they mean to handle it. You all brought masks?"

They nodded, more or less as one. A young man to his left, star name Capella, grinned and said, "For all the good they'll do."

"It's all we've got," Bolan reminded them. "The masks should handle any airborne gas, but I won't lie to you. You know the score. If you get any on your skin, you're history."

No one replied; they didn't have to. What was there to say? It took two trips for the young waitress to deliver all their food, and no one spoke while she was at it, mulling Bolan's words, the fact that they would soon be walking into mortal danger. Still, none of them seemed afraid, in any normal sense. He never doubted for a moment that these four young men were ready to lay down their lives on behalf of The Path.

And he wondered whether it would be his hand

that snatched away their lives. Would any of them live to see another sunset in L.A.? Would he?

He thought about the L.A. subway, shiny and new beside the ancient system in New York, or even San Francisco's BART. The underground network had been still under construction when it got a jolt from Hollywood, destroyed in a sci-fi extravaganza dealing with a volcanic eruption in the downtown business district, but today's potential catastrophe was no Hollywood nightmare. There were no guarantees of happy endings, and the dead—if any—wouldn't rise again and go to lunch when the director shouted, "Cut!"

This was for real, and if the plan went south on Bolan, if he lost control, Los Angeles would never be the same again. Life would go on, of course, for some. But whatever security the "better" classes felt, living with crime rates that were through the roof already, would be shattered overnight. If it could happen here, mass murder in the City of Angels, it could plainly happen anywhere.

As for the Arab sponsors of the deed, they still remained the focus of his concern. When he found out how many men and weapons they were bringing to the game, then he would have a better grasp how he should react.

Until then, Bolan knew, his gamble was the riskiest in town.

Nevada

THE CABIN near Lake Tahoe was another hideaway Hermes and Circe had acquired through a subsidiary of Stargate Incorporated, using some of the donations from their followers to buy the land and structure, with the deed recorded in the name of an associate who had no recognized connection to The Path. Circe had wanted to remain at Big Sur for a few more days, but Hermes knew that safety—for the moment, anyway—lay in mobility. It made him feel more comfortable, on this day when all the world would have its eyes on California, to be sitting just a mile or so from the Nevada border.

Gazing at the placid lake, Hermes imagined a world without man in his present, degraded state, once the Ancients returned and the planet had been purged. The notion conjured images of landscapes never seen before by human eyes, with constellations overhead that were unknown to earth's astronomers. He hungered for the day when rightful balance in the universe would be restored, and the humans who remained, purified by fire, could rove among the stars at will, communing with their kindred races, dancing to the music of the spheres.

Soon, now, he told himself. It wouldn't be much longer. He had waited all his earthly life, but all the waiting was about to end.

Those who survived would thank him when the smoke cleared. They would recognize their debt to Hermes for enabling the Ancients to return. They would build statues of him in the central mall of every futuristic city on the planet. Hermes would be worshiped as a god—which, after all, was only fitting. He had earned whatever homage might be paid to him by those whom he had led from darkness into perfect light. Who else deserved it more?

He missed Ares a bit, for they had traveled far together, carrying the message to an often heedless world. Still, he couldn't deny the message of the Ancients that had come to him when he was called upon to judge between the two conflicting stories told by Ares and Nimrod. The right would triumph in a test of strength and will—and so it had.

Ares had lost his focus near the end, or, rather, he had come to focus overmuch upon himself. As chief of security for The Path, the field commander of Thor's Hammer, he had been invested with a fair amount of autonomy, but Ares had clearly overstepped his bounds with the attempt on Nimrod's life. He had bypassed The Two on a command decision, dealing with the fate of a chosen one, and that was ultimately unforgivable.

By usurping authority, he had betrayed more than The Two, more than The Path.

He had betrayed himself.

"It's beautiful," Circe said, coming up behind him on the cabin's porch and slipping one hand into his, her eyes turned toward the lake. "I hope we still have lakes and trees and rivers, afterward."

"We will," he promised, "only better than before. Primeval lakes and forests, all the way they were supposed to be. It won't be long now."

He knew that in his mind, believed it in his heart. A new earth had been promised by the Ancients, and he trusted them to keep their word. No strife between the races, no political disputes or squabbles over territory.

"Will it be all right this time?" she asked, squeezing his hand. It wasn't like Circe to ask for reassurance, and he took it seriously.

"We've made every preparation possible," Hermes reminded her. "Don't forget our other plans. How can we fail? The Ancients won't allow it."

"I just hope we've made the right decision," she went on. "About Nimrod, I mean."

"He won the contest," Hermes said. What more was there to know?

"Still..."

"What?" he asked her, suddenly concerned. Circe possessed the power to make him stop and think again, even when he was certain of the course that he should follow. Not that she had ever tried to second-guess the Ancients. Still, she seemed to have the knack of clarifying things, somehow.

"I can't help wondering, that's all," she said. "As long as Ares served us—served The Path, I mean—he never let us down before. I just keep thinking that there may have been, well, some mistake."

"Ares had every chance," he said. "In fact, if you recall, he flaunted our instructions even at the end. There was no honor in the way he tried to kill Nimrod. No courage. He was bound to pay the price."

"But what if he knew something that we're not aware of?" Circe asked.

"Then he was duty-bound to tell us first before he acted on it," Hermes said. "It seems to me that Ares had begun to place himself above the cause. I hate to say it, but the evidence speaks for itself."

She didn't answer him aloud, but gave his hand another little squeeze, still facing toward the lake. Hermes wondered again, as he had wondered on occasion in the past, if there was—had been—more between Circe and Ares than mere comradeship in the faith. He felt no jealousy, per se—they weren't married, after all; whatever may have happened, he hadn't been sinned against—and he could put such thoughts behind him now. His eyes were focused clearly on the future, looking forward to the day of victory.

But they weren't there yet.

"It's hard, sometimes," Circe remarked. "Waiting, I mean. I wish that I could snap my fingers, and the tribulations would be all behind us."

"You're a dreamer, love," Hermes said, not unkindly. "What would anybody learn from that? The easy way has never been much of a teacher."

"No. You're right, of course. It's just that I've grown tired of all the suffering."

"You know the rule," he said.

"I know the rule," she echoed in agreement.

He spoke the first part of the mantra anyway. "Things always get worse..."

"Before they get better," Circe finished it, turning toward Hermes with a smile that was tempered by sadness. "It doesn't stop me dreaming, though."

"Nor should it," he replied. "We're meant to dream, dear one. Enjoy it. It's a gift."

His own dreams had been tending toward the dark

side lately, but he didn't mind. You had to travel through the dark, he realized, before you reached the warm and perfect light.

California

DAYLIGHT CAUGHT UP with Andy Morrell and Celeste Bouchet on Interstate 15, a few miles east of Rancho Cucamonga. Tired of desert driving as he was, Morrell was still glad to be moving, going somewhere—anywhere. He didn't even mind the fact that he was heading into a potential war zone, where a relatively minor error on the part of Michael Blake could unleash deadly nerve gas at the city's very heart.

The only part of it that really troubled him, the part he couldn't seem to get around, was risking Celeste's life at the same time. He tried to tell himself there had been no alternative, but that was nonsense. He knew he could have left her back in Barstow, forcing her to rent a car and follow him alone, without a clue as to the target of the planned sarin attack, but what would he have gained? There was no question in his mind that she would follow him, as she had promised. He couldn't stop her, short of having her arrested, and there was no chance of that, unless he spilled his guts and told the local lawmen everything he knew.

As if they would believe him. Aside from breaking confidence with Hal Brognola, spilling a tale like that to sheriff's deputies in Barstow was as likely to result in his being held for psychiatric observation, as detain Celeste.

This way, he told himself, he could keep an eye on her, attempt to keep her out of trouble. He hadn't had much success in that respect so far, granted. Celeste was nothing, if not independent and strong-willed. She knew her mind, no doubt about it, and she meant to see this mission through, regardless of the danger to herself. Morrell admired her courage, but he found himself increasingly worried about the danger she would face. Thousands of lives were riding on the line, a possible catastrophe unequaled in the nation's history, and still his thoughts came back to her, the woman dozing within arm's reach.

Celeste had gotten to him, even though he realized she was not interested in him that way. It could be the difference in their ages, something physical, perhaps the circumstances of their meeting.

Or it could be Michael Blake.

Morrell had seen the way Celeste looked when she spoke of Blake. He didn't know if she had truly focused on the feelings yet, herself, but much of what she felt for Blake was plainly written on her face each time they spoke about the man and his odds of getting out alive.

And what *he* felt, when he beheld Celeste looking that way, was something very much like jealousy.

He was crazy, Morrell told himself, out of his ever-loving mind. The last thing that he needed—that he wanted—was a complication of this kind, right now. If he lost focus on the job at hand, then—

What? he asked himself. It wasn't as if *he* had any front-line role to play in the grim drama already unfolding in Los Angeles. He was retired from active service, as Celeste had pointed out. The wise thing would have been for Andy to step back, let Blake and Hal Brognola handle it, without his interference. Blake could handle it, he thought. If not, what difference would it make to have a single, former G-man on the sidelines?

None at all...unless he was more actively involved.

Brognola had explained the basics of the plan. The sarin was supposed to be released on L.A.'s subway downtown, during the lunch hour. Morrell had no idea of the exact location chosen for the strike, but he had done a bit of homework on the target zone. He knew, for instance, that the L.A. subway system had been plagued with problems from day one: collapsing streets, cost overruns, work slowdowns and assorted accidents. The system was a relatively small one in comparison to San Francisco's; it was tiny, little more than embryonic next to London's or New York's. Downtown, for all intents and purposes, had to mean the Main Street line, which ran below the Hall of Justice, city hall, plus several hundred office buildings and high-priced department stores. At lunch hour, the subway and the streets above would be jam-packed with men and women hastening to restaurants, on shopping errands or to some illicit rendezvous, none of them ready for a tide of silent death to sweep down on them, smothering their hopes and dreams.

One tunnel, then, perhaps two miles in length; two trains to choose from—or would the assassins strike at both? Morrell couldn't watch both; he would be forced to make a choice, risk missing out on all the action, but there was no way for him to narrow the odds. The last time he had spoken to Brognola, Michael Blake himself hadn't been sure exactly where the terrorists would strike. Apparently the Middle East wild cards were averse to sharing final details of their plans, even with those who were about to make the slaughter possible.

So be it.

He would leave Celeste at some motel, make up some excuse to leave her on her own, pick out a subway train—whichever one appealed to him, once he was underground—and ride it for a while. If he saw Blake, or spotted some suspicious character, Morrell would wait and see what happened next, do what he could to head off a catastrophe. If nothing happened on the first train, he would switch, head back downtown, and hope for better luck the second time, repeat the circuit if he had to, hunting total strangers in a crowd that would run into the hundreds, maybe thousands.

Talk about your basic wild-goose chase, he thought, and couldn't stop the smile that creased his features, catching the expression in the rearview mirror. It wasn't like any smile he could remember wearing in the past, almost a grimace, as he pictured tunnels choked with bodies, others dropping on the street above as wisps of sarin found their way topside. He'd be among the dead if he ran out of luck, eyes open, glazed from staring at the dark heart of the universe.

What secrets waited for him there? With any luck at all, Morrell was hoping he wouldn't have to find out—at least, not yet. He had no martyr complex, no compelling wish to throw himself on top of a grenade to save the troops, but he would do whatever was required of him this day.

Meaning whatever he demanded of himself.

Approaching L.A. from the east on Highway 10, he started looking for motels. The first one that he found would do. It didn't have to be the Ritz, as long as he knew that Celeste was safe.

As safe, at any rate, as anyone could be that day, at any point around Los Angeles. He only hoped that the City of Angels wasn't about to be transformed into a city of the dead.

ANOTHER DAY, another damned plane ride, Brognola thought, as he stepped off the red-eye from Washington at L.A. International. He moved along the jetway to the terminal, surrounded by other rumpled, bleary-eyed travelers like himself, all of whom plainly would have preferred to be at home in bed. Brognola's carryon contained a fresh shirt and a change of underwear, his shaving kit, a rolled-up Kevlar bulletproof vest.

The latter piece of gear had been his wife's idea, despite the fact that he assured her he would have no part in any confrontation that occurred. She knew him well enough by now to know that any promise made to her when he was safe at home might be forgotten in the crunch when duty forced his hand.

Brognola meant to keep his word this time, however. As it happened, he would likely have no choice. His call to the attorney general had set crucial wheels in motion, and the gears were turning even now. The troops were doubtless on alert, perhaps already being briefed on their objective in as much detail as possible.

Which wasn't much, he realized. Barring a last-minute communication from the Executioner, it was impossible for them to be precise. Strike teams would have to be distributed around the downtown area, prepared to move out on a moment's notice—and concealed somehow, to keep from tipping off the terrorists or starting any kind of panic in the lunchtime crowd.

His welcoming committee was an agent from the FBI's Los Angeles field office, young enough to draw the crack-of-dawn details that agents with seniority were better able to avoid. He put on a semi-cheerful face anyway, and met Brognola with a smile that stopped within a hair's breadth of sincerity.

"Good morning, sir," the young man said. "I'm Special Agent Forsythe."

"Tell me, Forsythe, what's so good about it?" Brognola asked.

"Sir?"

"Forget it, son. Let's take a ride."

"Yes, sir."

The car was standard Bureau issue, unmarked only in the sense that it didn't have "FBI" emblazoned on the sides in letters two feet high. The federal license plate was all you needed to distinguish it from a civilian vehicle, assuming that you missed the radio antenna sprouting from the trunk, the handset mounted underneath the dashboard or the spit-and-polish look of its young driver.

"Will you be needing a hotel room, sir?" Forsythe asked.

"I hope not."

Staying overnight would mean the plan had gone to hell, most likely with disastrous results. Ideally he was looking for a quick and clean solution to the deadly job at hand, but long years of experience had taught him to expect the worst.

In this case, though, Brognola couldn't say exactly what the worst scenario might be.

How many people would be killed, he wondered, if the sarin was released on schedule? It was anybody's guess, how many thousands of Los Angelenos worked and shopped downtown on any given weekday. If the canisters were opened in a subway tunnel, it would help contain the gas to some degree, but how many would be penned beneath the teeming streets, deprived of air?

He tried to put the numbers out of mind. Fretting about the body count would get him nowhere. There was no way to alert the public, short of touching off a panic that would also give their adversaries more than ample time to slip away. If they were routed now, before they made their move, the terrorists might just as easily decide to leave the sarin behind, as a going-away present for their enemies. It wouldn't matter much where they released it, in the last analysis—a high-rise rooftop or a hotel lobby, in a sidewalk trash can or the back seat of a taxicab.

How many canisters? How much nerve gas?

Again, Brognola did his best to let the numbers go. It was enough for him to recognize the grim potential of the business, without having every detail spelled out in advance. It might be bloodless slaughter, but it would be slaughter all the same.

And only one man had a chance to stop it now.

The SEALs could only move once they were pointed toward a target and unleashed. By that time, Brognola thought, it could be too late.

"Where to, sir?" Forsythe asked, as they pulled out of the parking lot.

"The Federal Building for a start."

Beyond that, they would have to wait and see.

CHAPTER EIGHTEEN

The Arabs all wore business suits that looked like they were purchased from a Goodwill store, without regard for style or fit. The colors ran toward brown and gray, with a couple of navy blues thrown in for variety, the seven of them looking more like shoddy door-to-door solicitors than businessmen or tourists. Bolan would have been disgusted if he had been hoping for the mission to succeed. In fact, however, he was grateful for their lack of taste, since it would help him spot them in a crowd when it was time to take them down.

Each one of them was carrying some kind of automatic weapon underneath his jacket, most with handguns tucked into their waistbands, either at the back or on the side opposite the larger guns. As baggy as the jackets were on some of them, he had no problem picking out the hardware by the bulges underneath. Each man carried a garish shopping bag that clashed outrageously with their ill-fitting suits.

They loitered in the sporting goods department of a store on Temple Street, a block west of the L.A. County Building, dawdling near a rack of long guns, fending off an eager, twenty-something sales clerk who was trying hard to make a sale. Bolan picked out the two who had been on the tour of the Roswell lab and sidled over to the one who had appeared to be in charge that day.

"You're right on time," he said.

"Of course." The Arab glanced around, as if in search of Bolan's team. "Where are the rest?" he asked suspiciously.

"They'll join us on the way," Bolan said. "There was no point ganging up and calling more attention to ourselves."

The leader of the Arab hit team stiffened, on the verge of taking offense, then blinked a few times rapidly and nodded, almost to himself. It was a lesson filed away for future reference.

"I didn't catch your name the other day," Bolan said.

Once again the Arab peered at him, as if examining an unfamiliar life-form. Finally, deciding for himself that there was no trick to the question, he replied, "I am Amal."

"Nimrod," Bolan stated, knowing better than to take a stab at shaking hands. "If you're all done here, you can come with me."

The others had surrounded Bolan and Amal while they were talking, and the Arab scanned their faces while Bolan made a point of focusing entirely on the leader of the pack, ignoring the rest.

When he had finished counting heads, Amal nodded stiffly and said, "We go."

Hercules was waiting for them on the sidewalk, with a gym bag slung over one shoulder. The bag contained a canister of sarin gas, wrapped in a sweat suit that would cover it on casual inspection, the parcel resembling workout gear until you dug a little deeper.

There were no more introductions as Hercules joined them, falling into step on Bolan's right, Amal at his left hand, the other Arabs tightly clumped behind them. Moving east along the sidewalk, Bolan thought they had to resemble something from a grade-B movie—which, of course, could only help to guarantee that they would pass unnoticed in Los Angeles.

He checked his watch and saw that it was just 11:10 a.m. A few more minutes, and they would reach the subway station, following the stairs down to the gate. Bolan had purchased tokens in advance, more than were needed for the job, and he would dole them out to all concerned once he had learned the final details of the plan.

That was the hell of it, he thought, not knowing, even now, exactly what the Arabs planned to do. Of course, he knew they meant to dump the sarin underground, but would they all be on one train or did they plan to split up to maximize the spread and body count? There had been nothing more for him to tell Brognola on the telephone that morning, and he only hoped that the emergency response team was a large one, sharp of mind and well-equipped.

The other three from Bolan's team, each carrying a gym bag of his own, were waiting for them underground. They drifted toward the new arrivals, homing in from different corners of the station.

"Okay, we're here," Bolan said, jingling tokens in his pocket. "What's the play?"

"Two men per bag," Amal replied. "One for security, the other to release the sarin."

Even with his voice pitched low, Bolan imagined big ears perking up on every side of them, eavesdropping. Counting heads and bags, he said, "You're one man short."

"I take one by myself," the leader of the hit team said. "It is not a problem."

"Maybe not," Bolan replied, "but I'll cover you regardless, just in case. My other people can divide and cover yours. We'll flip to see who doubles up."

"I'll go with you," Hercules said before the others had an opportunity to choose among themselves.

Reluctant as he was, Bolan still nodded in agreement. One man, more or less, would make no difference in the long run. It was the others that concerned him, splitting into teams to spread themselves around.

Still, short of drawing his weapon and taking on eleven guns at once, surrounded by a mass of innocent civilians, there was nothing he could do about it at the moment. He would simply have to bide his time and hope that when the proper moment came, he would be swift enough to pull it off.

"All right," he said. "So how's it breaking down?"

AMAL SAYOOB WAS PLEASED to be about his task at last. They had stopped in the men's room of the subway station to switch the canisters of sarin from the gym bags carried by four of the Americans to the shopping bags his soldiers carried. The remaining three men on his team retained their brightly colored bags because they couldn't otherwise conceal the gas masks hidden there.

The team had been divided, four men boarding the northbound train, while Sayoob and his remaining soldiers, plus their escorts, boarded the train heading south. Sayoob himself would have preferred to face the coming trial alone, but he was not disturbed at having the Americans along to watch. They might learn something of how a true warrior dealt with his enemies.

Assuming they survived.

The shopping bag rested on the metal floor between his feet. The man known as Nimrod sat immediately to his left, the other, younger one, across the car from where Sayoob was seated, barely visible between the swaying bodies of the noonday riders. Still, he knew the young man—both of them—would be there for him if he needed them.

But would he?

There was bound to be an awkward moment when he reached inside the shopping bag and put on the gas mask. He hadn't asked the two Americans if they were properly equipped for the release. It didn't matter to him in the first place, and he also took for granted that they were professional enough to come prepared. If not, well, they could die along with all the rest.

It would be those few moments, while he slipped on the gas mask and reached back inside the shopping bag to lift out the canister of sarin, that he would be most vulnerable to attack. Sayoob possessed an understanding of Americans, which led him to believe that most of them were cowards and self-centered fools, for whom "getting involved" was an eternal fear. Still, there were always some exceptions to the rule. It was entirely possible that someone in the subway crowd would see what he was doing, note the mask before he had a chance to reach the canister and make some move to intervene.

In that case, it was up to Nimrod and the other one to help him, use their guns if necessary, even if it meant a stampede in the car. What difference would it make? Where could they hide from silent, creeping death?

The second team was two cars back in line, each car connected to the next by a flexible umbilicus, designed for transit in emergencies. They would be glancing at their watches, even now, and peering through the windows of the car, watching out for the Beverly Boulevard station. When they saw the signs, and when the train began to slow, it would be time.

Sayoob had come up with the final plan himself. It would be perfect, he had determined, if they waited for the train to stop before they spilled the gas. The plan had three great benefits: first, while the subway riders were intent on getting on or off the train, they would be that much less inclined to notice strangers slipping into gas masks and reaching into shopping bags. Second, the open doors would let the sarin spread beyond the narrow confines of the subway cars and into the station, thus insuring maximum casualties. And finally, the stopping of the train would give Sayoob and his commandos something of a chance to slip away in the confusion, possibly to save themselves.

Survival was the least of Sayoob's concerns at the moment—indeed, he had always cherished an image of himself as a martyr, laying down his life for the cause—but he would seize the opportunity if it arose. More to the point, his soldiers, while unquestionably dedicated to the mission and their stolen homeland, had been more at ease since he spelled out the details of the plan and showed them that there was at least a chance they would escape.

The train was slowing, and Sayoob glanced up, craning his neck to see the station's sign. Not yet, he thought, and settled back into his seat. The next one.

He considered lifting the shopping bag into his lap for convenience, but decided it would only make his moves more obvious to those around him. As it was, he would be leaning forward, head down, when he took the gas mask from the bag and put it on. Assuming those around him noticed him at all, the extra moment of confusion might be all he needed to secure the mask before he turned the nozzle on the sarin canister.

He had considered whether he should leave the canister itself inside the shopping bag, but then it had occurred to him that such a method might somehow restrict dispersion of the gas. Instead, he had decided that the better way would be to take the canister in hand, open the nozzle with a twist and quickly roll the canister away from him along the metal floor. There was a three-second delay before the gas was vented under pressure, in a rush.

Sayoob believed that it would be enough.

If not, well, then he would be treated to the gift of paradise, a just reward for one who gave his all in God's sacred cause.

It was a no-lose situation, as the smug Americans would say. Whatever happened, he would have his victory, and he would be remembered by the soldiers who came after him. Who else had done more for the movement than Amal Sayoob?

No one.

The Arab smiled, content to know that he was on his way to making history.

ANDY MORRELL WAS STARTING to believe that he had picked the wrong train...again. He had been riding back and forth, a mile or so in each direction since eleven o'clock, switching trains and heading back the other way when nothing happened on the one he had selected.

It was frustrating, this technique, if he could even qualify it as a search. For all he knew, the faceless men he sought could be a few yards distant in another car, and he would never know until it was too late. Until the silent, choking cloud of gas enveloped him and stole away his breath.

What would it feel like, dying in that way? Morrell had done some basic homework, and he knew enough to be appalled at the idea. Asphyxiation was the least of it, when you considered the internal hemorrhaging, the muscle spasms that would make him thrash and tremble like a stranded fish, the voiding of his bowel and bladder in a fetid rush.

Not that the other passengers would mind, of course, since they would all be in the same condition. The good news was that death from sarin inhalation was a relatively swift demise, as such things went. His last minute or two of consciousness would be pure hell on earth, but it wouldn't drag on for hours or days, as might have been the case with other toxic agents, breaking out in bloody sores or watching, helpless, while his hair and teeth fell out.

It could be worse, he thought, and caught himself from laughing out loud.

Not that his fellow passengers would care about a giggler in their midst, from all appearances. A few of them were paired off, talking trash or business, heads together to be heard above the subway's noise, but most were seemingly preoccupied with self. Headphones were worn by roughly one in five, a hedge against distraction from fellow travelers. Others—even those who had been forced to stand, while handing on to straps or poles—were focused to exclusion of all else on magazines, newspapers, paperbacks. It seemed a miracle that any of them knew which stop was theirs, but Morrell chalked it up to practice and experience.

He spent the whole time scanning faces, checking bags and briefcases. Uncertain how the sarin was to be delivered, still he realized that it couldn't be carried in a pocket, or conveniently beneath a coat. Some kind of carryon would be involved—a bag, valise, or box, whatever. Even women had to be suspect, since an aerosol dispenser could fit easily inside the average purse.

He had believed, at first, that it would be a help, knowing the terrorists were Arabs. Now that he was actually on the train, though, he could see that it was no damned help at all. Los Angeles was such an ethnic stew that every third or fourth face on the train could just as easily have been one of the men or women he was looking for. And then, there would be members of The Path involved, as well. The only one he could truly hope to recognize was Michael Blake, and meeting him by chance, among the hundreds who were piling on and off the train at every stop, would take much more than luck.

It would require a bloody miracle.

The SIG-Sauer P-226 pistol on his hip was a comfort to Morrell, even though he knew the men he hunted would undoubtedly be better armed. He had a Colt Detective Special in an ankle holster for backup, but if it came down to that, the extra six shots were unlikely to make much difference. Still, it helped to know he had the backup weapon handy, just in case.

It was a damned fool's errand, this pursuit of men whom he had never seen, no doubt armed to the teeth with guns, and never mind about the canisters of nerve gas. He couldn't explain the need for action that propelled him toward this moment any more than he could quantify his unexpected feelings for Celeste Bouchet. Brognola had his people standing by somewhere behind the scenes, and there was nothing he could do to help them. On the contrary, his presence on the train, his half-baked plan, might well endanger them and jeopardize their strategy.

He should get off at the next station, mount the stairs to the street and flag the first cab he could find to drop him back where he had left his rental car. If he was smart, that was.

Morrell stayed where he was, deciding he would give it one more stop, and then make up his mind about what happened next. It wasn't noon yet, and he had been told the strike was scheduled for midday, although he had no way of knowing how precise the terrorists would be. They wanted a rush-hour crowd, that much he knew, but lunch hours downtown might well be staggered anywhere from eleven to two o'clock or so.

It had occurred to him that Blake might try to take them out *before* they reached the underground, but if that was the case, his mission was a truly hopeless case. There was no hope at all of finding those he sought, if he was forced to search L.A. at large.

The train was slowing for its next stop, and Morrell rose to his feet, prepared to disembark, switch to another train and start from scratch. He was already moving toward the door as it slid open, stuck behind a pair of broker-types who could have used more fashion sense and less cologne. The rush of passengers unloading had collided with another group coming aboard, the traffic briefly stalled, and it was that delay that saved Morrell from missing those he sought.

Two Arabs boarded, one behind the other, both

decked out in cheap, ill-fitting suits, with gaudy shopping bags in hand. It was the shopping bags—one of them electric orange, the other bright chartreuse—that caught his eye and made the two stand out from all the other swarthy passengers he had surveyed so far. On instinct, Morrell sidestepped, giving up his place in line to leave the car, and grabbed the nearest upright pole.

He wouldn't sit this time. If these men were the terrorists he took them for, each heartbeat would be critical to his reaction time. The fraction of a second he would waste in standing again, once he was down, could mean the crucial difference between survival and agonizing death.

Were they alone? What of the cultists who were in on this disaster-in-the-making with the Arab terrorists? Did they have backup somewhere in the car?

Morrell resumed his scan of faces, shifting closer to the Arabs where they sat together near the exit. Standing several paces back, a young man with a gym bag slung across one shoulder seemed more interested in the two Arabs than the pretty blonde who stood beside him, ample cleavage jiggling with the motion of the train.

So what? he thought. It took all kinds.

But he was on alert now, hackles rising as he braced himself, feet wide apart, preparing for the move that could mean life or death for everyone aboard the train.

If he was wrong, Morrell would be embarrassed at the very least, and might wind up in jail. If he was right, however, and he took no action, he would soon be dead, with countless other souls to keep him company.

It was no contest, he decided.

No contest at all.

BOLAN KNEW he would have to time his move precisely. There was no second chance with the sarin, no margin of error with the three-second time-delay nozzles. If Amal had time to reach the canister, whatever Bolan did from that point would be too little and disastrously too late.

He had no sound suppressor for the Beretta slung beneath his arm, meaning the first shot fired would start a panic in the car that might result in injury, or even death for some of those around him. Bolan meant only for two of them to die, as expeditiously as possible, but anything could happen once the battle had been joined.

The train was slowing for its next stop, telling Bolan he was nearly out of time. Amal was staring at the hot-pink shopping bag between his feet, brow furrowed in a scowl, deep-breathing as he braced himself for what must follow in a few more seconds.

Now or never, Bolan thought.

He reached inside his windbreaker, but not for the Beretta in its shoulder rig. His right hand clasped the satin-finish buckle of his belt and gave it a tug and twist to free the two-inch, double-edged push dagger from its leather sheath. Folding the buckle in his palm, the blade protruding from between his fingers, Bolan half turned toward Amal and spoke the Arab's name. Before the grim face turned his way, he struck with lightning speed and deadly force below the Arab's jaw line, flush against his neck.

The blade was in and out before the man knew what was happening. He blinked and made a little choking sound, a jet of crimson spouting from the slashed carotid artery. The Arab's lips moved, no words coming out, and then he did the unexpected, lunging toward the bag and deadly canister between his feet, hands groping for the nozzle, desperate to take someone with him as his life ran out.

Bolan struck again, his blade and knuckles blood-slick from the first blow, catching Amal below his chin, arresting his forward momentum. Somewhere off to Bolan's right, a woman screamed, her blue dress speckled violet from the spray of blood. Others were gaping at the sight now, drawing back from Bolan and his victim, even though they had nowhere to go.

Fresh out of time, he left the dagger planted in Amal's windpipe, reaching for the Beretta in its arm-pit holster. As he drew the piece, more screaming from his captive audience, he caught a glimpse of Hercules, directly opposite. The young cultist was gaping at him, startled into immobility by Bolan's stunning act of treason. Then he had the gym bag in his lap, tugging open the zipper, digging for the weapon that was hidden there.

Bolan swung the Beretta in front of him, the sub-way riders scattering before him like a flock of chickens in a hailstorm. Some of them went down, clutching others as they fell, a thrashing, cursing pile of bodies on the floor, but it was all the room that the Executioner needed for his shot.

He stroked the pistol's trigger once, twice, drilling both rounds through Hercules's startled face. Heroic name aside, the young man died like any mortal, blood and grisly tissue splashed across the window at his back. The rapid gunshots echoed like a double thunderclap inside the crowded subway car, eclipsed at once by frightened shouts and screams.

Bolan was on his feet before the other riders could react with anything beyond chaotic noise. He grabbed the shopping bag, dripping with blood, and reached the exit at the south end of the car in half a dozen strides. The door swung open when he threw his weight against it, and he cleared the noisy coupling between the cars in two more steps, bursting into the next car back.

A hundred faces swiveled toward him as he stepped into the second car, all gaping as they saw the gun in Bolan's hand. He bulled his way ahead and watched them scramble, left and right, clearing a path along the middle of the car. He took advantage of their fear and raced along the full length of the car, painfully conscious of the fact that he was running out of time.

They were all running out of time.

"I STILL DON'T LIKE THIS, sir," the SEAL team leader said.

"It's duly noted," Hal Brognola answered. "Can your people handle it or not?"

"It's handled," the Navy commando told him stiffly. "Sir."

"Not yet, it's not," Brognola groused. "When we've recovered all four canisters of sarin with the seals intact *and* bagged the team, *then* we can say it's handled. Not before."

Beside him in the Tac van, Special Agent Forsythe watched the bank of black-and-white video monitors that were plugged into transit security, one camera for each subway station between Bartlett and Second Street—a half-dozen in all. There were no cameras on the trains, which left them nearly blind.

Except that Brognola had spotted Bolan going in. A fleeting glimpse, surrounded by perhaps a dozen faces that the big Fed didn't recognize, most of them toting bags of one kind or another. He had watched them split into trios, three men each in different cars, six to a train, pointing them out to the commander of the SEAL team.

"Which one's yours?" the SEAL had asked.

"The tall one, there," Brognola answered. It was one thing, pointing out a face to keep his friend and number-one soldier from getting picked off by mistake. As for the rest of it, whatever happened in the next half hour, Bolan's true identity and link to Stony Man wouldn't be jeopardized.

Not even if he died.

The odds against his old friend, this time, were as bad as Brognola had ever seen them. It wasn't the number of his enemies, but rather their capacity for killing hundreds, maybe thousands, with the mere twist of a nozzle. Once the sarin was released, it would require a special decon team to neutralize the gas. No single man could pull it off, much less without the proper gear. Once any single canister was opened in the subway tunnel, Bolan stood no better chance against the killing tide than any other victim in its path.

"You have men on both trains?" Brognola asked the SEAL team leader.

"That's affirmative."

"I don't want anybody taking out my man by accident," Brognola said.

"My guys don't make mistakes, sir."

"I sincerely hope not, son." Brognola's face and tone were grim.

"Suppose it goes the other way?" the SEAL inquired.

"It won't," Brognola said. "He has his targets marked. He doesn't miss."

"I'm thinking, sir, that if he spots a team of strangers, armed—"

"Forget about it," Brognola replied. "He knows damned well that anybody else down there with guns is on the home team."

"Well..." The Navy man didn't sound totally convinced. "I hope that's right, sir."

"You know your men," Brognola informed him. "I know mine."

"I guess we've got no problem, then," the SEAL replied.

And that was overstating it to hell and gone, the Justice man realized. They had all kinds of problems—problems up the old ying-yang, in fact, and no mistake. On top of the civilians in their way and the terrorists themselves, there was a danger no one even spoke about, though it was obvious to one and all. In sum, it wasn't only a deliberate release of sarin that they had to think about; an accidental spill down there—a bullet puncturing one of the canisters, for instance; even someone dropping one, so that the nozzle snapped or twisted—it was all the same downstairs, whatever set the toxin free.

"Your men know what to do, right?" Even as he spoke, Brognola knew that he was on the verge of insulting this man, but he had to nail down the loose ends himself, or he wouldn't be satisfied.

The SEAL commander didn't take offense—or if he did, he managed to conceal it. "No one moves until your man kicks off the party, sir. I'll hear about it when that happens—" he reached up to tap the earpiece of his headset with an index finger "—and I'll tip my people on the other train."

"Okay. I guess now all that we can do is wait." He had another thought and turned to Forsythe. "Is the decon team in place?"

"Yes, sir." The young G-man's face wore an expression stuck somewhere between concern and curiosity. At last, he said, "It wouldn't make a difference, sir."

"What wouldn't?" Brognola inquired.

"If you were down below."

The big Fed scowled and said, "It would to me."

CHAPTER NINETEEN

The big man came at Bolan from his left, exploding from his seat and firing off a haymaker at Bolan's jaw. It would have been a better try if he had managed not to screech like something from the sound track of a Bruce Lee movie, thus announcing his intent and giving Bolan time to brace himself.

A glance told Bolan that his adversary's hands were empty, meaning he was just a would-be hero, not a member of some backup team that Bolan knew nothing about. He was a danger, all the same, if for no other reason than that he was slowing Bolan, preventing him from getting to the other terrorists before they had a chance to vent their canister of gas.

With both hands full, he had an extra disadvantage as he turned to face his enemy and stepped inside the big man's swing. He dared not drop the canister of sarin, and there was no time to holster the Beretta. Thinking fast, he drove his shoulder hard into the big man's gut and swung the pistol into his groin. The impact drove a bleat of pain from startled vocal cords, and his momentum did the rest, the big man toppling over Bolan's shoulder, landing heavily upon his back, with force enough to empty his lungs. A short chop with the pistol, at his hairline, kept the slugger down.

"Get him!" another would-be hero shouted, rushing from the left, and Bolan knew he had to stop the game right now, before the others mobbed him. Squeezing off a Parabellum round into the ceiling of the car, he drove the brave guy back and raised another chorus of screams.

"We're stopping soon," he told them, hoping that a few, at least, had wits enough to comprehend what he was saying. "When the car stops, everyone get out and back up to the street as fast as possible."

Somebody called out "Why?" but there was no time for a duck-and-cover seminar. Instead of answering, he turned back to the exit at the south end of the subway car.

How long until the train stopped at the Beverly Boulevard station? It was a matter of minutes, at best, Bolan knew. The other members of the hit team were supposed to vent their sarin canister the moment that the doors slid open on their car.

He hesitated for a precious moment on the platform of the coupling between cars, crouching slightly, peering through the window set into the door that served the next car in line. He couldn't see the Arabs or their escort—was it Perseus?—but it appeared that no one in the car had picked up on the sounds of gunfire, yet.

Small favors, Bolan thought, gripping the handle of the shopping bag in the same hand that held his pistol, while his free hand gripped the outer handle of the door.

Its opening produced a blast of noise within the insulated car, drawing all eyes toward Bolan where he stood, half crouching in the doorway. They hadn't focused on the pistol, yet, when he glimpsed the startled face of Perseus, off to his right, peering across a stocky black man's shoulder.

"Nimrod? What—"

The younger man saw Bolan's pistol, then his eyes darted to the shopping bag that he had lifted from Amal. One glance was all it took for Perseus to know that there was something badly, desperately wrong.

Although his view of Perseus was blocked by other bodies, Bolan saw the young man's shoulder dip and knew that he was reaching for his gun.

There was no room to risk a shot from where he stood. Bolan went low and to his left, ducking below the cultist's line of sight. It didn't stop the younger man from squeezing off two quick shots, though, and Bolan heard a scream of pain as someone took the bullets.

Bastard! Bolan realized the wild fire was predictable. Why would the cultist care about a few stray casualties, when he already planned to murder everyone aboard the train?

Bolan rose, holding the pistol in front of him and scanning for a target. All he needed now was one clear shot—and failing that, a miracle.

MORRELL WAS SURE about his targets now. The furtive glances, whispered comments back and forth between the Arabs, the protective attitude toward those outlandish shopping bags between their feet—it all came down to nervous guilt in the ex-agent's eyes. Those two were dirty.

He edged cautiously—and casually, he hoped—between the riders who were standing in the aisle until he reached a point directly opposite the seated Arabs. Reaching out to grip the nearest pole, he caught a sidelong glare from what appeared to be an aged Rastafarian and forced a smile in return.

How long until they reached into those bags and came out with machine guns—or, worse yet, with canisters of nerve gas, hosing down their fellow passengers? It would be tantamount to suicide, he realized, but when had that thought ever stopped a True Believer? In Morrell's view, it was often part of the attraction: hopeless losers looking for a way out of their worthless lives, finding the one escape hatch that could make them heroes—maybe even legends—at the very moment of their deaths.

His jacket was unbuttoned, hanging loose. He slipped his free right hand inside and found the thick butt of his pistol, gripped it firmly, flicking off the thumb-break snap that held the gun secure inside its holster. Were the targets *really* bending forward, reaching for those shopping bags? Could he afford to wait?

Morrell whipped out the P-226 and thumbed back the hammer. It was a jerky, awkward draw, but got the job done, all the same. He braced the pistol in both hands and bellowed at them like a copper in the movies: ''Freeze, goddammit! Don't you fucking move!''

The Arabs froze, mouths open, gaping at him. He

could see the aged Rastafarian retreating, just the ghost of movement, in the corner of his eye, and put the old man out of mind. He had the two men covered, and it wasn't good enough by half, but what else could he do?

He could cap them and search for the others, some demented spirit whispered from inside his skull. If anything was certain at the moment, Morrell knew that these two men weren't the whole strike team. While he was holding them at gunpoint, others, in a different subway car, could be releasing toxic clouds of sarin gas that very moment. Hundreds could be strangling where they stood, right now, while he was—

Something—someone—slammed Morrell between the shoulder blades and knocked him forward. He collided with a woman who was all of five feet tall and looked to weigh around 250 pounds. She had been staring at him since he shouted; now she gave a little squeal and belly-bucked him backward, bouncing him off the pole that he had clung to moments earlier.

He felt his left leg buckle, folding under him, and saw the Arabs moving, reaching for their shopping bags. There was no time to wonder who had shoved him: someone in the crowd, who hoped to save the day and get his face on *Hard Copy*. If he thought about that now, he was as good as dead. The whole damned carload of strangers was as good as dead.

He shot the Arab nearest to him, wincing as the shot drove spikes of pain into his ears, immediately followed by a ragged, panicked chorus of whimpers, curses and screams. His bullet slammed into the dark man's shallow chest and slammed him back into the plastic seat, blood spouting from the entry wound. He slumped against his partner, but the other Arab shoved him ruthlessly aside, fumbling his suit jacket open to reach some kind of weapon slung beneath his arm.

A gun, Morrell thought with a sudden flash of hope. Whatever he was reaching for, be it a pistol or bazooka, the ex-agent didn't give a damn, as long as it wasn't the sarin.

Morrell was lining up his pistol for a second shot, braced on one elbow, aiming the pistol one-handed, when it happened. He heard the shot all right, but knew he hadn't pulled the trigger. When the bullet ripped into his upper thigh, an inch or two below the ball-and-socket of his hip, the pain was instantaneous and stunning, but it somehow didn't take him by surprise.

Backup, a small part of his mind observed, while he was busy biting off a scream. So, what the hell did he expect?

He jerked the trigger, firing at the Arab, knowing he would miss before the Parabellum slug breezed past his target, drilling through the window just behind him. Still, it made the other man duck, frustrating for a heartbeat his attempt to draw the gun from underneath his coat.

Morrell was turning, even as his second gunshot echoed through the subway car, pain jolting through his body as he made the move. He swung the pistol around, scanning for targets, flinching as another shot rang out, the detonation thunderous, seeming almost in his face.

The bullet struck the pole beside him with a sharp, metallic ringing sound. A jagged splinter of the slug or pole sliced into Morrell's cheek, an inch or so below his eye. The pain was nothing in comparison to that which burned in his leg and hip, but he recoiled from it, regardless, slumping onto his side.

Where was his adversary?

As if in answer to the silent question, Morrell saw a young man shoving past the riders several paces back, approaching him. The stranger had a semiauto pistol in his hand, and it was pointed straight at the ex-agent's face.

BURKE HAMMOND HAD BEEN with the SEALs for two years, and while he felt prepared to fight in any given situation—Sea, Air, Land meant just exactly what it said—the last place he had ever thought he would go trolling for the enemy was on a stateside subway train.

What made the exercise that much stranger, was that they were next to naked: no war paint, no uniforms, no scuba gear or parachutes, no combat boots, no heavy weapons or grenades. They had a little body armor—Second Chance vests underneath their sport shirts—but beyond that, they were traveling too light for comfort: small handguns in ankle holsters, stubby MP-5 K submachine guns hidden in one kind of bag or another.

They normally wore headsets fitted with no-hands microphones on a job like this, but that kind of headgear would have made them too conspicuous. Instead, each SEAL had come on board the subway with a set of miniearphones clamped onto his head. The "tape deck" clipped onto each belt, however, was in fact a small receiver that would channel orders from the team's control. The hell of it was that they couldn't talk back to the boss, keep him advised of what was going on.

Which, at the moment, was precisely nothing.

Hammond considered himself a patient man but this was getting on his nerves, and no mistake.

"All teams, listen up!" the gruff, familiar voice spoke in his ear. "We've got shots fired, the southbound train, third car. Teams five and six, move in ASAP, and keep an eye out for that friendly while you're at it. Everybody else, look sharp and watch your asses."

Hammond muttered, "Roger that" from force of habit even though he didn't have a microphone, and got up from his seat. A quick glance toward the far end of the car told him that Lassiter was also moving, weaving through the crowd as quickly as he could, without provoking any fistfights.

Lassiter and Hammond were Team Six, two out of twenty-eight men split between the north- and southbound trains. No shots were audible from where Hammond sat, but you could write that off to the acoustics of the train. If you were standing in the tunnel and a gun went off, it would have sounded like the crack of doom on Judgment Day, but every car was insulated, more or less, and there were baffles in between, those awkward passageways reserved for engineers and other staff, to keep the noise in one car from disturbing riders in the next.

So far, he thought, the system seemed to work just fine.

Already halfway to the exit at the north end of the car, he wondered whether this would be a false alarm, or something else. He didn't know where the report of shots had come from, whether it was accurate, or if the shooter—granting that there *was* a shooter—would turn out to be one of the faceless targets they were hunting. Hammond thought it was unlikely that some shooter unconnected to the mission would decide to open fire on board the subway, just when they were staked out to receive expected terrorists, but stranger things had happened.

Four men, he thought, which left the other ten in place, covering different cars. Did that suggest uncertainty on the commander's part?

Screw that!

The old man knew what he was doing. You could take that to the bank and cash it in, regardless of the situation. If he wasn't absolutely sure about the target, that was just good sense, until he had a firm report.

And how would he get that, when none of them could talk back to him from the train?

His was not to reason how or why, and all that shit. Hammond was nearly to the exit, and he heard some peevish voices raised, as Lassiter closed the gap behind him. Neither one of them had drawn their weapons yet—another deviation from the norm—but Hammond had both latches open on the imitation leather briefcase he was carrying, one stiffened finger all he needed to hold the case shut as he reached out for the door handle with one hand, ignoring the sign that it was an Emergency Exit Only!

Shoving through, he left Lassiter to secure the door behind them, concentrating on the second door in front of him. There was a window in it, smudged and grimy, but he saw enough to make the short hairs on his neck stand. Two Arab-looking types were seated halfway down the car, on Hammond's right, each hunched protectively above a party-colored shopping bag. There were no guns in evidence, no sign of any shots fired in the car. Most of the passengers surrounding the two Arabs wore the kind of bored expressions that you saw on any public transportation vehicle. And, yet…

Hammond was weighing whether they should barge into the car, when suddenly, a tall man entered through the doorway at the other end. The SEAL had a quick glimpse of him, between heads craning for a better view, and thought this just might be the so-called "friendly" they had been alerted to avoid. Hammond couldn't tell if he carried anything—a bag or weapon—but the riders nearest to the other door were lurching backward and away from him, as if in fear.

Except for one, that is.

A youngish, white-bread type was pushing *toward* the new arrival in the car, and in another heartbeat, Hammond glimpsed the pistol in his hand. A heartbeat later, the shooter opened fire.

"Let's go!" Hammond snapped.

Lassiter, behind him, replied, "Roger that!"

Hammond withdrew his MP-5 K from the briefcase, cast the bag aside and shouldered through the door into the car.

MUSTAFA AL-WADI HAD NEVER panicked in his life, and he wasn't about to panic now. It was apparent that the tall American had managed to betray them somehow, and the shopping bag he carried told Mustafa that he had to have killed Amal Sayoob. The how and why of it was immaterial. He only knew that he couldn't allow the infidel to stop them now, when they had come so far toward vengeance on behalf of all their countrymen.

Fazir Hussein, beside him, had the sarin canister, and he was reaching for it when the white man who had been assigned to guard them drew his pistol, blasting at the traitor from a range of twelve to fifteen feet. Hussein was reaching into his shopping bag, prepared to vent the nerve gas, when al-Wadi grabbed his arm and snatched it back.

"Not yet, Fazir!" he snapped. "We must have open doors!"

Hussein bobbed his head in agreement, while scowling in what might be anger or fear. He left the shopping bag alone, though, and reached underneath his gray suit jacket for the Spectre submachine gun tethered there.

Al-Wadi drew his own weapon, glancing back to his right, where the traitor called Nimrod had dropped out of sight. Their escort fired another shot, but missed his target, punching the bullet through a tall, blond woman's shoulder. She was screaming as she fell, but al-Wadi was distracted from the side-show, as the *other* door burst open, at the south end of the subway car. Two more men burst in, both armed with submachine guns, and he realized that they were in a trap.

He swiveled toward the new arrivals, thumbing off the Spectre's safety, tracking on the forward target. He was good with guns and always had been, dropping his first man at the tender age of sixteen. These two looked competent enough, but he wasn't intimidated by them. He had been prepared to die on this job from day one, before he left the camp in Jordan. All that mattered now was taking out his enemies.

The first short burst al-Wadi triggered from his Spectre was, in fact, a hit. The bullets stitched a line across his target's chest, but only one of them—a shot that winged him—drew any blood. The man wore some kind of vest, but while it stopped the slugs from ripping out his heart, the stunning impact still propelled him backward, slamming his shoulders flat against the wall.

Assuming that the second gunman also wore a vest, al-Wadi dipped the muzzle of his SMG and fired another burst, this time directed at the target's legs. The new arrival tried to dodge him, but too late. Al-Wadi was rewarded by a splash of blood and tissue from the man's legs, a cry of pain as he slumped backward, triggering a burst into the ceiling of the subway car.

Al-Wadi triggered off another burst before his adversary hit the deck. This time, the first few bullets thumped into the man's protected chest, but two or three ripped through his neck and face. Blood sprayed across the door behind him, scarlet runners dribbling down the glass and dull steel finish. As he crumpled to the floor, there was no doubt whatever in al-Wadi's mind that he was dead.

And that left two, unless the white man detailed to protect them did his job. Assuming that he would at least delay the one called Nimrod, possibly with the assistance of Hussein.

As if in answer to that thought, another burst of gunfire reverberated through the car. Al-Wadi turned and saw Hussein unloading on the passengers at large, without regard to whether they posed a threat or not. Al-Wadi struck down the weapon, heard wild rounds strike the floor and ricochet, imagined bullets punching through the shopping bag and canister of gas beside him.

"Dammit! Save your ammunition for the enemy!"

"These *are* my enemies!" Hussein responded, lurching free of the restraining hand.

"The ones with weapons, fool!" Al-Wadi snapped at him. "Down there!"

He shoved Hussein, not gently, so that he was facing the direction where Nimrod had last been seen. The other white man fired another shot, just then, and drilled a fat man through the buttocks. Putting on a grin, Hussein brought up his SMG and started blasting toward the far end of the car.

Al-Wadi swung back toward the closer door in time to see his dazed opponent struggle upright, clutching at the wall with one hand, while the other held his submachine gun out in front of him. The white man's teeth were clenched in pain, but he had both eyes open, clearly focused on the enemy.

Upon al-Wadi.

He was close to a killing shot, but al-Wadi fired on instinct, unloading nearly half a magazine, some fifteen rounds, from less than twenty feet away. The vest stopped some of them, but it couldn't stop all of them. Blood spurted from his face, his throat, his right biceps. The enemy's machine pistol spit out a few more rounds, all wasted, only one of them passing within a yard of where al-Wadi sat.

Half satisfied, he turned away from the corpses, looking for another infidel to kill.

AT LEAST THREE GUNS were blasting at him now, although, in the chaotic firing, Bolan could have sworn at least two more machine pistols had joined the chorus briefly. Were they in the hands of enemies or friends? Would it make any difference in the crowded subway car? Could any of the troops Brognola drew as backup even recognize Bolan, much less distinguish him from those they meant to tag?

The first thing Bolan had to do was shave the odds, while making sure no bullets found the sarin canister inside the garish shopping bag he carried. And the only target he could even glimpse, so far, was Perseus, aiming another shot at Bolan with his semiauto pistol. The Executioner ducked back just in time and heard the slug slap into flesh or fabric, he couldn't be sure exactly which. In either case, it drew a squeal of pain from the recipient.

The time had come for him to take a chance, and Bolan seized the moment, lunging out from under cover, staying low. The next round fired by Perseus was closer, nearly parting Bolan's hair, but firing it compelled him to expose himself, stepping away from the half-dozen passengers who had been serving him as a reluctant shield.

Bolan squeezed off a round from his Beretta without aiming, knowing it wouldn't find a vital organ, even as his fingers tightened on the trigger. Still, he scored a flesh wound, staggering the young man, crimson spouting from his side. He stumbled, windmilling one arm for balance, while the other waved his piece in front of him and triggered two more rounds in rapid fire.

It was the opening that Bolan needed, and he took advantage of it, following his first shot with another, more precisely aimed. The bullet drilled his adversary through the solar plexus, slammed him over backward. A third shot found him as he fell, beneath his chin, and snapped his head back.

That left the Arabs, plus whomever else had come into the subway car since Bolan entered.

He still had two-thirds of the initial load in his Beretta, plus the two spare magazines in pouches underneath his arm. That gave him close to fifty rounds, but he couldn't afford to waste them, not if he intended to eliminate the enemies at hand, go on to find the rest and make his way back to the surface of the earth. It seemed impossible when Bolan spelled it out that way, but he would have to take it one step at a time.

That way, he just might make it out of there alive.

Almost before dead Perseus had crumpled to the floor, two submachine guns were unloading on his killer, driving Bolan back to cover, hosing down his corner of the subway car with bullets. Windows shattered, men and women screamed, the plastic seats were shot to hell, but there was still enough cover for Bolan—animate and otherwise—that he wasn't directly in the line of fire.

Infuriated with his enemies for pumping rounds into a crowd of innocent, unarmed civilians, Bolan still knew it would mean his death to leap in front of them—the death of everyone on board, if even one round hit the canister of nerve gas in his liberated shopping bag. Still, he couldn't just crouch there, hidden, while the slugs ripped into those around him.

Rising from his huddle to a crouch, he marked a moving target to his right—it wore a suit; one of the Arabs, then—and almost had it lined in his sights when swift deceleration of the train pitched him off-balance, backward to the floor.

The train was stopping, dammit! He could hear the squeal of its hydraulic brakes beneath him. In another moment, an electric signal from the driver's seat would open all the doors at once.

And it would be too late.

CHAPTER TWENTY

The wound in Andy Morrell's thigh was pumping blood, but there was nothing he could do about it at the moment. With the grim young cultist lurching toward him, lining up another shot, he knew his life was measured out in fractions of a second if he didn't take some swift, decisive action to eliminate the threat.

His right arm felt like lead as he raised the P-226, triggering a quick double-tap more by instinct than conscious volition. The first shot tore into his adversary's stomach, while the second drilled his chest a hand's width left of center, puncturing a lung. The man fell backward, limp fingers losing their grip on his pistol, man and weapon hitting the floor together.

No time to waste now. Turning toward the second Arab, Morrell found him kneeling in the middle of the aisle, struggling with the reluctant action of a small submachine gun. He wore no gas mask, and Morrell assumed, since both of them were still breathing, that his target hadn't loosed the sarin yet.

He gripped the pole beside him with his left hand, braced his right arm on the left and found his target with the pistol's sights. He still had two-thirds of a magazine, but as it turned out only one shot was required. The pistol bucked against his palm, and he saw a neat black hole open in the Arab's forehead. The man dropped backward on his haunches, slumping over in an awkward sprawl.

Screams echoed through the car as Morrell used his free hand to unbuckle and remove his belt. The riders in the car were close to panic, and he knew he couldn't calm them, but he hoped to hell that he could shut them up.

"Police!" he shouted, lying through his teeth. "Stay quiet now, and everything will be all right."

It was another lie, perhaps, but it appeared to do the trick, at least in part. Most of the screaming stopped, though there was still a lot of fearful muttering and grumbling from his fellow passengers.

Morrell ignored the questions that bombarded him, placing the pistol in his lap, looping his belt around the wounded thigh, an inch or so above the bullet hole that spilled more blood with every heartbeat.

Going fast, he thought. No time to dick around.

He drew the belt as tight as he could stand it, found he couldn't buckle it and did his best to tie it off. It was a piss-poor tourniquet, he realized, but it would have to do.

Wedging the pistol into his waistband, looser than normal now, without his belt, Morrell gripped the stainless-steel pole in both hands and hauled himself upright, pushing off with his good leg, gasping at the pain that pulsed and radiated from his wound.

He had to move despite the pain.

These weren't the only terrorists. If these two were the whole damned team, he would have bet that Michael Blake would be there with them, would have taken them himself, before Morrell could make his move. That meant at least one other team, one other canister of sarin.

Were they on this train? The only way for Morrell to find out would be to search for them, and that meant moving from the pole where he was leaning like a drunkard, clinging with both hands.

Pushing off, he tried one step and then another, almost buckling as his right leg wobbled under him, flaring with agony. He reached for the pole again, but found his balance with effort, just before his fingers grazed the metal. Moving toward the second Arab he had shot, walking like some B-movie monster from the crypt, he concentrated on each step he took, prepared to lunge and catch the next pole down, one of the plastic seats, whatever was required to keep him up and moving forward. Never mind the blood that he was losing, even with the lousy tourniquet. If there was sarin in the air, he wouldn't have the opportunity to bleed to death.

He reached the dead man and the gaudy shopping bag, bent to check its contents, almost slumping forward on his face. There was a fat, black-painted canister inside the bag, a nozzle at one end, like something from a scuba outfit or a hospital room.

He picked up the bag by its rubber handles, lifted it and drew the pistol from his waistband as he straightened. Proceeding toward the nearest exit from the car, he spread his arms for balance, waddle-clomping toward the door.

He made a half-assed Frankenstein, he thought, and would have laughed out loud if it hadn't been for the dizziness, the pain, his fear, the urgency of hunting down and neutralizing any other terrorists aboard the subway train.

The taunting little voice inside his head reminded him that he was bleeding to death, dying.

Maybe so, but he wasn't about to sit and wait for it to happen. He might not go out in style, but he would go out *trying,* bet your ass.

He reached the door and fumbled at the handle with the hand that held his gun.

MUSTAFA AL-WADI COULDN'T believe his good luck, as the subway train began to slow for its next stop. Beverly Boulevard was coming up, *his* stop. A few more seconds and it would be time for him to unleash silent death upon the infidels.

But did he have those seconds he required?

Fazir Hussein squeezed off another burst, directed toward the north end of the car. There were more screams, more bodies flopping in the aisle, across the seats, and still, al-Wadi couldn't tell if Nimrod, their betrayer, had been hit.

He triggered off a short burst of his own, more from a need to do something than out of any hope that he would find his mark. He saw a fat man stagger, clutching at his side before he fell.

Curse it!

Craning for a look outside the car, he saw a sign

for Beverly Boulevard flash past the window. Almost there, and he would have to be prepared.

Hussein no longer gripped the precious shopping bag between his feet. He had, from all appearances, forgotten it when he joined battle with the traitor. It was just behind him now, almost within reach of al-Wadi's hand. He reached out for it, stretching, fingers capturing one of the rubber loops that served as handles for the bag. He dragged it over to him, watching as Hussein emptied the magazine and dropped it, digging underneath his jacket for a spare. He found one, and was beginning to reload, when furtive movement at the south end of the car demanded al-Wadi's attention.

Nimrod!

In the very moment when he recognized the danger, it was already too late to save his comrade. Still, he shouted a warning. "On your left, Fazir!" he cried, seeing the pistol clutched in Nimrod's fist.

Hussein was turning toward the enemy, bringing around his Spectre SMG when Nimrod fired, the flat crack of his pistol shot almost a muted sound after the noise of two unsilenced submachine guns. For half a heartbeat, there was hope that he would miss the shot, despite the range. Hussein might take him then, if he was quick enough about it.

Any hope in that direction vanished as the bullet caught Hussein below his short ribs, burrowed through, blood squirting from the exit wound in his back. The wounded man slumped backward, flinging out a hand to catch himself, firing his SMG one-handed.

Hussein was quick and bold, but he was also gravely wounded, clenching teeth around his pain as he slumped backward and sat heavily, prevented from collapsing only by the plastic seat that stopped him short. He used the brace to hold himself upright, firing wildly with his right hand, groping backward with his left to find the shopping bag that held the canister of sarin. His fingers closed on empty air, flexed blindly for a moment, while he kept on pumping bullets toward the north end of the car. Finally he risked a backward glance and saw al-Wadi crouching just beyond his reach, the shopping bag between his knees.

It might have been surprise that flickered in his eyes, or even anger, but it passed within a heartbeat, draining from him with the blood that pumped out through his mortal wound. Hussein gave up on reaching for the bag, saw clearly—and perhaps for the first time—that he wouldn't be able to complete the mission, leaving the dispersal of the toxin to al-Wadi. With a grimace the dying Arab braced his free hand underneath him, propped his other elbow on the seat that held him upright, struggling to his feet like some ungainly child.

Al-Wadi used the opportunity, the cover that his crippled friend provided, to edge backward farther from their enemy and closer to the door. The subway train was definitely slowing now, about to stop, and while he couldn't see the signs outside, he had been counting stops before the shooting started, matching them against a map inside the car, and knew that this had to be his station.

He would need only a few more moments, just enough to slip out of the car, an instant to release the gas, perhaps with time enough to don his mask. Survival was of no importance to him, though, as long as he could carry out his mission and wreak bloody havoc on the infidels.

As if on cue, Hussein lurched to his feet just then, firing another short burst from his submachine gun, while his left hand reached to clutch the nearest upright pole. He slipped a little, almost lost his grip with his bloody fingers, but he saved it at the final instant, leaning on the steel pole for support.

Al-Wadi felt the subway train begin its final shudder, coming to a halt. He scuttled backward, brandishing his submachine at some riders who were also creeping toward the door. "Stay back!" he snapped. "I will kill you all!"

It was supposed to be a warning, but in fact it was a statement of intent. He didn't wish to waste the time required for shooting them when Nimrod was so close, so deadly, but he meant for them to die in moments, all the same. As soon as he released the gas, they would be doomed.

Another moment, now. Another moment...

BOLAN WAS READY, waiting, when the wounded Arab fired his last burst from the small Italian SMG. He knew the gun was out of ammunition, for the simple reason that the dying man stopped firing when he did. Clearly the terrorist was bent on fighting to the death, but he had lost all discipline in terms of fire control, the Spectre gobbling ammo at a cyclic rate of some 850 rounds per minute. When the magazine ran dry, the Arab slumped against the pole that held him upright, fumbling in his pocket for a spare.

It was the break that Bolan needed. He rose, squeezing off a shot that drilled the terrorist between his eyes and took the starch out of his legs, leaving him crumpled in a heap. There was no shopping bag nearby, and Bolan cursed under his breath, already moving forward, seeking the dead man's partner, as the train came to a stop. The doors whisked open, and he glimpsed a flash of color, saw a dark, hunched figure in a rumpled suit rush through the opening to gain the outer platform.

Bolan sprinted after him, Beretta in his right hand, a bagful of hideous death in his left. The crowd outside was scattering, the first sight of a crazed, armed stranger all it took to make Los Angelenos run for cover. Bolan saw the target pause, glance backward, and he was just about to nail him with a head shot, when the Arab hosed the subway train with bullets from his compact SMG. The Executioner was forced to duck and roll, regaining his feet in time to see his adversary sprinting toward the staircase that would take him to the street.

There hadn't been time for him to vent the sarin, but he would make time once he reached the open air. Bolan couldn't permit his enemy to reach the street. He had to be stopped below ground, where there was at least some chance of containing the nerve gas, neutralizing it. If that meant firing with civilians in the way, endangering bystanders, he would have to take that chance.

Thirty yards in front of him, the Arab froze with one foot on the first step of the staircase. Bolan looked past him, wondering why he would stop, and saw two uniformed LAPD patrolmen coming down the stairs, apparently oblivious to what was going on a few yards distant. Were the noises of the street above so loud, Bolan wondered, that these two didn't hear reports of gunfire emanating from the station platform?

Both patrolmen had their weapons holstered when they saw the Arab at the bottom of the staircase, scowling, with a submachine gun in his hand. They tried to separate and draw their guns, moving in opposite directions as they had been taught at the police academy, but there was no time for textbook maneuvers. Bolan's quarry sprayed them both with bullets, still firing one-handed, dropping one cop where he stood, the other tumbling headfirst down the concrete stairs.

Bolan was lined up for another shot, when half a dozen panicked subway riders ran across his line of fire. The last one tripped on something Bolan couldn't see and went down on his face, but it was already too late to make the shot. Killing the two young cops apparently had soured Bolan's prey on the idea of going topside. He had found another sanctuary, and was running all out down the platform toward the nearest men's room.

The Executioner risked a shot and believed it found the mark, the way his target flinched and nearly doubled over, but the man kept running, Bolan pounding after him. He disappeared into the rest room, fired a short burst at some target in his path, the echoes of that gunfire rattling around the subway station like the sound track from a gangster movie.

Bolan was close behind him, slowing for a heartbeat as he reached the open door, then lunging through regardless of the risk, because there was no time to spare. Subconsciously he knew this was the best scenario he could have hoped for, if the sarin was released outside the subway car. The men's room wasn't sealed airtight, far from it, but it would contain the nerve gas better than the station platform could.

There was no outer door, per se, since the men's room was open around the clock, but just inside a tiled partition blocked his view of urinals and toilets. What he *could* see, from that vantage point, was a long mirror mounted on the wall above a row of sinks, and nowhere in that glass could he pick out the image of his prey.

Where had the Arab gone?

Ducking around the corner, Bolan knew the man he sought had to be in one of half a dozen toilet stalls. No feet were visible beneath the gray-painted partitions separating the commodes, but there was nowhere else for him to hide—no other exit from the rest room, not even a cubbyhole below the sinks.

A dead man sprawled in front of Bolan, stretched out in his blood on the concrete floor, a briefcase lying inches from the fingers of one outflung hand.

A shifting, scraping sound from one of the toilet

stalls reminded Bolan that he had no time to waste on dead men. Moving forward, he began to unload the Beretta, pumping two rounds into the door of each successive stall, about chest-high. The doors were made of sheet metal, no match for Parabellum rounds unleashed at point-blank range. As he was firing, emptying the pistol's magazine, he told himself there could be no civilians in the stalls; he would have seen their legs if they were in there.

Not necessarily.

The first shots from the Arab's SMG would certainly have frightened anyone enthroned behind those drab-gray doors, but what if Mr. X was thinking fast and raised his feet to keep from being seen?

Forget about it! Bolan ditched his weapon's empty magazine and slapped a fresh one into place and thumbed down the catch that let the slide snap forward, chambering the first round off the top. He had to stop the gas from being vented here and now, at any cost.

The Arab slid down from his perch in a cubicle to Bolan's right and dropped the shopping bag between his feet. There was a sharp, metallic clank on impact, Bolan praying that the nozzle wasn't damaged, that there had been no time for his adversary to release the gas.

He started to pump bullets through the gray door—one, two, three—and took a long step backward, as the Arab cut loose with his submachine gun, firing blindly through the drab walls that surrounded him. The Executioner kept firing, hoping desperately that no wild shot from either gun would strike the canister.

Bolan pumped two more rounds into the cubicle before his enemy collapsed, shoes sliding blood-slick on concrete as the Arab slumped clear of the toilet seat. The subgun slipped from the dead man's grasp and clattered on the floor. One of his legs, extending, nudged the shopping bag beneath the bullet-riddled door, its toxic burden rocking heavily inside.

Bolan approached the dead man cautiously, crouching to verify the kill, before he drew the shopping bag aside. That made two he had managed to deactivate, but what about the other two aboard the other train?

Too late, he thought, knowing that there was nothing more for him to do. Whatever happened with the other terrorists, the last two sarin canisters, it would be left to other hands. He only hoped that Brognola had mobilized sufficient troops to do the job, and that he had the decon team on standby, close at hand.

The CBW experts might be needed yet, Bolan thought, as he stowed his pistol, hoisted the two shopping bags and made his way outside in search of sunlight and fresh air.

ANDY MORRELL SUSPECTED he was dying, but he wasn't finished yet. The right leg of his slacks was blood-drenched, and he knew that he had left a crimson trail behind him, through the last two cars he had traversed. Now, with his sweaty face pressed up against the smudgy window of another door, he saw the men he wanted, sitting close together on the right-hand side, some twenty feet away.

If only there was time to take them out before one of them reached into that bright blue shopping bag and turned a nozzle, to unleash the very breath of hell.

He couldn't pick out the third man, assuming he would be one of The Path's fanatics, and there was no time to waste examining bland faces through the glass. Morrell barged through the doorway, shopping bag and canister suspended from his left hand, slapping heavily against his good leg, while he aimed his pistol with his right.

There was no subtle way to do it, so he went in shouting, "Get your hands up, assholes! I mean now!" The weary croaking of his voice surprised him, but his targets got the message, sitting frozen in their seats, although they didn't raise their hands.

Morrell was waiting for the third man to reveal himself, and when the movement came, off to his left, he was already turning toward the sandy-haired young man, the P-226 bucking in his fist. He saw the bullets find their mark, blood leaping from the stranger's chest as he pitched backward, going down.

In twenty-five years with the FBI, Morrell had fired only one shot in anger, and that shot had missed its target, running through an auto graveyard in the dead of night. Two agents on the far side of the lot had made the collar, leaving Morrell with a stack of paperwork that kept him several hours overtime. Now, here he was, retired, a mere civilian, bleeding from a gunshot to the leg, and he had killed four men within the past five minutes.

And he still had two more to go.

Morrell swung toward the Arabs, found one of them on his feet, a submachine gun coming out from underneath his jacket, while the other thrust both hands into the shopping bag between his feet. It was no contest, and he shot the seated target first, his bullet drilling through the Arab's scalp and skull to find his brain. The man was dead before he knew what hit him, slumping forward, crumpling the bright blue bag beneath his body as he fell.

The subway car was filled with screaming, cringing men and women, aghast at what they had already seen, as the second Arab opened fire. The first half-dozen rounds were wide, off to the left, Morrell returning fire as rapidly as possible. When he was hit, the hot 9 mm Parabellum slugs stitching a ragged line across his abdomen, the impact hurled him backward, but Morrell kept firing as he fell, oblivious to pain, the weightless sense of being airborne, squeezing off his last three rounds before his shoulders slammed into the metal wall behind him.

Sliding to the floor, Morrell could see his final adversary stretched out on the floor, the submachine gun wedged beneath his torso, pinned against the deck. It startled him to realize that he wasn't in any major pain, especially when he glanced down and saw the fresh blood soaking through his shirt.

All eyes within the subway car were focused on him, taking in his wounds, the awkward angle of his twisted legs, the pistol in his hand, its slide locked open on an empty chamber. If there was another terrorist on board, Morrell knew there was nothing he could do to stop the nerve gas being vented. He couldn't begin to reach the backup weapon in his ankle holster, even if another target had been visible.

He heard the doors swish open, and a woman screamed as four men armed with automatic weapons burst into the car. One spotted Morrell, rushed over to him, shoved a submachine gun's muzzle in his face and slapped the useless pistol from his hand. Morrell knew there was something he should say, but he was having trouble with the words, his lips and tongue numb as if a dentist had injected him with novocain.

"Gas canister," he finally managed, wondering if anything he said was getting through to the young man standing above him. "There," he added weakly, pointing in the general direction of the two dead Arabs with a right hand that weighed tons, almost too much for him to lift. It dropped back to his side a moment later, and he barely felt the impact of his knuckles on the floor.

"Got it!" one of the SEAL commandos said, and Morrell saw him lift the shopping bag, holding it at arm's length from his body. "It's secure."

"I've got another one," the nearer SEAL announced, hoisting the bag Morrell had clung to, somehow, even as he fell. "We're done," he said.

And so was he, Morrell thought, smiling as he closed his eyes.

"ALL CANISTERS accounted for," Brognola said, his gruff voice sounding distant through the telephone receiver, even though he was no more than half a dozen blocks away from Bolan in the L.A. federal building. "Same thing on the strike force," he went on. "We've got eleven DOAs, not counting the two SEALs."

Bolan stood in the open booth and watched the traffic flowing past. "Plus one."

"It's a damned shame about Morrell," Brognola said. "I still don't know what made him wade into the shit that way, but it's a good thing that he did. We could have lost it on the second train, without him being there."

"Who told Bouchet?" Bolan asked.

"I did. She took it pretty hard. I didn't know they were that close."

Bolan wasn't surprised. He had experienced the need for creature comfort that was often spawned by tension and the proximity of death. He had been thinking that he ought to call Bouchet, himself, but now decided it could wait.

"One thing," he said into the telephone, "my cover's shot. There's no way Locke and Braun would ever buy me coming through another scrape like that."

"So what's the plan?" Brognola asked. "We still don't have a line on where they've gone to ground."

"I'll have to backtrack," Bolan answered, "starting with the Roswell lab. Is there some way for you to keep the names and final body count out of the papers for a day or so?"

"That shouldn't be a problem. Listen, though..."

Brognola hesitated, searching for the proper words. "The tab on this is getting too damned high for my taste. Maybe we should let the Bureau handle it from here."

"No good. They were getting nowhere when we started, and they still can't prove a thing against the leaders of The Path without a witness who'll agree to testify. I don't much like the odds against their finding one."

"I just feel like the whole damned thing's about to get away from us," Brognola said. "We came *this* close to losing it today."

"Close doesn't count," Bolan reminded him, "except—"

"In horseshoes, right," Brognola said. "I know. I just keep thinking that we're only born with so much luck, and it's been stretching pretty thin the past few weeks."

"We make our own luck, Hal. I can't just let this go."

"No, I didn't think you could. So what about some backup? I can still reach out for Able Team or—"

"No," Bolan said, interrupting him, "but I could use some private wings. Is Jack available?"

"Should be," Brognola said. "I'll know within the hour. Do you have a number I can call?"

"I'm on the move. I'll call you."

"About those other canisters..."

"Check locker number fifty-seven," Bolan told him, "at the Greyhound station. They're secure, but you'll need someone who can pick the lock."

"No sweat. I'll get right on it."

"You should also have Bouchet stand down," Bolan said. "She's done everything she can. It's butcher work from here on out."

"The lady won't like that," Brognola said.

"Don't ask her. Insist."

"Sounds like a plan. Say listen, uh, before you go..."

"Don't sweat it," Bolan said, reading his old friend's mind. "I'll watch my back."

"Watch everything, okay? I have a feeling that these bastards still have something up their sleeves."

"That's why I'm hanging in," the Executioner replied.

"Okay. I'm reaching out for Jack as soon as we hang up."

"Stay frosty, Hal."

"You, too."

Bolan returned the telephone receiver to its cradle and went off to find his war.

Don't miss the exciting conclusion of
the Four Horsemen Trilogy.
Look for SuperBolan #66,
Termination Point, *in June.*